BLOOD IN THE SAND

KELLY CLAYTON

Published by Stanfred Publishing 2015

ISBN: 978-0-9934830-1-1

Book design: Dean Fetzer, www.gunboss.com
Cover design: Kit Foster Design, www.kitfosterdesign.com

For Grant
Forever and always
My love, my heart, my life.

Prologue

Jersey, Channel Islands

If Kate Avery had wanted to die, she couldn't have picked a better day. Her bills were paid, and she'd finally updated her will, no easy task for a childless widow of a certain age. The gardener had even been there the day before. The large plot was bordered by curving wide beds overflowing with trees, from weeping willows to palms, lush flowers and thriving plants in every hue of nature.

Kate sipped a glass of wine as she relaxed on the wide balcony that ran the entire length of the first floor of her beach house. Leaning back, she rested her head against the padded cushions of her high-backed wicker chair and admired the view. As she looked past the turquoise water of the swimming pool and across the wide expanse of manicured lawn, her aged eyes were drawn to the sea, which was visible beyond the high garden wall. The property was separated from the beach by only a narrow coastal road. From her vantage point, Kate had an uninterrupted view of the bay, all the way to the lighthouse, which stood sentinel on its rocky outcrop.

The last of the sun's rays sparkled off the water; diamondsharp pinpricks of light, almost blinding in their intensity as they dazzled and shimmered with the undulations of the waves.

Kate lazily tracked a lone sailing boat as it drifted along the horizon. She adored this view—the sea an ever-changing, living canvas that made her a little fanciful and dreamy.

The setting sun slowly sank deeper, a hot, fiery ball almost too bright for the eyes to bear. The entire sky resonated in colour and blazed in a bleeding kaleidoscope of crimson red, orange and yellow. The sky was momentarily lit by streaks of fire until, all too soon, the vibrancy faded and only dusk and the approaching night remained.

She sighed with pleasure at the beauty and simplicity of nature and poured herself another glass of red wine, suppressing any twinge of guilt. She was seventy-eight years old and had surely earned the right to do as she pleased, when she liked.

She leaned over the round glass table, wincing as her joints ached a little, and pulled across the plate of cheese and biscuits she'd put together earlier. She'd just have a little bite of supper then do her bedtime check of the doors and windows before snuggling into bed with her current book.

Kate's senses were befuddled by the wine, her hearing dulled with age. A prickling at the back of her neck was the first indication that she was no longer alone. She turned around, just as the intruder's dark-clad arm snaked out and restrained her in a firm, tight neck hold. Too shocked to move, Kate was immobile for mere seconds, but as she recovered her senses enough to struggle, she felt a sharp, flashing sting in her abdomen.

Her attacker held her tight as the injector pen was depressed and liquid rushed into her bloodstream. The air was filled with a pungent, cloying smell. She feared it was insulin. If that was the case then she was in real trouble. Her blood sugar level would be relatively low anyway, as it had been hours since lunch and just about time for dinner.

The panic alarm! Her eyes flicked towards the open doors. If she could only reach her bedroom and activate the alarm. *Why hadn't she kept it with her?*

She cursed her naivety as she struggled, vainly trying to dislodge her attacker's hold. She was running out of time and could almost feel the insulin rushing through her bloodstream.

Within seconds, her glucose levels were dropping in reaction to the massive insulin dose. The familiar signs came one after the other. First the tingling in her mouth, numbing the tongue, then the light sweat coating the back of her neck, followed by the slowing of brain function, the disorientation. All this took mere seconds, and Kate knew it would be minutes before she lost consciousness.

She may be seventy-eight, but Kate still felt she had more to experience. She'd yet to see her nephews' own children marry, had never held their yet-to-be-born grandchildren in her arms. Kate didn't want to die.

Blood in the Sand

Through the dense fog that pervaded her mind, past the dark cloud that was her consciousness, one thought forced its way to the distant part of her that retained a modicum of awareness. *Samuel.* Never particularly religious, she now clung to the hope that she would see her beloved husband once more.

Her attacker easily picked her up and held her tight in their lethal embrace. In the next moment, she was lifted higher and suspended over the balcony. Her vision was blurred and her confusion wouldn't allow her to process what was about to occur. Strong arms threw her over the balcony with a vicious shove, and in her last conscious moments, Kate saw the terra-cotta patio tiles loom closer before awareness fled.

When the last finally came, Kate Avery didn't know where she was or what was happening. Her thought process slowed and stuttered as the insulin flow to her brain dulled her senses even further. It was never a good day to die.

CHAPTER ONE

Dressed in dark jeans and a casual T-shirt, Detective Chief Inspector Jack Le Claire sat hunched over the desk in his cramped office. The case files were piling up fast, and he needed all the time he could get to review the incidents that had occurred in the past week.

He knew he was considered young for his position, having just turned thirty, and so felt the urge to work that bit harder to show the doubters that the confidence in him was justified. He ran a hand over his jaw, wincing as he felt the rough stubble. He hadn't shaved this morning, and now he was paying the price.

Perceptive eyes reviewed the computerised files, and he let out a sigh as he noted nothing of interest. This was hardly London. A dark part of him couldn't help but acknowledge that he was bored, that he missed the thrill of working homicide and feeling that he could make a difference in the everyday savagery of the city streets. Perhaps he should have stayed in London, brazened it out and carried on doing what he knew he was best at—being a bloody good homicide detective. He brushed the thought aside. He had left London for a reason and wouldn't go back—the memories wouldn't let him. He'd made his choice, and now he just needed to accept it. But he was policing in an almost paradise—was that all he was good for?

He typed in the case number that corresponded to a thorn in his side. There had long been rumours that unlicensed gambling rings were operating, frequently shifting location and always one step ahead of the local police. There were rough elements involved and, recently, signs that London syndicates were pushing their way in. Scanning the latest updates posted by the officer in charge, he sighed in exasperation. Nothing-these guys never took a misstep, always covered their tracks and apparently threatened anyone who came into contact with them. As evidenced by a local hotelier they'd invited in for questioning. There were suspicions that he was allowing his property to be used for after-hours gambling. When he came in to see the police, his eyes were black, his arm in a sling and his mouth firmly shut.

He moved on through the latest files. One of the cases caused him to take a second look. An elderly widow had died unexpectedly. The initial police report was due to be sent to the coroner later that day. The cause of death was massive trauma to the brain. The woman had taken a huge dose of insulin and fallen from her first-floor balcony. After he read the routine report, Le Claire clicked through the images of the balcony that the old lady had fallen off. A close-up had been taken of the table, littered with the debris of a quiet evening at home—well-thumbed glossy magazines sat alongside a bookmarked paperback, an open bottle of red wine was paired with a used glass and an untouched plate of cheese and biscuits. An uncapped injector pen lay beside its lid. His mind was still processing the images as he clicked on a shot of the balcony from the garden. And then he stopped and went back to the previous image. He enlarged the sizing, bringing the injector pen into sharp relief. Where was the needle? The top of the pen was empty. A needle would need to have been attached for the insulin to have been administered. Disliking loose ends, he made a note for someone to check and see if any of the other images showed the needle. It had probably fallen to the ground.

\#

Grace Howard waited in the small airport arrivals area. Her flight from New York had landed in London at dawn. A short car journey between airports and a flight across the English Channel had brought her to the island of Jersey, where she now waited for the promised car to meet her. Usually an avid people-watcher, Grace had little interest today. All she wanted to do was get to her hotel with as little hassle as possible. Her nerves were frayed and her enthusiasm dimmed.

She scanned the busy arrivals hall for a board with her name on it. Belatedly, she realised she didn't know the details of the car company booked by her aunt's lawyers. She would give it ten minutes and then get into one of the waiting cabs. She was exhausted, grieving and not in the mood for waiting.

Her attention was drawn to a tall man who had just walked in. She took in the athletic build and broad shoulders before she noticed what he was carrying. A wide smile lit his face when he noticed her, making his eyes crinkle and his high cheekbones rise even farther. His eyebrows lifted in enquiry as he indicated the sign in his hand. The name board was a tattered piece of A4 paper, her full name written in block capitals with what looked suspiciously like a fading magic marker. Her eyes focused on the man holding the name card, and she momentarily held her breath.

He was young, maybe in his early thirties, with mussed-up dark blond hair. Startlingly blue eyes, a strong, classical nose and a full mouth certainly meant he drew his share of attention. Still smiling, he walked towards her. "Miss Howard, I presume?" he asked, his tone more flirtatious than Grace would have expected from a professional driver.

He took her luggage, and they headed outside to the car park. Given the small size of the airport, it was a bare five minutes before she was escorted to an old but immaculate bright red Jeep Wrangler.

She couldn't contain her surprise, and her laughter rang out. "This is your car?"

"I beg your pardon. This happens to be a 1989 Wrangler, lovingly restored with original parts. What on earth is funny about that?"

"Well. I didn't mean it was funny *ha ha*, just funny strange. I guess if I had thought about it, I would have expected the car company to send a sedan or something—but it's fine. It's absolutely no problem."

"Ah, I'm afraid I should have introduced myself properly. I'm Sam Avery. Kate's late husband was my Great-Uncle Samuel. I'm named after him, though you probably guessed that by now. Kate was an amazing woman and meant a lot to my family, and we share your loss. Please accept my deepest condolences."

"Thank you. I can't believe she's gone."

Sam opened the passenger door and offered his arm to Grace, who took it gratefully as she eyed the running board she'd need to hop onto to get into the car. She held on and jumped up, slightly stumbling as a jolt of electricity shot through her at his touch. Sam grabbed her by the waist to steady her, and Grace felt a searing heat where his hands lightly held her. Her nerves must be shot to pieces. She drew a self-conscious hand over her hair, trying to smooth what she knew was a sleep-mussed mess.

She settled into the passenger seat as Sam started the car and headed out of the airport.

"Is this your first visit to Jersey, Grace?"

"Yes, it is." She took a steadying breath and continued, "I had heard a little about it from Aunt Kate on her visits to the States, but I've never been here. Actually, this is the first time I've been out of the US. After college, I went straight into practice."

"Practice? Which is it? Doctor, lawyer or accountant?"

"Nothing as useful as a doctor, I'm afraid. I'm a private client tax lawyer."

"Ah, yes. I recall Kate mentioning it."

"And what is your line of work, Sam?"

"I'm a property developer. We run projects in the UK, as well as on the island. My grandfather and Samuel started the business, and now it's me and my dad."

"The island seems pretty small."

"I guess it is. Nine miles long and four miles wide; however, we do have a population of 100,000. Jersey is a huge melting pot. People come here from all over the world: British, French, Portuguese, and Eastern European and farther afield from Asia and even a few Yanks."

"Well, you've got one more Yank for a few days." Grace stilled as she thought about the reason for her trip.

#

Sam sneaked a quick glance at his passenger. He had recognised her straightaway. She looked a little like a young Kate did in her wedding photos. They shared the same thick honey-blonde hair and heavy fringe, although Grace's hair waved past her shoulders whilst Kate had preferred a short bob. Grace's mouth was wide and quirked up at the sides, as if smiles came easy to her. Her hazel eyes looked tired after the long journey, but that didn't detract from her appeal.

If anything, the fatigue and grief gave Grace a fragile air, and Sam had a sudden impulse to protect her from the trials of the next few days. He shook his head to brush away that notion—he hardly knew the girl, and he had enough on his mind as it was.

#

The Jeep wound its way through a tree-lined valley, the road curving in a tight spiral. The farther they travelled, the more built up it became with whitewashed terraced houses and tiny pastel-coloured fishermen's cottages jumbled together. At the bottom, they turned onto the coast, and Grace marvelled at the narrow two-lane roads, low buildings and slower pace of traffic. There was a continental vibe, with restaurant tables spilling onto the pavements, all set around a small harbour.

They travelled on in silence as the Jeep moved inland.

Sam took a sharp turn to the left, and they started a steep descent. The air felt a little heavier as the sun was hidden behind the arches of tree branches that interlocked over the road.

The canopy of green became sparser as they wound down the hill until they passed an ancient church, where the tree line ended and the sun blazed down on them.

Grace gasped as they rounded the corner. The horseshoe-shaped bay had a pristine white sand beach, a perfect surround for the turquoise waters that gently lapped the shore.

"St Brelade's Bay. Truly one of the wonders of the world, or it should be."

A few moments later, Sam turned his car to the right and entered the grounds of an imposing hotel building. Parking in the free space nearest the entrance, he jumped out and, to Grace's surprise, came round to the passenger door and offered her his hand to get out of the car. Grace almost drew back at the fury of sparks that set her whole body alight. As soon as she exited the car, she quickly moved away, although she could still feel the heat of his flesh.

"I'll grab your bag, Grace. Let's get you checked in."

#

Several hours later, Grace admired the views of sparkling sea and sandy beaches as the taxi sent by her aunt's executor hugged the coastline on its journey into the main town. The closer they came to what she assumed was St Helier, modern office blocks sprouted between the island's more traditional buildings.

The car stopped in front of a large glass-fronted building, the driver beckoning her towards the entrance. The heat of the early afternoon sun warmed her back, and she felt the rays slightly burning her face.

Grace quickly walked into the welcome coolness of the air-conditioned foyer. After checking in at the front desk, she was led along a long corridor and ushered into a room at the end. She had a brief glimpse of a modern, stylish office before a man came forward and, to her surprise, enveloped her in a bear hug.

Grace stiffened and pulled back. Seeing her unease, the man released her. "Forgive me, my dear. I am afraid you caught me unawares. Kate was a dear friend first and a client second, and seeing you is like seeing a young Kate walk into the room. I am Paul Armstrong, Miss Howard, but please let us be on first-name terms?"

At Grace's nod, Paul gestured for them to sit on the brightly coloured chairs set on either side of a low glass table.

"Paul, as my father explained in his email, he is heading up a class-action lawsuit and is due to give the closing arguments this week. I am afraid he had to concede it would be inappropriate for him to leave New York at this time. He asked me to pass on his sincerest apologies to you."

"Not a problem. Kate specifically wanted you to be here."

As they sat, Grace glanced around the room, taking in the eclectic decor and artwork. A long, lacquered wooden sideboard lay along one wall, and it was covered in framed photographs, many showing a much younger Paul Armstrong with a smiling older couple. Grace's heart flipped as she immediately recognised them—Kate and Samuel Avery.

Paul noticed her gaze. "I knew Kate and Samuel for years. I started out doing some legal work for the company and ended up with two lifelong friends."

Grace asked the question that had been occupying her mind since that tragic early morning call from her father.

"What actually happened to Kate? My dad wasn't that clear, but I was told she fell off her balcony."

With a huge exhalation of breath that resonated in the quiet of the room, Paul sat back in his chair, hands clasped over his slightly protruding stomach. "Kate was having a light supper. The police found the remains of a plate of bread and cheese and half a bottle of wine. Their opinion is that she was befuddled by the wine and mistakenly took too much insulin."

Paul took his glasses off and carefully wiped them with a cloth from his pocket. "The inquest will take place over the next couple of weeks, but I understand the initial thoughts are that if the fall hadn't killed Kate, the insulin dose would most certainly have done so—at the very least she would have been in a coma."

Grace reared back in disbelief. "I cannot believe that she would have been so careless. She ate like a bird and only needed tiny doses of insulin."

"I'm afraid we just have to accept that Kate had a terrible accident, a tragic overdose of the very stuff that was meant to keep her well and alive. We've lost her."

The finality in Paul's tone was made all the more poignant by his watery eyes. They were brought back to the present by the opening of the office door.

Sam Avery walked in. The smile on his face widened as he saw Grace, and she resisted the urge to grin back. Sam reached out to take the older man's hand in a firm handshake. "Paul, good to see you."

Grace took the opportunity to size up Sam. She had to admit that he was looking good. His dark chinos and open-necked shirt were suitable for the weather, the meeting and, of course, for mourning.

The top two buttons were undone, and Grace could see the fine blond hairs highlighted against his tanned skin.

"Grace, are you all right?"

"Sorry, I was just wool-gathering."

Grace caught what looked like a smirk cross Sam's face, as if he knew exactly what wool she'd been gathering, and felt a hot blush creep over her face.

Paul stood and crossed the room. "Perhaps we'd best take this to the conference table?"

He gestured for them to sit side by side whilst he took the chair at the head of the table, placing him at a right angle to his guests. A thin, buff-coloured folder lay in front of the lawyer, the name "Kate Avery" typed on a white label affixed to the top righthand corner.

"Kate and Samuel had *mirror wills*. Their estate passed to the survivor in its entirety. Most of their assets were jointly held anyway. On the subsequent death of the survivor, the assets—that is, the movable assets—were to be split into two portions."

Grace was politely interested. Her father, and Sam's, had been the couple's dearest relatives. No surprise that the two men would be the beneficiaries of Kate's estate.

Paul coughed and poured himself some ice water from the jug on the table. He took a sip and then continued, "So as I was saying, two portions. One for you, Sam, and one for you, Grace."

"What!" The word burst forth from each of them, and Grace knew the puzzled look on Sam's face matched her own.

"Kate and Samuel knew their nephews were successful and wealthy. They wanted you to have choices. Each of you has taken up your father's profession. Hopefully it's because that's what you wanted to do. If not, Kate and Sam's legacy gives you the monetary freedom to decide how you want to spend the rest of your lives."

Paul named a sum of money, the amount each had inherited, and Sam's whistle of disbelief almost drowned out Grace's gasp. It was enough to live on comfortably for quite some time.

"Sam, you're a good lad, always have been. Grace, you seem to have something of Kate about you. They wanted all they worked so hard for to be enjoyed by their two favourite people."

Paul rifled through the papers in front of him, evidently looking for something in particular; however, he seemed a little flustered. He cleared his throat several times as he pulled a sheet of paper out of the pile.

"There is one final matter: Rocque View. Kate and Samuel had many happy years in their home. Kate left a letter about the place. It's best if I read it to you:

> *My dear children,*
>
> *If you are reading this letter, then I am undoubtedly dead. I've always wanted to say that. It sounds like it belongs in one of those mystery specials on the television.*
>
> *You are, I assume, in the company of Paul Armstrong, a good man, and you'd do worse than to take his advice should any be required.*
>
> *Paul will have told you of our main bequest. All I ask is that you live your lives exactly as you want to. 'No regrets' was always my motto, and I have to say that I definitely don't have any. Not everything I did was successful, or even warranted, but I do not regret anything I have ever done.*
>
> *Of the many possessions Samuel and I gathered during our lives, the most precious by far is Rocque View. It has made for the most wonderful home, but it was much more than that. It has a sense of peace and quietness, a calm that is so at odds with the frantic pace at which we tend to live our lives.*
>
> *I don't want to keep you waiting, so let me get to the point.*
>
> *I ask this favour of you.*
>
> *Please live at my home for three months and let it weave its spell over you.*
>
> *If at the end of that time, one of you wants to keep the place, then a sum of money has been set aside to compensate the other. If neither of you wants the place, then it goes on the market, and both of you will split the sale proceeds and the separate cash account.*
>
> *Please think about what I have asked and don't be hasty. Good-bye, darlings. I know you'll make the right decision.'*

Paul laid the letter down on top of the open file, the rustling of the papers deafening in the unnatural silence of the room.

Grace and Sam began talking at once.

"It's impossible. I already have a beautiful apartment."

"But I live in New York."

"I can't take care of a house that size."

"But I don't live here," Grace almost shouted, her frustration rising.

Sam raked his hand through his hair, causing tufts to stand on end, making him look much younger. "Paul, it's obvious that neither Grace nor I want the place, so maybe it's best just to proceed with the sale?"

"It isn't that easy, I'm afraid. Kate's letter merely skimmed over the finer details of the legal arrangements she put in place."

"Legal arrangements?" queried Grace.

"Yes. To Kate and Samuel, that house was a labour of love; it was their child, where they poured their creative energy. Kate's detailed instructions are based on the simple fact that she couldn't bear anyone but family to at least try living there. So if neither of you want the place, if you can't see your way to even giving it a go, then Kate's instructions are very clear."

Paul paused, again looking uncomfortable as the silence lengthened and grew in weight. "The house is to be bulldozed, levelled to the ground. The gardens are to be dug up, where permitted by covenant, and the whole acreage sold as a building plot."

Sam was quick to protest. "You can't do that! Kate loved that house; my uncle adored it. He oversaw every single item renovated in that place. He made it beautiful for Kate, and now it's going to be senselessly destroyed. How can that be right?"

"Whether it is right or not—and I'm not saying I disagree with you, Sam—those were Kate's wishes, updated just a few weeks ago. I don't need your decisions right now. Take a day or two."

"So let me get this straight, unless we agree to live in the house for three months, the place will be completely destroyed?"

"I am afraid that is correct."

Grace glanced at Sam. "Obviously, I can't..."

"Yes, I can see that."

"Could you..."

"I'm going to have to, aren't I? My great-uncle worked too damned hard for it to be bulldozed like some derelict eyesore."

Relief flooded through Grace. "Thank you. That's settled. Sam will move in for the three months."

"That won't do, I'm afraid. Kate was quite explicit. You both have to stay in the house, together, at the same time, for three months."

"That is an outrageous suggestion." Grace's voice betrayed her shock, and she could hear the tremble in her words.

"Yes, my dear, but it is still what Kate wanted."

Sam rose to his feet. "We need time to think this over, especially Grace, who, lest we forget, actually lives on a different continent."

"Of course. The funeral is tomorrow, and you have until the day after to make up your mind." At the startled looks of his guests, Paul raised a hand. "I am sorry, but those were Kate's instructions. I cannot do other than follow them." Turning to Grace, he said, "I'll order a car to take you back to the hotel."

Sam cut in before Grace could accept. "No need. I'll give you a lift. We need to talk."

Paul placed a hand on each of their shoulders, a comforting gesture. "Think carefully. It would be a crying shame to see that fine house destroyed. I'll see you both at the church tomorrow. Grace, what time shall I send the car?"

Sam interjected again, "I'll pick her up."

Night had fallen, and a single lamp illuminated the bedroom. He stood by the window as he thought and calculated and considered.

Crossing to the wardrobe, he selected a plain black suit and crisp white shirt. Hooking the coat hangers over the bedroom door knob, he added a dark silk tie before laying out a good watch and some discreet cuff links. He carefully picked a piece of lint from the shoulder of the suit jacket. He stood back and, satisfied, got ready for bed.

Once the funeral was over, he could finally start making plans.

CHAPTER TWO

Grace had risen at first light, the early morning rays promising a glorious day. It should be raining, she had thought, and if rain was too much to ask, then a cold, grey day would be perfect. One of those colourless days where everyone and everything was just that bit grimmer.

She wore a plain black dress, matching tailored jacket and a pair of high-heeled court shoes. Her only accessory was a small enamelled brooch shaped like a butterfly, which she had pinned onto the lapel of her jacket. Kate had given it to her on her sixteenth birthday, and just touching it made her feel a little closer to Kate.

Her thoughts drifted to the day before. Sam had driven her home, but in contradiction to what he had told Paul Armstrong, they had little to talk about. Her life was in New York; there was no way she could take a leave of absence from her job. And what about Carter? She couldn't leave him. She had no intention of living on this island, even for three months, so really, there was nothing to discuss.

With that, she checked her wristwatch; Sam would be waiting for her.

#

Sam's car skirted the main town and kept heading east. As they drove along the coast, he pointed to a long, private drive on their left.

"That is the entrance to Rocque View. A reception has been set up there for afterward. I understand Kate was very explicit as to how she wanted everything handled."

The car slowed as Sam pulled over on the roadside, tight against a high granite wall. He helped Grace out of the car, and as she felt his strong fingers clasp hers, she almost recoiled at the electricity of his touch. She wasn't usually so sensitive. It had to be the situation, the melding of grief and sorrow that was wreaking havoc with her senses.

Sam locked the car and let out a long, low whistle.

"What is it?" asked Grace.

"Look at this line of cars." He pointed to the parked vehicles, around fifty, maybe more. "It looks like it's going to be busy."

They walked through a thick stone archway and followed the narrow, tree-lined path towards the ancient church. Grace spotted an older couple standing at the side of the pathway, watching their progress towards the heavy wooden doors. The woman was discreetly made up; her carefully highlighted hair was pulled back and framed a face that belied its years, but in a natural way. The man was tall, and the similarity with Sam was striking.

They both smiled warmly, although sadness clouded their eyes. As the couple moved towards them, the man hugged Sam tightly, just as the woman pulled Grace into her arms.

"I'm Susannah, Sam's mother, and this is my husband, Richard. We'll talk later. Come, let's say good-bye to Kate."

Kate Avery's funeral lasted thirty-five minutes, a little over thirty seconds for each year of her life.

#

Grace gasped at her first glimpse of what had been Kate's home. Tall iron gates towered over the car as it swept through the white stone columns flanking the entrance. A black marble sign had the house's name picked out in contrasting white. Wooden fencing enclosed the grounds, running parallel to the hedging, which further screened the property from view.

The car slowly travelled up the winding drive, wide borders on either side ablaze with brightly coloured flowers, vivid foliage and towering evergreens.

As they exited the car, Sam's parents parked beside them. Sam led Grace around to the front of the house, which overlooked the sprawling gardens and faced the sea.

Blood in the Sand

Three storeys high, the house was still wider than it was tall. Walls of glass afforded panoramic sea views that could be enjoyed from the balconies that ran the length of each floor.

At the ground-floor level, wide bifold doors had been swept open, granting access to a large room that was entirely white, from the painted wooden ceiling to the stone fireplace and the white floor tiles flecked with tiny light-reflecting crystals. The huge sofas were off-white linen, the only colour in the room coming from the brightly coloured dust jackets lining the floor-to-ceiling bookcases.

Sam spoke quietly, "I understand that Kate had already picked the caterers and the menu. Paul said she updated them every year or so."

A genuine smile crossed Grace's face at this last example of Kate's determination to plan the perfect party. She had wanted an elegant send-off, and that was exactly what she was getting.

Sam lifted two glasses of champagne from a passing tray and handed one to Grace. She took a sip from the crystal flute, the pale pink liquid slipping down her throat in a rush of effervescent bubbles.

Grace and Sam were quietly talking to Susannah, who had just joined them, when the older woman became distracted by something that had caught her attention.

"Oh dear," murmured Susannah. "Brace yourself. A tornado is headed in our direction."

A tall woman, her cap of shiny dark hair perfectly styled, strode up to them, a brittle smile pasted on her face. Her black pencil skirt sat a little too high on suntanned legs, her toned calves showcased by her vertiginous high-heeled pumps. The V-neck of her tightly buttoned jacket exposed an expanse of cleavage, the soft creping of skin betraying her age in a way her carefully preserved and enhanced face never would. She reached out and tugged Grace towards her, enveloping her in a quick, awkward hug. The woman kissed each of Grace's cheeks in turn and then held her at arm's length.

"Well. You are a sweet one. There's a bit of Kate about you, but that can't be helped. She really did not age well at all. You need to look after yourself as you get older."

Grace wasn't quite sure if she'd been insulted. She figured that a low blow had definitely been aimed at Kate but wasn't too sure about herself.

"Darling, I'm your Aunt Harriet"

"*Great*-aunt isn't it?" Sam said.

A fierce look came into Harriet's eyes as she snapped, "Oh, it's you. Make yourself useful and get me a drink."

Sam moved closer to Grace as he gestured to a passing waiter.

Harriet grabbed the proffered glass and greedily drained half of it in one gulp. She moved slightly so that she effectively blocked Sam and was closer to Grace. "My dear girl, you look exhausted. Must be jet lag—poor you. You didn't have time to go and get your hair done either."

Grace self-consciously brought her hand up to smooth her hair. She hadn't realised she looked so bad.

"Let's have a quiet chat." Harriet steered Grace away from the Averys.

Glancing back, Grace saw Sam move as if to follow them, but Susannah placed a warning hand on his arm. Harriet manoeuvred Grace across the lawn towards a wooden bench set under the branches of a spreading oak.

Grace found her voice. "It's a pleasure to meet you Great-Aunt."

Harriet's finely plucked eyebrows shot up, and she quickly looked around to see if anyone had overheard. "No need to stand on ceremony. Call me Harriet. I am, after all, much younger than Kate and Emily. First your grandmother, now Kate and I'm the last one left—all on my own."

Grace felt a tug of sympathy. Harriet sounded sincere in her grief.

"Anyway, I take it you won't be here for long. No doubt Paul Armstrong still deals with Kate's affairs and will get on with the reading of the will. I presume it's to be later today, when everyone else has gone?"

Grace felt the first stirrings of trouble ahead. "Actually, I think Paul pretty much dealt with it yesterday."

Harriet's head snapped up. "Yesterday? Who was present? What did the will say? Tell me!"

Harriet grabbed Grace in a vice-like grip. Long nails dug into the flesh of her upper arms. Grace felt a moment of real fear as she saw the feral look in Harriet's eyes—primitive, stripped of all civility. Grace took an involuntary step back.

"Sam and I were there, but I think you should speak to Paul Armstrong if you'd like to know more."

Over Harriet's shoulder, Grace saw the Averys approach. Harriet advanced on Grace. It seemed as if whatever sense of decorum she may have possessed had fled at this unexpected turn of events. Her face a cold mask, she demanded, "Tell me what the will said. What's my cut? I got the house, didn't I? Tell me."

Richard Avery laid a gentle but firm hand on Harriet's back. "For God's sake, Harriet, don't make a scene, not today of all days."

Harriet shrugged Richard's hand away, stepping past him as he tried to block her. Almost running, she bumped into other mourners in her haste to find Paul Armstrong.

#

As Harriet rounded the pool she saw the lawyer standing with an elderly couple. Furiously pushing past them, she demanded, "What is all this nonsense I hear? That you allowed those two," she almost spat the words as she threw a scathing glance towards Grace and Sam, "to hear the contents of my sister's will without me being present? I was her nearest relative. I'll report you to the Law Society for this." Harriet's voice finished with a screech.

"Harriet, this is neither the time nor the place for this discussion. Come into the study, where we can talk in private."

"No!" Harriet's voice had risen, drawing the attention of all those milling around the gardens. People looked away, embarrassed by the display, and an unmistakable tension had entered the air. "I have a right, every right, to know what she left me. I want to know now!" Harriet was snarling by this point, her face contorted in anger as an unbecoming flush stained her cheeks.

"Very well, Harriet. You asked for this. The will has been read in the presence of the beneficiaries. You weren't invited as you are not a beneficiary of Kate's will, meaning that, no, you don't have any rights. That's all I have to say. Please allow those here to do what they came for. To mourn Kate."

He walked away. Harriet stood completely still, her mouth gaping open.

"Harriet, love. You all right?"

Harriet turned at the voice. Ray Perkins was running to fat, the buttons of his expensive black suit straining almost beyond endurance. However, the fat hid a layer of muscle and covered up what not long ago had been a well-toned body. The material stretched across his wide shoulders, and his loosened tie and limp collar gave him a dishevelled look. Harriet sighed; he'd looked pristine this morning, but it never lasted long. The expensive watch and fine clothes were at odds with his rough manners, but Harriet didn't care. His balding head and poorly healed broken nose seemed menacing—although his attitude towards Harriet was anything but.

"Oh, Ray, did you hear what that awful man said. Did you?"

"Yes, I did. You've got rights. We've talked about this before— seems to reason as you were Kate's closest relative. Come on. Let's get out of here."

Harriet let Ray put a protective arm around her as he led her towards the drive. "I'm due something from that bitch's estate, and I mean to get it. I had expectations."

"I know, love. We both did," replied Ray as he wearily led Harriet off the property.

#

Paul Armstrong joined a shaken Grace, Sam and his parents.

"Well," Grace broke the uncomfortable silence. It was her great-aunt after all. "She is definitely not happy. I've never met Harriet before and rarely heard her mentioned. I don't believe she was at all close to my grandmother."

Susannah snorted. "She wasn't, dear. Harriet is a first-class bitch, and your Aunt Kate couldn't stand her. This is the first time she's set foot at Rocque View in years." Susannah's acid tone contrasted with her previous warmth.

"Forgive me. Harriet is still your family, and my comments were uncalled for. I must admit that I do have quite strong feelings towards Harriet, but I should have kept them to myself."

"It's fine, Susannah. I've only just met Harriet, but I think I'm developing similarly strong feelings myself. Who was the gentleman she left with?"

Susannah gently shook her head. "I don't think Ray Perkins has ever been called a gentleman before. He and Harriet have been in a relationship for a while. He owns a car sales business and seems to do well, but he's never quite polished off his rough edges. From what I can tell, they deserve each other."

#

Le Claire looked up from his computer screen as his office door banged opened. Detective Sergeant Dewar pushed her way into the room, balancing files, two Styrofoam drink holders and a paper bag of something that smelled hot, baked and fattening.

She had a rounded face with a stubborn chin. Of average height, she wasn't slim but nor was she fat; she was toned and muscled, her chestnut hair chopped short. And she had the potential to be one of the best—if she'd think things through a little more. That would come in time.

"Afternoon, sir—I better set this lot down before I have an accident."

"Here—let me help." Le Claire took the cups from her, sure that one would be a filter coffee for him—the other would be an extra-strong tea for Dewar.

Dewar settled herself in the chair in front of Le Claire's desk and, opening the bakery bag, handed him a napkin-wrapped cheese-and-ham pizza slice. "I thought you might not have had time for lunch, sir."

He hadn't. "Thanks. Now what have you got for me?"

Dewar had just bitten off a chunk of her own pizza and hastily swallowed her food. She opened the file she had brought in. "I looked at the incident report and all the related images. I also spoke to the attending officers, but the needle had definitely been removed from the injector, and there was no sign of it on the balcony."

"Okay. It's probably nothing, but let's just make sure. I don't know much about diabetes. You?"

"Not the insulin-dependent type. I can speak to someone."

"Find out what you can—especially about dosage. See who the deceased's doctor was or if she was seeing any specialists. I know

21

the report has gone in, and God knows I don't want to ruffle any feathers, but just make sure you tie up any loose ends and get the file closed to my satisfaction."

CHAPTER THREE

Grace sat on her hotel balcony, hugging a cup of coffee as she gazed at the bay in front of her. The sun was starting to sink lower in the sky, and she idly watched the waves brushing against the white sand.

She had stayed and paid her respects to Kate for an hour or so, but the conversation with Harriet had unnerved her. She felt the need to talk to someone from home—just to feel grounded and remind her of the life she would return to in a few days. She reached for her cell phone to call Carter, her fiancé. Grace had been engaged to Carter Lawson III for six months and had known him since the cradle. He was handsome in that distinctive East Coast way, a walking advert for Ralph Lauren. His dark blond hair was always neatly trimmed, a perfect frame to set off his square-jawed good looks.

She recalled that Carter was going to some lodge upstate to meet a client who was interested in buying the property and developing it into an upmarket resort. The lodge was in the mountains, which meant Carter probably wouldn't have a cell phone signal. He had told her as much and said there wouldn't be much point in her calling.

Her mind made up, she called the operator for the number of the lodge. The name was Pine's something—Pine's Peak. After she pressed the last digit, there was a pause, then a tinny, muted ring tone, making her feel absurdly far away from her familiar life.

"Good afternoon, Pine's Peak Lodge. How can I help you?"

"I'd like to speak to one of your guests, please. Carter Lawson."

"I'm sorry, ma'am. Mr Lawson has just left."

"Do you know when he'll be back? Did he say?"

"No. But they did say they were going to Antonio's bar. It's down the mountain a way, so maybe they'll be a while."

How typical of Carter, straight to work and looking at the competitors. "Thanks. He must be with his client already. I'm glad I didn't disturb him."

"Oh no, ma'am. It was just the two of them, Mr and Mrs Lawson."

"Mrs Lawson?" Grace hadn't known Carter was being joined by his mother, although they were close.

"Oh, of course, his mother," Grace clarified.

"You must have the wrong lady, ma'am. Mrs Lawson is a young lady. She's got long black hair, all curly like, and the cutest butterfly tattoo you ever saw."

Gina!

Grace felt like she'd taken a direct hit to her stomach, her solar plexus contracting as she released her caught breath. The moment was suspended. It couldn't be true.

What was Carter doing with her assistant? She couldn't take this in. Surely there had to be a good explanation. "Of course, thank you for the information."

As Grace went to hang up, the desk clerk shouted down the line. "Hold on! Don't go. Mr Lawson just walked back in."

Grace heard the clerk call out Carter's name, followed by a muffled reply. As the handset was passed across, she heard his aside to whoever was there. "Darling, it'll be the office. Damn it, I told them not to disturb us. Why don't you go fetch your wrap, and then we'll have that cocktail."

Grace heard the unmistakable throaty laugh of her PA.

"Hello. Who is this?" Carter spoke into silence. "Come on. This had better be good. I'm on vacation," he finished testily.

Grace couldn't find her voice. Instead, she let out a long, shuddering sob.

"Hello?" Carter's voice became hesitant, and a wary note crept in. "Grace? Oh God, Grace is that you? I didn't want you to find out this way. I was going to tell you when you got back. It just happened. I still love you, but I'm not in love with you."

"You utter bastard!" Grace slammed down the phone.

#

Blood in the Sand

The lone figure sat in a shadowed room. A shaft of fading light insinuated its way through the closed wooden shutters to fall across the paper-strewn desk. Tiny particles of dust danced in the beam, momentarily capturing his attention, a distraction from his calculations, the tallying of assets and a reckoning of how much they'd bring and how quickly.

The shrill tones of the ringing telephone made him jerk; the sound an unexpected intrusion in the heavy silence of the room. His hand reached out, hesitated as the caller ID was displayed, then, summoning courage, he answered the call. But he didn't say a word, simply waited for the rasping voice to make its commands known.

"Good man. You just listen. We both know I'm not interested in anything you have to say."

His intake of breath was the only response.

"You know the score. You're late, and I want what you owe me. You don't pay, and I go public, whisper a few words here and there, and that business of yours, shaky as it is, will collapse. All those creditors will be calling in their markers right, left and centre. You've got until the end of the month. I won't wait any longer."

He couldn't help himself. "Please just give me a little bit longer. I've something planned—it's a dead cert."

The harsh tone coldly cut across him. "I'm not interested. Just get me my money by the end of the month. You know the consequences if you don't come up to scratch. You know me— never an idle threat."

There was a loud click as the call was disconnected. Beads of perspiration marked his brow as the man cradled his downcast head in his hands. What was he going to do?

He couldn't find that amount of money in a few weeks. The mocking voice had been right—if all the creditors called in their accounts, it would be bankruptcy; if that happened, he'd never get his hands on the greater prize in time.

He really only had one option. Now, with the stakes even higher than before, he would do whatever it took. For hadn't he already gone farther than he had ever thought possible?

#

The next morning, Sam made his way to Paul Armstrong's office. He'd had a call from the lawyer to say that Grace wanted to see them both. As it was Saturday, Sam only had one appointment lined up. Later that day, he was to meet with a potential investor for a large project on which they'd had a setback. He felt slightly sick. They had to get the funding. If not, all they'd worked for could be at risk.

Grace was already there when Sam arrived. She sat on one of Paul's colourful armchairs, her paleness accentuated by her plain black dress. She looked more subdued than he had seen her before, staying quiet whilst Paul poured coffees and got them settled. Sam was intrigued. Grace did not seem at all like the self-confident woman he had seen over the past few days. She looked a little lost and vulnerable.

Paul spoke up. "Grace, you wanted to say something?"

"Yes, I do. I already gave you my decision that, torn though I was, I just could not agree to Kate's conditions and stay in Jersey."

Grace paused. Sam and Paul waited patiently for her to speak. "Well, my circumstances have changed, and I need a break from New York. If it isn't too late, I'd like to accept Kate's conditions or," Grace's smile was fleeting, "was it more of a challenge she issued? If it was, then that is fine by me. I'm picking up the gauntlet."

There was a heavy pause, broken only when Paul let out a long breath of relief. "I am delighted. So very, very delighted."

Sam still hadn't said anything. Something wasn't right, he just knew it. The woman in front of him seemed a shadow of herself.

"Sam, what do you think of this, then?" probed Paul, still beaming with pleasure.

Sam spoke as he turned to face Grace. "It is good news—but certainly surprising. You seemed quite adamant before. What made you change your mind?"

"Oh, just something... nothing really."

Grace couldn't meet Sam's eyes or Paul's either, for that matter.

Paul brought them back to the practicalities. "Well, Sam, no doubt you can move in at short notice. Grace, when will you be coming back from the States?"

"I'm staying. My things can be sent over to me, and my mother can have someone close the apartment for a while."

Paul raised his eyebrows. "Well, in that case, you can move in when you like. I'll have the gardener and cleaner kept on for the moment. All the bills are being sent here, so all you have to do is move in."

"Okay, I'm packed already, so today is fine by me."

#

Le Claire had to walk through the open-plan office to get to get to his own small private space. Wooden desks were jostled together, computer screens whirred through data and piles of papers looked as if they would soon topple over. The smell of strong coffee and pastries hung in the air—the debris from hastily consumed breakfasts by early-shift officers were strewn across tables.

"Hey, Le Claire—over here."

Le Claire suppressed a wince as he recognised the cocky voice. DI Bryce Masters was a walking advert for the States of Jersey Police. His suits hung beautifully on his tall, broad-shouldered frame. His black hair was always perfectly gelled into a modern style and his megawatt smile aimed to best advantage. He had even appeared in a few TV slots advertising police-driven community initiatives. Masters was also a smug bastard who frequently cut corners but always had a charming smile and a ready answer to get him out of trouble. Le Claire couldn't stand him.

"Masters, what's up?"

"Just wondered why you aren't busy? I mean, that girl of yours has been poking about in the strangest places. Some old dear gets drunk and falls off her balcony, and your DS is wasting her time, and ours, by asking stupid questions."

Le Claire didn't know what thought to process first—that an experienced female sergeant was being referred to as a "girl" or the fact that Masters had been involved in the case in question. Or maybe he'd just think about what an utter chump this guy was.

"Now, now, Masters, don't be falling foul of the new discrimination laws. As for the questions—I don't believe there is any law against making sure the department's cases get closed properly." Le Claire let the subtle reminder hang in the air. He outranked Masters.

"Bit of a comedown for you isn't it? From London gang wars to old grannies tippling on the sherry brandy and taking a nosedive."

Masters's ill-mannered description and mocking laughter followed Le Claire as he walked to his office. He would not rise to the bait—he couldn't. For if he did, he'd lash out, and that was something he definitely didn't need on his record again.

"Sir—wait, sir."

Dewar had burst into the offices like a whirling dervish and was making a beeline for him. It never seemed to amaze him that Dewar, who certainly wasn't overweight, clumped around on loud, heavy feet, especially when she was in a determined mood.

Dewar followed him into his office. "I spoke to one of the specialists at the Diabetic Clinic sir. Apparently, Mrs Avery had recently had her annual checkup. There was nothing out of the ordinary. Given the amount of insulin that was in her bloodstream, she'd need to have injected almost a whole vial. The doctor I spoke to said that he couldn't see any way that could be done by accident."

"What are we looking at? A suicide?"

"Perhaps. However, one thing did seem puzzling. The doctor said that the insulin would have worked quickly on Mrs Avery. She was careful with what she ate and kept her mealtime dosages relatively low. She was taking, on average, twelve units with her supper. The amount of insulin she must have taken would have started shutting down her senses pretty quickly. He can't see how she could have been alert enough to unscrew, remove and discard the needle."

"But we know it was removed. Well done, Dewar. Keep digging. I don't like loose ends."

#

Grace checked out of the hotel and took a cab to Rocque View, giving her a chance to marshal her thoughts. She had three months to consider what to do next, but her old life wasn't an option, certainly not the Carter part.

Sam's Jeep was already parked in the courtyard, as was a dark blue BMW, which she assumed belonged to Paul. Before she was properly out of the cab, Sam had appeared, paid the driver, gotten her luggage out of the boot and closed the car door after she'd exited. Grace was too tired to make any objection to his high-handed ways.

Paul walked round from the gardens, gave them each a set of keys and wished them well. To Grace, he said, "Why don't you come to dinner at my place next Saturday? You'll have had a week to settle in. Sam, you're invited too."

A middle-aged couple walked up behind Paul, and he formally introduced Grace and Sam to Mr and Mrs De Freitas, the couple who looked after the house and gardens on a part-time basis.

Belying her Portuguese surname, Fiona De Freitas was a fifty-something Irish colleen. If her russet hair and sparkling green eyes didn't give away her birthplace, it was born out as soon as she opened her mouth and spoke in her soft brogue.

"Sam, good to see you. Miss Howard, please accept our condolences. Kate was a marvellous woman."

"Please call me Grace, and thank you for the kind words."

"I come and clean the house once a week, and Luca spends a couple of mornings in the garden. He'll also do any odd jobs you have." Her husband, Luca, looked to be in his early fifties, a sturdy man of average height with tightly curled black hair that was tipped with silver. His swarthy complexion was darkened from working in the sun.

"Our telephone number is on the board in the kitchen. Just call if you need anything. We only live five minutes away."

Paul and the de Freitas said their good-byes and left Grace and Sam alone.

"Right," said Sam. "Let's tour the house and pick a bedroom."

"A bedroom?" Grace squeaked.

"Sure, a bedroom for each of us. What did you think I meant?" As this remark was accompanied by a broad wink, Grace figured Sam was teasing. So she ignored him, again.

#

Sam dragged Grace around the house until her head was spinning.

In addition to the ground-floor lounge, there was also a large and airy bedroom suite and a glossy utility room, which had a door leading to a courtyard filled with trees and shrubs.

On the first floor was a large kitchen that opened onto a modern spacious lounge with magnificent sea views, along with a master bedroom suite, cloakroom and study.

However, it was the magic of the top floor which literally took Grace's breath. A long corridor opened onto a small central sitting room. Off each end lay a bedroom suite. The front wall of the sitting room was made entirely of glass, overlooking the gardens and the sea beyond.

Sam broke into her thoughts. "Why don't you have one of these rooms? That way you have the sitting room and a little more privacy. This was the final part of Kate and Sam's remodelling and really was the icing on the whole project."

"Thanks, this will be perfect."

"Okay, I'll let you get settled in. I've dumped my bags in the first-floor bedroom. I'll unpack later. I've got to go to a meeting now, but I'll be home soon. You'll be okay, won't you? On your own, I mean."

"Of course. See you later, Sam."

#

As she started to unpack Grace's attention was caught by an old, faded photograph that sat atop the dresser. A smile of recognition lit her face. She must have been about four years old in the photograph, which looked like it had been taken near her maternal grandparents' summer place.

Kate had come to visit and had dutifully taken her small great-niece to the beach. A whisper of memory struggled to the surface, the image clearing as Grace recalled the day captured in the photograph.

Grace was babyish and plump in a frilled bathing suit, Kate demure in a plain black one-piece. They wore huge, floppy sun hats and dark glasses. At the time, Kate had seemed so old to Grace.

Blood in the Sand

With the passing of the years, and her own maturity, Grace saw that Kate, then in her fifties, had been a handsome woman, physically fit and in her prime. Samuel hadn't accompanied Kate on the vacation, and Grace supposed he had either been busy with his business or renovating this house. Whatever the reason, Grace had relished being the centre of her great-aunt's world for a few weeks. She smiled as she looked at the pose struck by her younger self, a mirror of Kate's.

Kate had said they were bathing belles, with hands on hips, shoulders lifted and pouting mouths air-kissing the camera. A rush of memory almost overwhelmed Grace. It was as if she could actually smell the tang of the Atlantic breakers, feel the shingled beach between her toes, the cooling breeze blowing her curls across her face.

Grace gently ran a finger over the photo, tracing the lines of her aunt's beloved features. Kate had loved her, truly loved her, and in wanting Grace to spend time at Rocque View had surely wanted her to enjoy all it had to offer. Perhaps it was also a challenge? Could Grace, a product of her mother's influence, just simply enjoy life?

CHAPTER FOUR

Grace lay on her new bed, wrapped in a bath towel, gazing through the long windows towards the sea. As she was on the second floor of the house, her view was simply endless—clear blue sky and the sparkling turquoise sea.

The bed, the pillows and the duvet were so soft and cocooning that Grace was drifting off. Perhaps she needed a couple of hours of sleep, blocking out the situation with Carter and numbing the pain for a while. Her closing eyes flicked open at the jarring noise of her ringing phone. Grace hesitated as she saw the caller ID, but she decided she'd best get it over with.

"Hello, Mother."

"Is that all you have to say, Grace?"

Her mother's clipped vowels and precise diction dripped ice through the phone.

"Well..." Grace began.

"Can you even begin to imagine how I felt when I heard your voice mail? What on earth possessed you to break up with Carter, and you say you're staying in England? Nonsense!"

"Jersey, Mother, not England. Jersey isn't part of the UK; it's a dependency—quite separate."

"Who the hell gives a damn!"

Grace was shocked at this lack of control, the display of passion. That never, ever happened. Within moments, her mother had regained her coolness.

"Forgive me, Grace. I am quite naturally upset. I trust you'll see the error of your ways and be home soon to sort out this terrible mess. Poor Carter must be so distraught."

"I'm not coming back. I told you in my message that I'll be staying in Jersey for a while."

A furious huff of breath preceded her mother's next words. "Don't be ridiculous. What about Carter? What about work?"

"Carter is having an affair. He wants to be with his lover, who happens to be my assistant. I obviously can't face them, so going back to work is out of the question. Are you satisfied?"

There was a long silence on the other end of the phone.

"Mother, are you still there?"

"Yes, yes, I am. But isn't staying away just playing into this woman's hands? You're leaving the coast clear for her. You must come home and fight for Carter."

"No." Grace didn't think she had ever said that to her mother before, so she said it again for good measure. "No, Mother. Carter hasn't been stolen. He wants her, not me, and I am happy to leave it at that."

"But—"

"Will you help me with closing my apartment temporarily, or should I call someone else?"

"No, Grace." Her mother's voice sounded weary. "I'll take care of everything. I just don't understand you, I really don't."

"Maybe that's the problem, Mother."

And with that, Grace hung up.

#

Dressed in loose cotton pants and an off-the-shoulder baggy T-shirt, Grace made her way downstairs. As she passed the open kitchen door, she glimpsed several foil-covered dishes on the counter. She lifted the cover off a large platter and saw a fabulous salad. Sam must've been busy.

Grace wandered outside. Sam was nowhere in sight. The water in the pool sparkled in the early evening sun. A cloth-covered table had been set for two on the terrace. The colourful pottery and glassware made for informality. A silver ice bucket held a bottle of white, and an open bottle of red wine had been left on the table to breathe. Pink-and-turquoise-striped cotton cushions were scattered on the chairs.

Although Grace wondered at Sam's motives for creating such a perfect setting for... well, whatever he had in mind... she felt a twinge of guilt as she realised how busy he'd been whilst she'd been relaxing.

"Did you manage to get yourself settled in?" Sam walked out of the house. His hair was damp, and he wore faded jeans and a plain T-shirt.

"Yes, thank you. However, I feel incredibly guilty that you've gone to so much trouble. Thank you." Grace indicated the beautifully laid table.

"Afraid I can't take any of the credit for this. Mum called earlier and asked what we were doing tonight. When I told her we didn't have anything planned, she said you—not me, mind, but you—shouldn't have to lift a finger after all you've been through. She dropped off some seafood and salad. She must have set the table and put the wine out at the same time. She's nothing if not thorough."

"Wow. What a mother! Mine would've ordered in catering and sent the maid over but still would have wanted all the glory."

At Sam's gentle laugh, Grace wondered where that comment had come from. She normally never criticised her mother. But now her old life seemed a bit regimented, maybe a little false and—this gave her pause—maybe also a little bit cold.

"Mum's reward will be knowing she did something nice for us, that we'll have an easier night because of her efforts."

Grace arched an eyebrow. "Hmmm, you sure you're not a mummy's boy, Sam Avery?"

"I might be, Grace. I just might be."

There was a brief silence, and the peace of the garden seemed to envelop them. The rustling of the gentle sea breeze through the leaves of oak, birch and bay trees was overlaid by the intermittent background sounds of nature and the neighbourhood all around them.

Sam broke the quiet. "Why don't you pour us both a drink, and I'll nip upstairs and get the food."

Grace happily agreed and, taking a seat at the table, poured two generous glasses of the straw-coloured wine.

#

Several hours later, Grace and Sam sat laughing together as they surveyed the debris on the table. They'd moved on to the cheese and a seriously good red.

Sam indicated the long, slouchy outdoor sofa that lay at one end of the pool. "Let's go and sit on the comfy chairs."

As the sun had sunk lower in the sky, Sam had switched on the garden lights, which were hidden amongst the dense foliage, casting shadows and illuminating the trees with an ethereal glow. The pool lights had also come on, shining brightly underneath the water and catching the ripples, reflecting undulating shimmers of light against the white walls of the house.

Grace rose to her feet and followed Sam, aware that she was a trifle unsteady. She'd had three glasses of wine, and that was one more than usual.

Sam carried both their glasses, stems entwined, in one hand as he reached out and offered his free hand to Grace. She took his a little self-consciously as he drew her towards the sofa. Grace released his hand with a murmured "thank you" and sank onto the well-padded seat. She propped a couple of jewel-coloured cushions behind her back and, shuffling to get comfortable, toed off her shoes and brought her bare feet up to tuck them by her side.

Sam sat on the other side of the couch, his long, jean-clad legs stretched straight out in front of him. He leaned back and gazed up at the clear sky.

"So, tell me, Grace, what's wrong? Why did you stay? Why the change of heart?"

Grace laughed, a short, sharp, brittle sound.

"That just about sums it up nicely, Sam. It *is* all about a change of heart; but not mine. No, not mine."

Grace's tone was wistful as she reached across to the coffee table and grabbed her glass, taking a sip of her wine.

"Whose change of heart was it?"

Grace was tired. She'd lost Kate—someone she had truly loved. Her love life lay in ruins. She had a suspicion that she may have messed up her career, and suddenly she didn't have a damned idea as to who she was. If she wasn't the future Mrs Carter Lawson, up-and-coming lawyer, then who was she?

Her whirling emotions, coupled with the liberating effects of the wine, lowered her reserve and loosened her inhibitions and then, finally, her tongue.

"Carter. It's Carter's heart that has changed."

"Carter?"

"My fiancé," Grace faltered. "Ex-fiancé, I guess."

She held out her left hand and examined the emerald ring, a large square-cut stone surrounded by twelve flawless diamonds. The ring certainly made a statement, even if it was a false one.

Her voice was hollow. "This will have to go back. It was his grandmother's."

"What a cheapskate. He couldn't even buy you a new ring, had to pass on an old hand-me-down."

Grace looked up in surprise, a smile escaping her. "Very droll. Anyway, this secondhand beauty will no doubt shortly be required to grace the hand of my ex-assistant."

"So his cheating crossed over into your workspace—what a moron!" Sam's disgust was evident.

"Yes. So I have no fiancé and no job—I can't go back to work there; the fallout would be huge. Anyway, that's why I've stayed. Not because I wanted to, or even because I felt I had to, but because I don't have a life to go back to—not anymore."

"I am sorry to hear that, Grace, but their loss is our gain. We're doing the right thing by Kate. I think I would always have regretted it if we hadn't at least tried to follow her wishes."

"I know. Even though my mind is in a muddle, I am happy that we're doing what Kate wanted."

"It's only a few months. Then the house can be sold, and you can do whatever you want with your life."

What did she want? A feeling of uncertainty and not a little trepidation swept over Grace, which she quickly brushed aside. Suddenly, she felt so very tired. A culmination of the upheaval of the last few days and several glasses of wine saw fatigue sweep over her, and her eyelids started to close.

Noticing, Sam rose and gently pulled Grace to her feet.

Grace felt a tingle as Sam's fingers clasped her own. Wanting to break the physical contact as soon as possible, she jumped up a little too quickly. She stumbled, and as she reached out to steady herself, she crashed solidly against Sam's chest.

With lightning-quick reflexes, Sam's arms came around Grace, his steady palms resting on her back, waiting until she had regained sound footing.

Grace pulled away and tilted her head back. As she opened her mouth to apologise for her clumsiness, Sam's arms tightened, his hands pressing deeper against her back as he bent his head and pressed a soft kiss on her lips.

A fleeting brush of lips, so quick Grace could scarce believe it had happened. Sam pulled back and stared into Grace's astonished eyes. To her dismay, he ignored the obvious question in them.

"Good night, Grace. You must be shattered. Go to bed. I'll clear up." With that, he gently steered her towards the house.

#

Long after the house lay in darkness, a dark figure prowled through the garden. The silence of the night was broken only by the occasional ruffling of the breeze through the leaves.

The full moon flooded the garden with a preternatural light, forcing him to hug the shadows as he slowly crept around the perimeter. He stopped occasionally to inspect the ground, but the light prevented him from searching too far. He hadn't been able to resist, not now that he was so close to the end. All the planning and conniving had been worth it—or would be soon. He always had a Plan B.

CHAPTER FIVE

The next morning, Grace sat on the first-floor balcony with a cup of coffee, pen and notebook in hand as she jotted down a list of the clothes she'd need to buy. She had called her mother back and asked her to send some things, but they probably wouldn't arrive for another week, so she'd have to buy the essentials. She glanced at her watch. Susannah Avery had called and asked her to join them for Sunday lunch at their favourite restaurant, and Grace had happily accepted. She had at least a half hour before she would need to start getting ready. Sam wasn't even back yet. He had gone for a run and said he'd be back in plenty of time to get ready.

A movement through the trees to her right caught Grace's attention. A car was coming up the drive. She rose and went to investigate, her curiosity piqued.

She opened the front door just as a shiny silver convertible drew to a halt in the courtyard. A pretty brunette jumped out of the car, leaning back into the passenger seat to grab a large leather tote. Straightening, she came towards Grace with a beaming smile and outstretched hand.

"I'm Emma Layzell from Layzell Estates. We're property agents. Are you Grace Howard?"

"Yes, I am. How can I help you?"

The response was blunt. "Rocque View. I have a client who is extremely interested in acquiring this property."

"Come in, Miss Layzell. There's no need to have a discussion on the doorstep."

Emma Layzell followed Grace into the downstairs lounge.

"Call me Emma. I'm actually due to update the client and thought it would be good to have a quick one-to-one with you to check the current position."

"And you would understand the current position to be... ?"

"I've sent a letter to the executor and advised that there is an excellent offer on the table. But I thought it best to speak to the new owners as well."

Grace wondered if the girl was fishing for information. "And how would you know who inherited this house?"

"The buzz is that you and Sam Avery inherited everything. You live in the States, and Sam has an amazing beachfront penthouse. In any event, this place is too big for him as a bachelor. So I did my sums, and two plus two equals a quick sale and a nice lump of cash for each of you. Yes?"

"No. I'm afraid your calculations are a little off. What do you mean by your comment that people know about the contents of my aunt's will?"

Emma laughed in genuine amusement. "This is Jersey. Nothing stays a secret for long, especially when your Aunt Harriet is involved."

"What do you mean? Do you know Harriet?"

"To be perfectly blunt, I know her as well as I'd like to. Your aunt is quite prickly, and, if I'm honest, I usually give her a wide berth. She was holding court at a champagne bar in town last night. She was telling anyone who'd listen that she'd been done out of a fortune by two snivelling brats. That'll be you and Sam."

Emma turned serious, laying a hand on Grace's arm. "Don't be concerned. Most people know that Harriet is a total bitch, and the Averys are a well-respected family. No one's going to believe anything bad about Sam."

"What do you mean by that?"

Emma looked as if she had said too much. "I am sure it was just Harriet being her usual self—mean and spiteful and lashing out. Saying she heard Sam needed money. Nothing really."

From Emma's closed-mouth expression, it was obvious that she wasn't going to say more. She stood to leave, and Grace escorted her downstairs.

As Emma's car drove away, Sam came jogging up the drive. His baseball cap, pulled low, shadowed his face, but Grace took her fill of his muscular form in running shorts and a sleeveless tee.

"What did Emma Layzell want?"

"Rocque View, apparently. You know her?"

"A little. What did she say?"

Grace quickly told Sam all.

"I'm sure the buyer will still be there in three months." Yes, thought Grace, there was that at least. The end was in sight, but then what would she do?

The restaurant was already busy when they arrived. A few inside tables were occupied, but it was those out on the long, wide terrace that were filling up fastest.

A middle-aged woman approached them, a beaming smile on her round face.

Sam gestured to Grace. "Ellen, this is Grace Howard, Kate's great-niece.

A look of sympathy flashed across the older woman's eyes. "I am very sorry for your loss, my dear. I saw you at the funeral. Why don't you head out and have a drink at the bar? I've reserved some places for you. Richard, perhaps you'd lead the way?"

As Sam and Grace followed Richard onto the terrace, Ellen placed a hand on Susannah's arm, and, heads bent, the women quietly shared a few words.

Susannah soon joined the rest of them on the long sofas that overlooked the wide expanse of golden beach. As she sat down and accepted a glass of white wine from the waiter, her face was tight. She took a sip of her drink and, carefully making eye contact with Grace, addressed all three of them. "Ellen just told me that Harriet has booked a table for lunch today. Our table is for one o'clock. Harriet's is for one thirty." She reached out and placed a comforting hand on Grace's arm. "We can leave and go somewhere else if you'd like. It's no problem at all."

Susannah's announcement was met by silence as all eyes turned towards Grace, who slowly shook her head. She wasn't going to hide. "No, I don't think so. Thank you, Susannah, but I don't see why we should have our arrangements changed just because of Harriet. If it's okay with you, I would rather stay here."

The day had taken an unexpected turn. There was a palpable sense of tension as the subject was changed and they quietly conversed about inconsequential matters.

Grace had occasionally heard her grandmother and father speak of the troublesome Harriet in the past. Her late grandmother had usually become agitated and a little bewildered at the latest antics of her youngest sister, which were succinctly detailed in Kate's frequent letters.

Grace felt a knot in her stomach, which she desperately tried to ignore as she sought to keep her thoughts away from what the apparently volatile Harriet might do once she saw them.

#

The food ordered, Ellen led the foursome to a beautifully laid table that sat in a prime position overlooking the beach.

Grace spoke to Susannah, who was sitting across from her. "It is very rude of me not to have done so already, but I must thank you for a lovely meal last night. It was really kind of you."

Susannah beamed in pleasure at the compliment. "Thank you, dear, but I can truthfully say it was my pleasure. Sam is so independent that I am afraid I couldn't resist taking advantage of your being here to spoil you both a little."

An icy voice interrupted their gentle conversation. "How unsurprising—the conspirators all together."

Harriet's voice, dripping venom, was louder than needed and carried across the terrace. Several other diners glanced in their direction and then looked away, not wanting to become involved in the unfolding scene.

Susannah was quick to respond. "I doubt it's a surprise, Harriet. Richard and I lunch here most Sundays, as you well know."

Harriet ignored the return volley and focused her attention on her direct targets: Sam and Grace. "I just thought you'd like to know that I'm not happy about being cut out of Kate's will. I'm instructing lawyers. Kate can't have been in her right mind."

Harriet leaned towards the table, menacingly hovering over Grace. "I'm going to tie the estate up so tight that you won't get a penny until I get what is due to me. You won't be able to sell Rocque View, and you can keep your sticky little fingers away from everything else. I deserve a fair share."

Richard's voice cut across her. "That's quite enough, Harriet. It was Kate's decision and indeed her right to leave her estate as she felt fit. She owed you nothing. In fact, you benefited more than enough from her generosity over the years. Kate stopped bailing you out a long time ago—she knew she was throwing good money after bad. Go to the lawyers, do your worst. It's all we'd expect of you anyway. Now please just leave us alone."

An unbecoming flush had slowly stolen across Harriet's face, her mouth pinched in rage at being dismissed so easily.

Grace said nothing. She was struck silent, trembling slightly at the anger radiating from her relative.

A gruff voice said, "Come on, Harriet. I said this was a bad idea. Never mind them." Ray Perkins steered her away to their table, which was tucked away at the far end of the terrace.

Susannah managed a smile. "Good on Ellen. Look, she's tucked Harriet as far away from us as possible."

A sudden commotion drew their attention. Ellen had approached Harriet and her escort and was leading them inside the restaurant. A minute or so passed, and then a grim-faced Ellen approached the table and quietly said, "Harriet was totally out of order. I won't have her coming here and causing a scene and spoiling the day for everyone. She'll have to get her lunch—and her kicks—somewhere else today."

Susannah reached out and affectionately patted Ellen's hand. "That is so kind of you. Thank you."

"Not kind, more like self-preservation. Harriet's a nasty drunk, and knowing her, she wouldn't have finished lunch sober."

#

A young man approached their table as they sat sipping coffee. He was tall with an athletic build and dark hair cut close at the sides but slightly longer on top. An aesthetically handsome face with a generous mouth was toughened by shadowed stubble around the jawline and the merest hint of a moustache, all set off by a deep suntan. His eyes scanned the table as he spoke. "How is everyone? I hope there wasn't an issue with Harriet Bellingham. I couldn't help overhearing."

Sam responded, "We're fine, James, just family business."

Grace flicked a glance at Sam. Coldness had entered his voice.

The man smiled affably. "Oh, okay". He turned to Grace, and there was sympathy in his eyes.

"Miss Howard, I didn't get a chance to speak to you at the funeral. I'm James Grayling, and I was so sorry to hear about your Aunt Kate. She was a wonderful lady."

"How did you know my aunt?"

"My business is restaurants, and Kate often used one of my town premises to run some charity events. She was a lovely lady to work with. It's been good to meet you. I assume you'll be going back to the States soon?"

"I've changed my plans. I'll be around for a while."

Surprise briefly crossed James's face, and Grace saw a flicker of interest. "That is wonderful news. If it's okay, can I give you a call sometime and we'll grab a bite to eat?"

Grace was slightly taken aback. The last thing she needed was a date. Did he mean a date? No, surely he was just being friendly. "Sure. I'm staying at Rocque View."

Grace fished in her bag for a card with her cell number and handed it to James.

"Great. I'll be in touch." James briefly glanced at the card and pocketed it. "I had better get back to my friends. I hope you all enjoy the rest of your day."

As James strolled away, there was a brief silence. Sam's face was unreadable as he said, "Well, you've got a date. He's quite well-off, I hear. Suppose he's handsome enough, if you go for those sort of bland looks."

Susannah laughed, a motherly, understanding sound, and turned to Grace. "Sam and James were at school together. I don't think they've ever got over their boyhood rivalry."

"Anyway," Grace said with finality, "it isn't a date. That is the very last thing on my mind."

CHAPTER SIX

Harriet lay sprawled on her sofa. She'd had a bitch of a day. She'd let that cow Ellen know exactly what she thought of her. Throwing her out of the restaurant like that—damned cheek. As for those two little suck-ups, Sam and Grace, they'd known which side their bread was buttered on. Why else would they have acted as if they actually liked that old biddy Kate?

And then there was Ray. They'd had words in the taxi on the way home, and he'd dropped her off at her place and said he may—*may*—see her later. She knew better. He'd come crawling around soon.

The doorbell rang, the shrill buzzer disturbing the quiet of the room. Harriet stumbled against the wall as she went to the intercom. Her solitary late lunch had been a bottle of merlot, and she was now well on her way to the bottom of another one, which would be all the dinner she'd have tonight.

She recognised the voice instantly. This should be interesting.

As she waited for her guest to arrive, Harriet caught a glimpse of herself in the ornate mirror that covered most of one wall in the long, narrow hallway. She looked old. With an all too rare clarity, Harriet saw—and understood—the bitterness that had driven her life etched into her face. All the Botox and nips and tucks in the world couldn't fully disguise that. But she'd try anyway. As soon as she got some money from Kate's estate—and she better—she was having the works done.

Harriet brushed her melancholy aside and tidied herself up. Running a finger under each eye, she rubbed away the smudged eyeliner and mascara, slightly wetting her finger to erase the stubborn marks. She ran a hand over her hair, trying to regain some of the order from earlier that day.

Harriet went to open the door, eager to find out what her visitor would have to say.

#

Le Claire pulled up the collar on his jacket as he stepped outside the police station, warding off the slight chill that was in the night air. Shoving his hands in his pockets and hunching his shoulders, he turned to cross the alley that led to the main thoroughfare. He'd pick up a takeaway and head back here to collect his car.

He could vaguely hear a murmur of voices in one of the deep, arched doorways that led to the storage buildings. The telltale pinpricks of burning embers and the accompanying heavy smoke gave the game away. Smokers having a secret puff, relegated to the outdoors.

Le Claire made to carry on, but he stopped in his tracks when he heard his name.

"What's your take on Le Claire? I mean, I can't get my head round why he'd come back to the island. It's not like we get many murders here, and he was supposedly heading up a homicide division at the Met."

"Maybe he just fancied a change of pace. London's not all it's cracked up to be."

"Nah. There's something suspicious about it, if you ask me. I heard there was an accident, and he was involved."

"Really? Come to think of it, I heard he screwed up big time on a major case."

Le Claire heard the unmistakable sound of police-issued shoes grinding cigarette butts into the ground and instinctively moved farther back into the shadows.

"Whatever it was, he's sitting pretty, isn't he? With his family, he's never going to be short of cash, and he's got the connections to make any issue disappear."

"What it is to be a rich boy, eh?"

Le Claire heard the echoes of their laughter as they walked away. His mood darkened as the damning memories flashed through his mind and the familiar guilt overwhelmed him. It had been weeks since he had allowed himself to think about what happened in London.

He wasn't surprised at his colleague's comments. No one would dare say anything to his face, but there were always rumours and speculation—especially when the gossip was based on fact.

#

Derek Lang had a problem. He was the caretaker at Harriet's apartment block, and she had rung him the morning before, a Sunday at that, complaining about a broken blind. She had demanded that he be at her door at 8:00 a.m. the next morning to fix it! Derek was the maintenance guy, but he was only supposed to deal with fixtures and fittings, not the occupants' own furnishings, and no matter how he looked at it, that meant it wasn't his responsibility if her fancy blind was broken.

Derek Lang was a nice chap, a hard worker and trusted employee. He was also absolutely terrified of Harriet and her abrupt mood swings, which is why he found himself knocking on Harriet's door at 8:00 a.m., as ordered. When there was no answer to his persistent knocking, he debated what to do. Should he let himself in? He had emergency keys. Would Harriet go ballistic if he just walked in? She might still be in bed. At the thought of an irate Harriet in her nightwear, Derek paled. Maybe he should come back later? As he dithered and prevaricated, fear rose to the surface. Fear over what Harriet would say if he didn't get her blind fixed propelled him forward. Using his master key, he cautiously entered the apartment.

Leaving the door open in case he had to make a quick exit, Derek called, "Miss Bellingham? It's Derek, Derek Lang. I've come to fix your blind. Miss Bellingham?" As the last notes of his voice were reclaimed by the silence, Derek moved farther into the apartment. Perhaps she'd gone out early, and if that was the case, she would want the offending blind mended and Derek gone well before she returned.

As Derek walked into the lounge, he blinked his eyes to adjust to the half-light. The blinds were closed tight against the morning sun, and it was difficult to make out much in the shadowed room. The air felt heavy and smelled slightly fetid, as if the windows hadn't been opened in a while. As his eyes became accustomed to the dark, he saw something out of place in the usually pristine apartment. One of the wooden dining chairs was upturned and lying against a low table, which was perched awkwardly on its side. Knowing the layout of the apartment, Derek reached out and felt along the wall nearest the door. His fingers fumbled around until he felt the cold metal of the light switch. A quick click and the room flooded with light.

As his eyes took in the scene in front of him, Derek's recognition system faltered. His eyes were frantically sending a message his brain was neither expecting nor accepting.

Harriet lay on her back in the middle of the floor, her arms stretched out to the sides and her legs bent awkwardly beneath her. Her head was turned to one side, the vivid red marks on her neck in stark contrast to the icy paleness of her skin. A splatter of bruises covered one cheek.

Derek stood in Harriet's lounge and screamed like a teenaged girl, a fact he would later manfully deny.

CHAPTER SEVEN

Le Claire drove into a scene of mayhem. Police cars were scattered throughout the apartment complex's parking area. A barrier had been set up blocking general access to the building, and the insubstantial yellow plastic cordon tape sagged and stuttered in the breeze; behind it ranged a group of people whose TV cameras marked them as media. Did nothing ever stay quiet in this island?

"Sir, over here."

Dewar, an anxious look on her face, rushed over to him.

"What's the score? Tell me what's happened."

"The caretaker, a Derek Lang, called it in. Apparently, he was almost incoherent on the call, and he's no better now. He's in the back of the ambulance having a lie down. It's brutal, sir—the victim was badly beaten."

"Who's in there now?"

"The crime scene guys have done the preliminary work, and Dr Viera is waiting for you so the body can be removed to the morgue."

"Okay, let's get on with it."

The crime scene investigators were inspecting the lift area, so they climbed the two flights of stairs. A uniform stood on guard outside the open apartment door, standing stiffer and taller as Le Claire approached.

The place was swarming with police, apart from the living area where Dr Viera stood next to the body, his voice low as he recorded his initial impressions on his phone.

"Viera. You got here quick."

"I was driving near here when I got the call. Bad business, Jack—really bad." His voice was strained.

Viera was an utter professional but still young enough that he hadn't faced many violent deaths in his line of work. His curling

48

dark hair and swarthy complexion were matched with a build more suitable to a rugby player than one of the island's finest medical experts. Dr David Viera was both.

"What have we got?"

"Female, mid-sixties. Blunt force trauma to the head and ligature marks around the neck, with severe bruising to the facial area. You'll need to get a Home Office Pathologist involved for the autopsy, as we can safely say this wasn't an accident. As they'll have to be flown in from London, it will be at least tomorrow before they can get to work."

Le Claire turned as Dewar walked into the room—he never once mistook that heavy-footed gait. He spoke without turning around.

"Who was she? What have you found out?"

"I talked to the neighbours. Her name was Harriet Bellingham. She had lived here for about five years. She was divorced but had been seeing someone for a couple of years, a Ray Perkins. I didn't get the feeling she was universally popular."

"Whether she wins a popularity contest or not is immaterial. Who's the next of kin?"

"Apparently, the elder sister has just passed away. No other relatives in Jersey apart from a great-niece who has come from America to attend the funeral. The lady next door said she was a Grace Howard, and I believe she was staying at the L'Horizon. The neighbour said Miss Bellingham had a moan about that in case it was being paid for by the estate."

"Okay, call the hotel and try and track her down."

Le Claire noticed that Dewar's face looked even grimmer than normal. "Sir, I'm afraid there is a problem. You better come with me."

He followed Dewar into the hallway and through an open bedroom door. There was a man sitting on the edge of the bed with a policeman hovering over him. The man's face was flushed, and the red stain reached up and covered his bald head. His eyes were wild, and his breath was shallow and shaky. Le Claire looked to Dewar for an explanation.

"This is Ray Perkins, sir. Apparently, the caretaker called Mr Perkins before he made the 999 call. Mr Perkins was already here when the uniforms responded to the emergency call. He was in the room with the deceased."

Le Claire heard what Dewar was saying and also what she didn't voice. They had a contaminated crime scene.

#

Le Claire parked up at the station. He had instructed Dewar to meet him here, and they would drive to their next appointment together. First, he had to speak to his boss and so went straight to the senior management floor.

Detective Superintendent Michael Fleming was in charge of Crime Services and was Le Claire's immediate superior. In his late forties, he had a runner's build, a receding hairline and an uncompromising nature.

Le Claire entered the office after a perfunctory knock. "Guv, we've got a suspected murder. I've just come from the scene." He quickly updated him with the main particulars.

Fleming's face was grim and his tone abrupt. "I'm declaring you the SIO. Get an MIR set up and choose your team. You'll have the set budget for whatever you need, but keep it tight."

As the Senior Investigating Officer, Le Claire now had the authority to set up the Major Incident Room, second what manpower he felt necessary and give round-the-clock focus to solving, and closing, the murder enquiry.

It was a huge amount of responsibility and the first real challenge he had been faced with since the London issue. "Thank you, sir, I appreciate your confidence in me."

Fleming's face was unsmiling. "Just make sure it's not misplaced, Le Claire."

#

Susannah's car was loaded down with bags as she turned into Rocque View. "I have had a lovely morning. I do enjoy shopping, but it is so much fun when it is for someone else. As you can imagine, Sam has never wanted to willingly spend a day shopping with me!"

"Well, I have to say that if you had asked me my opinion beforehand, I would have said I'd be dreading trawling around the shops, but I have really enjoyed today. Thank you, Susannah."

The elder woman's pleased blush rode high on her cheeks. As they parked, Susannah's brows drew together. "What on earth do they want?"

Grace peered out the windscreen as she saw the black-and-white police car. What was going on? Not trouble, surely. What if something had happened to her parents?

The two women anxiously got out of the car as a man in a plain suit and a young woman in uniform turned from the front door. The man strode down the steps and came towards them. "Grace Howard?"

"Yes, may I help you?"

"Miss Howard, I am Detective Chief Inspector Le Claire, and this is Detective Sergeant Dewar."

Le Claire was dark-haired, and Grace figured many would consider him handsome. He was tall, certainly over six feet, with a lean and muscular build. Broad shoulders were shown to advantage by a well-cut, plain grey suit. His white shirt had crease lines along the front; either it was new or he had his shirts dry-cleaned and folded. His colleague was professionally immaculate from her neatly chopped dark brown hair to her shining shoes. Le Claire looked pointedly at Susannah, and Grace belatedly made the introduction. "Oh, sorry, forgive me, this is Susannah Avery."

Dewar ventured a brusque "hello," the Scots burr evident in the monosyllabic greeting as Le Claire stepped forward and asked, "May we take this inside?"

#

Grace led the way to the upstairs lounge. The air had turned heavy with an edge of tension—the police didn't turn up without a good reason. "Please take a seat."

Le Claire and Dewar remained standing as Grace and Susannah sat next to each other on one of the long sofas. Le Claire said, "Miss Howard, the manager at the hotel told us you were staying at this address. I am afraid I have some bad news. Your great-aunt, Harriet Bellingham, was found dead at her home this morning."

She couldn't find any words. Her brain wasn't processing what her ears were hearing.

Susannah was the first to speak. "What? Harriet is dead? I don't understand…"

Susannah's voice trailed off as an ashen-faced Grace quietly spoke, "This is shocking news, Chief Inspector. How did my aunt die? I had no idea she was ill."

Le Clare ignored the question. "Did you know Miss Bellingham well?"

"No. In fact, we met for the first time last week at my Aunt Kate's funeral." Realisation dawned. "God, who would believe it? Two sisters passing away within days of each other—and Harriet so much younger than Kate."

"I'm afraid that Miss Bellingham didn't pass away from natural causes. We have every reason to believe that she was murdered."

Grace's eyes widened. She heard a shocked gasp from Susannah. Grace paled and started to sway to the side. Susannah steadied her with a comforting arm. The policewoman went into the kitchen and returned with a glass of water. "Here. Sip some of this. It will make you feel better."

Grace gratefully took the glass and pressed it to her lips, taking small sips of the cold water. Slightly refreshed, composure returning, she said, "Please forgive me. It is just such a shock. I did not know Harriet well. I believe she had been estranged from her sisters for some time—that would be my Great-Aunt Kate and my late grandmother."

Le Claire nodded. "Well, if you are feeling up to it, we do have some questions." He looked pointedly at Susannah.

"Oh yes, of course. I should leave you. Grace, I shall be in the garden if you need me." As Susannah made to stand, Grace laid a restraining hand on her arm.

"Actually, Susannah, if it is all right with the Chief Inspector, I would rather you stayed."

Le Claire nodded his agreement. "That may actually save us some time."

Dewar stepped forward. "Miss Howard, when did you last see your Great-Aunt Harriet?"

"Yesterday. At a restaurant; I am afraid I don't recall its name."

"Bistro Blanc. It was Bistro Blanc," interjected Susannah, which won her a grateful smile from Grace.

Dewar continued, "Were you all there together?"

"No, but we did speak to Harriet—or rather, I should say she came to speak to us. I was with Susannah, her husband and their son, Sam. I am afraid that Harriet was not at all happy when last we saw her. In fact, she was incredibly angry."

Grace paused. The silence lengthened as Le Claire and Dewar patiently waited for her to carry on speaking. "As I mentioned, Harriet's elder sister, Kate, also passed away very recently. Kate Avery was a wealthy woman, and her estate was split equally between myself and Sam Avery, who was Kate's great-nephew by marriage."

Le Claire interrupted and turned to Susannah. "And Sam Avery is your son?"

"Yes, my husband was the nephew of Kate's late husband."

Grace sipped her water and then carried on. "Harriet was not pleased. In fact, I believe her expectations of receiving an inheritance from Kate were quite high. She seemed very disappointed that she was not a beneficiary of the will."

Le Claire seemed to carefully consider Grace's words. "When did Miss Bellingham first make these feelings known to you? At the restaurant?"

Grace's voice trembled at the memory of their first ugly exchange. "No, it was after Aunt Kate's funeral. Harriet was expecting the will to be read later that day. When I told her it had already been dealt with, she became enraged and went looking for Paul Armstrong, who was Aunt Kate's lawyer. They had words, and then Harriet left."

"And you didn't see her again until yesterday?" questioned Dewar.

"That's right. Harriet approached our table and made a bit of a scene. She left the restaurant shortly afterwards."

"Exactly what sort of scene did Miss Bellingham cause?"

Grace shook he head dismissively. "Nothing really, I guess. Harriet just let off some steam. She just made the atmosphere rather uncomfortable."

"In what way? What were her exact words?"

Grace frowned as she tried to visualise the distasteful exchange. "I cannot recall verbatim. I was shocked at such a vulgar display, and it took me a moment to catch up with what Harriet was saying. The gist was that she wasn't satisfied and was going to get some legal advice and block the estate whilst she sued for what she deemed to be her fair share."

Dewar's voice was even as she spoke, "That must have angered you, Miss Howard."

Grace looked at her in surprise. "No, not anger exactly, just disappointment that Kate's death was seen by her own sister as nothing more than an opportunity to get her hands on some cash. I don't know Harriet's circumstances, but surely she must have been desperate to take such a stance. I know the two weren't close, and if Kate had wanted Harriet to benefit, she would have said so."

Le Claire spoke up, "And what about you? Would it cause hardship for you if the estate was frozen until Miss Bellingham's claim had been reviewed?"

Grace's eyes sharpened as she realised where the questioning was headed, what avenues they were exploring.

With a snort of disgust, Grace responded, "My father is one of New York's foremost litigators. My mother is one of the East Coast Rotherams. Her family owns a chunk of New York State. I myself am also a lawyer. So no, the inheritance from Kate was neither needed nor looked for. However, as a lawyer, I uphold the right of the individual to dispose of their free property as they wish. I cannot see that Kate wished for Harriet to receive anything at all. Had the law decided otherwise, I would have conceded to any ruling."

Le Claire's only reaction was an almost imperceptible lift of one eyebrow. "Miss Howard, as an upholder of the very law we speak of, I am sure you appreciate that a woman has been murdered. We must do all we can, follow every lead, until the culprit has been apprehended."

Grace's anger deflated. "Of course, of course. Please accept my apologies if I seemed aggressive. You are right—my aunt is dead, and the important thing is to catch who did this."

Grace paused and thought about whether to say what she knew she ought to. She decided she couldn't hold back. "Inspector, I don't know who you have spoken to so far, but in my, admittedly short, acquaintance with Harriet, I don't believe she was particularly well liked. What has happened is dreadful, and I truly hope you swiftly catch whoever is responsible. I can't add any more but would, of course, be happy to assist in any way I can."

Sincerity rang in Grace's voice, and, seemingly satisfied, Le Claire turned to Susannah. "Mrs Avery, I have a few questions for you as well. How long had you known Miss Bellingham?"

"I have known of Harriet since Richard and I got married, which was almost thirty-five years ago. But we rarely came into contact with her."

Dewar stepped forward. "And why was that?"

"Harriet had not been close to Kate Avery for quite a while. I had not seen her at Rocque View in a long time. We occasionally bumped into each other in restaurants. That's it really. We didn't have the same circle of friends or interests."

"And when did you last see Harriet?"

"When we were at lunch yesterday."

Le Claire asked, "And do you have anything further to add to Miss Howard's account of the interaction with Miss Bellingham?"

"No. Harriet was aggressive and throwing threats around, but quite frankly, that was only to be expected. She wasn't going to take being left out of Kate's will without a fight."

"And how do you feel about being overlooked?"

"Overlooked? You mean the will? Richard would never have had any expectations. I know my husband very well indeed."

"Thank you, Mrs Avery. Now where can we find your son?"

"He'll be at our offices, Avery Developments, in town. But what has Sam got to do with any of this?"

Le Claire replied, "Just routine, Mrs Avery. Your son was with you at the restaurant and is also one of the two beneficiaries of what Harriet Bellingham believed was partly her inheritance. Thanks for the information. We'll be on our way."

Le Claire stopped by the door and glanced towards the balcony and pool area. "Miss Howard, your great-aunt who passed away last week, was that the lady who recently died from a tragic fall?"

"Yes, that's correct."
"I thought so."

#

They took their leave of the two women, who sat huddled together, silent and stunned at the tragic development.

As they settled in their car, Le Claire said, "Let's get going. We've got work to do in sifting through the Bellingham case. Get a move on with looking into Kate Avery's death. It's a bit of a coincidence that two apparently healthy sisters died within a week or so of each other. Especially when there is a lot of money involved. And you know I never like coincidences. But first, let's catch up with Sam Avery."

CHAPTER EIGHT

Sam Avery roughly ran his hand through his already tousled hair, then slapped the palm against his brow, elbow planked on his desk. He just needed the numbers to add up. Why didn't they add up?

He'd been sitting in his glass-fronted corner office for over two hours. He hadn't been able to schedule any of his usual meetings with architects, owners or contractors. Just him, a screen filled with red-lined spreadsheets and a massive headache.

Sometimes he wondered if he was ready to get more involved in the financial side of the business, a stepping stone towards one day taking over. His dad thought he was. That's why, Sam thought sourly, he was stuck in front of his screen today whilst his Dad had been out and about checking on their various projects. Sam smiled. He really couldn't resent him for having the opportunity to do something that years of managing the company had robbed him of. Engaging with their stakeholders and talking to people, motivating them, selling their business and reassuring clients. His dad had been doing a lot more of that over the past couple of years.

The buzzing of his telephone let him know that his personal assistant, Sarah, was on the other end of the line. Sam sighed. He had asked not to be disturbed.

He picked up the handset. "Hi, Sarah, what's up?"

"There is a Detective Chief Inspector Le Claire and his colleague to see you." Sarah then added helpfully, "They're from the police."

Sam raised an eyebrow. The police! What did they want?

#

Le Claire and Dewar were shown into the spacious office. At a glance, Le Claire took in the modern furnishings and expanses of glass—an expensive and well-designed space. He stepped forward. "I am DCI Le Claire, and this is DS Dewar. Thanks for taking the time to see us."

"Absolutely no problem, although I must confess I am curious as to what you want to discuss with me. Won't you take a seat? Can I get you anything? Tea or coffee, perhaps?"

Le Claire spoke quickly. "No thanks. We're fine." He caught Dewar's glare out the corner of his eye and just smiled in victory. Dewar would drink endless cups of tea were she given the opportunity. And then he'd be stuck with her continually wanting to nip to the loo when all he wanted to do was get on with the job.

Le Claire took the lead. "Mr Avery, I am afraid there has been a fatality. Harriet Bellingham was found dead at her apartment this morning. We have every reason to believe she was murdered."

"Harriet? Murdered? Christ. That can't be true. Who the hell would do that?"

Dewar's tone was dry. "That's what we'd like to know, Mr Avery. We know that you and your parents had lunch with Miss Bellingham's great-niece yesterday. We also understand that there was an altercation."

"Well, I'd say the altercation was more *by* Harriet than *with* her. Look, I feel awkward speaking ill of the dead, but Harriet simply unleashed a torrent of abuse before she was asked to leave the restaurant."

"What do you mean by abuse?"

"Harriet was very upset that she had been left out of her sister's will."

"And why would that be?"

"Kate had washed her hands of Harriet for good; she was sick of bailing her out. Harriet has married well a couple of times—and divorced even better. Yet she runs through money like there is a never-ending supply. I understand that Kate had refused to give her anymore. They had a big showdown several months ago, and I believe they stopped speaking. Any show of grief from Harriet was crocodile tears. Kate and Harriet had fallen out a few times before, but they usually made up as Kate was so soft-hearted. Harriet obviously felt she was due something and was threatening to get lawyers involved to sue for a share of the estate."

Dewar asked, "And that would have bothered you?"

Sam Avery smiled, but it didn't reach his eyes. "Only if Harriet won. That would have stuck in my throat. Kate obviously didn't want to leave Harriet anything. If she had, Kate's will would have made provisions for her sister. She was a careful and organised woman. Kate wouldn't have mistakenly left out a bequest."

"And if the estate had been frozen until any claim was resolved? I guess that would have angered you, maybe even caused you hardship?" Dewar's voice was low and sympathetic.

"That would not make any difference to me."

Le Claire took over. "Really? I would have thought the inheritance from Kate Avery came at just the right time. Hasn't the largest investor just pulled out of your redevelopment project at the old docks? That's what the papers say. Surely Kate Avery's money is enough to plug the gap?"

"Not that this is any of your business—certainly not in relation to Harriet's death—but whether I, or indeed my father, had been left anything by Kate would make not one bit of difference to the docks development. The business has a strict financing rule, one we have never broken. We would not have used any personal money to—as you say—plug the gap."

"And what is this financing rule?"

"We provide the ideas, the architectural plans, the contractors— everything, in fact—but we only ever put up a maximum of two-thirds of the project cost. That money has to be in the business already. We do not mix personal and business funds. That way the risk is shared, but we retain control."

"But what if you don't replace the investor?"

"Then the project doesn't go ahead. Not until the financing is raised."

"I have to ask where you were from 2:00 p.m. yesterday until 8:00 a.m. this morning." Time of death hadn't been confirmed yet, but Harriet had last been seen at 2:00 p.m., and Derek Lang had found her just after 8:00 a.m. this morning.

"Are you being serious? Jesus!" With a sigh, he answered. "Okay. Fine. Lunch was a long one. After the past week, I guess we all needed to let off some steam. We were at the restaurant until seven or so. Grace, that's Grace Howard, and I got a taxi back to Rocque View. We had some coffee, watched TV for a bit and called it a night around nine thirty."

"I was not aware that you and Miss Howard had started a relationship."

"I am not in a relationship with Miss Howard. And before you get any ideas, nor were we indulging in any sexual antics, even as a one-off. Under the terms of Kate's will, which is quite complicated, Grace and I must stay at Rocque View for several months to preserve the house. So I had to move in there as well."

"Thank you, Mr Avery. We'll take our leave of you, but if you do think of anything else that could be important, please let us know." Le Claire handed out his card. "All my numbers are there." Le Claire and Dewar left the building, but Le Claire did not turn towards the parked car. Instead, he indicated for Dewar to follow him as he turned to walk through town. "Come on, I think we better have a chat with Kate Avery's lawyer. I want to know more about Kate Avery's will—a lot more."

Sam came home to the sight of both his parents drinking coffee with Grace. "So this is why no one was at your house when I called."

Susannah replied, "We tried you at the office, but Sarah said you had left. And that the police had been to see you?"

"Yes, I take it you all know about Harriet?"

Grace said, "It's horrifying. I realise that Harriet wasn't that popular, but murder? That's in a totally different league."

Richard turned to his son. "Did the police say if they have any idea who could have done this?"

"Actually, I think I'm quite high on their list."

Susannah bristled. "What! That's outrageous."

Sam spoke calmly, "Everything will be fine. They are bound to look at me closely because of the will and Harriet's threats. They even tried to insinuate that I was desperate for Kate's funds to replace the docklands investor who pulled out." He turned to Grace. "Unfortunately, we are each other's alibi."

Grace's voice was thoughtful. "I know how intrusive the law can be, Sam, and actually we can only alibi each other until nine last night. I am afraid that, as far as the police are concerned, either one of us could have left the house and killed Harriet."

#

Emma Layzell sat at her desk and tidied the last of her client files away. That was the last item on her to-do list. Actually, it should have been on her assistant's to-do list, but she had offered to help out. There was nothing more to waste time on. She had to make the call she had been dreading since yesterday morning.

She dialled the number from memory. It was answered after only a few short rings. There was silence on the other end.

"Hey, how are you doing? You'd already gone out when I called yesterday." Emma kept her voice light and cheerful. She didn't want to set things off.

"How did you get on?"

Emma took a huge breath—best get it over with. "It's true. She isn't going anywhere for the moment. She sounded like she wasn't playing around."

"Keep at her. I don't know if I can trust what she says. Rocque View was always meant to be mine."

#

Le Claire was ploughing through a towering pile of paperwork when there was a knock on his door, and in walked the head of the crime scene investigation unit. John Vanguard was in his late forties with prematurely grey hair, a narrow face and laughing blue eyes.

"I'm not intruding am I?"

Le Claire checked his watch. "Very amusing, Vanguard. It's not as if I've been waiting the last five hours for you—is it?"

Vanguard threw himself into the chair opposite Le Claire. "I've just finished up. Had a quick shower and came straight here. We'll get the report written up, but I wanted to update you straightaway."

"What have you got for me?"

"No forced entry. The door was opened by the caretaker before he found the body. The peripheral areas didn't give up much. Apparently, there was no suspicious activity in any room other than the living area. And that's where the problem is."

"The boyfriend?"

"Exactly. The fact that he contaminated the crime scene means that it will be nigh on impossible for anything we now discover to be admissible."

"If he is the murderer, I'd already assumed it would be difficult to prove that any evidence he left during the murder wasn't simply left over from a previous visit."

"That is right, but we have a bigger problem. When you find your murderer—and I know you will—a clever defence lawyer could argue that *anything* we now find could have been accidentally transferred to the scene by this Mr Perkins. We took him off, bagged his clothes for analysis and ran the usual checks."

Le Claire couldn't believe this. "That's a load of bollocks. Perkins could only have been there moments before the uniforms arrived."

Vanguard rose and made for the door, a look of sympathy on his face. "I agree with you, but it isn't my opinion that counts. I'm afraid a contaminated crime scene gives up no evidence. Sorry."

Le Claire watched him go and considered what his next step should be. If the crime scene wasn't going to give him any clues, then he'd better go and find some the old-fashioned way.

CHAPTER NINE

The next morning, Grace rose with the sun. She threw on her new trainers and running gear and headed outside. In New York, she was a park runner. Here, she simply crossed the road to the white sandy beach, momentarily pausing at the bottom of the steep steps that led from the roadside. There wasn't a breath of air, just complete stillness shrouded in quiet. The sunrise blazed fiery streaks across the light grey sky.

She briefly closed her eyes and took a few long breaths and then broke into a jog down towards the shoreline. Once she reached the water, she ran parallel to the tide as it washed over the sand.

With her rhythm in place, Grace went into automatic mode and simply ran. Ran from the betrayal of Carter, the insensitivity of her mother, perhaps even from her entire life in New York. Doing everything expected of her; doing nothing that she wanted. Grace ran but felt a momentary disquiet as she wondered what she was running to.

She had yet to deal with the grief of losing Kate, to come to terms with the oddity of that beloved woman's final wishes. If she was honest, Kate had come to her rescue. Her last will and testament would seem odd to some, but to Grace it had meant a reason not to return to New York. It gave her a reason to break free. The thought startled Grace—where had that come from?

Grace abruptly stopped running and stood still. As if blinkers had been wrenched from her eyes, she saw with clarity that her previous existence had been a stifling and unsatisfactory half-life in New York. A life she had barely given a thought to over the last few days.

She didn't actually miss Carter. In fact, she realised she hadn't given him a thought. Theirs had been a relationship that was bolstered by social expectation and boosted by their shared background. Not raw emotion.

And she just felt relief that she was free of work. She had sent the HR partner an email tendering her notice and explaining that, with the Carter and Gina situation, she felt it best that she didn't return. Grace had felt a pang for all the work they would have to pass on to others and the explanations to be made to clients, but, for once, she didn't give a damn. She felt free, as if an abundance of possibilities lay before her and all she had to do was choose the ones she liked best.

Grace was going to start living—living *her* life *her* way.

#

Le Claire strolled into police headquarters, coffee cup in one hand whilst the other held his suit jacket in place, which was casually slung over his shoulder. The sun was shining, and he was feeling positive today. His mobile rang.

He reached into his trouser pocket and pulled out the phone. The caller ID made him pause. Then he manned up and answered.

"Sasha, what can I do for you?"

"Do for me? That is a change. I mean, what have you ever done for me?" He could almost hear the vitriol fall like a thick slab as she continued to let rip. "What can you do for me? You can bloody well pull your finger out and sign the divorce papers."

Le Claire blanched. How could he have forgotten the papers from the solicitor? Obviously, the end of his own marriage didn't rate high on his radar. "Sasha, I'm sorry, but I've been tied up on a case, an important case." As Le Claire heard the sharp, guttural intake of breath, he knew he had misspoken.

"You utter bastard. You can't even pay attention to the death throes of our relationship. It's always, always been about the damned force..."

"Sasha, stop this. I'm sorry I forgot to sign the papers. It certainly isn't that I don't want to. You've made it patently clear you don't want us to be together."

"Together! Is that what you call what we had, what we were?"

Blood in the Sand

Sasha's voice broke, and suddenly, as if she stood right in front of him, Le Claire could feel the rage, the strength, the poison leave her. When she spoke, his wife sounded defeated.

"Jack, sign the papers. Please? I just need to move on."

Maybe he had remembered the divorce papers. Perhaps he just hadn't wanted to sign them, didn't want to make that final, irrevocable step. The pain in her voice reached a part of Le Claire he didn't want awakened.

So he answered in the only way he could, "Of course. They're in my office. I'll sign them and get them back to the lawyers today. That suit you?" He winced as he heard the faintest hint of petulance in his voice.

His wife's voice was weary. "It doesn't suit me, Jack. It doesn't actually suit me at all. It's just how it has to be. Bye."

After she showered, Grace went to the kitchen. She saw from the window that the drive was empty. Sam must've left for the day.

She settled down at the kitchen table with a mug of coffee and some cereal. Firing up her laptop, she started to draft an email to her parents. Grace hadn't let them know about Harriet yet. For one, she had been busy with the Averys around, and she knew her parents wouldn't be emotionally involved—they hadn't known Harriet after all—but her dad was involved in a massive litigation case that was at a key juncture. An email would make it easier for them to take it all in. Grace also had to admit to herself that she was avoiding her mother, who had left several increasingly frosty messages on her voice mail, all demanding to know just what Grace was going to do about Carter. Grace was going to do precisely nothing about Carter. There was nothing to do.

The ringing of her phone cut into her thoughts. It looked like a local cell number. At least it wasn't her mother, so she answered.

"Hey, Grace, it's James. James Grayling. I heard about Harriet. Such a tragedy."

Grace replied carefully. How she had felt about Harriet was her business. "Yes indeed. Quite shocking."

"I just wanted to pass on my condolences and ask if you'd like to join me for some dinner tomorrow night? I thought it might do you some good to get out and see some different faces. I mean, you don't have to if you don't want to, obviously. But I thought you might enjoy some dinner and a few drinks." His voice trailed off nervously.

Be brave, accept new things. New life, Grace thought. "Why, yes, actually. That would be lovely. Thank you."

She could almost hear his sigh of relief. "Great. How about I pick you up at seven? Do you like Italian? Or maybe Chinese?" The questions fired out.

Grace laughed as she replied, "Yes, yes and yes."

#

"Sir, there you are. I've been waiting for you." Dewar came bounding up to Le Claire, exhibiting a puppy-like enthusiasm that was quite unlike her usual dour nature. She was even smiling.

"Well, Dewar, what has got into you today? Surely you aren't happy? Come on, spit it out. And then you can get back to your usual miserable state." Le Claire knew his voice was waspish, but after talking to Sasha, he had to vent on someone. Although he had to admit to feeling a little shame that he was picking on his defenceless subordinate.

Dewar's smile faltered and fell back into her usual grim expression. "I was trying, albeit obviously failing, to express joy, sir."

"Joy at what?"

"At unearthing a potential serial killer."

Le Claire stopped in his tracks. "What the hell?"

Dewar looked slightly shamefaced. "Well, maybe not an actual serial killer, but," her voice grew serious, "I think we have another murder. You were right about Kate Avery's death, sir. It just doesn't add up."

"What have you found?"

Dewar's eyes lit up. "For a start, I checked with the evidence room. They had taken in several of the items from the scene, including the insulin injector pen."

"And?" Le Claire could feel the stirrings of anticipation.

"Well, with it seemingly being a tragic accident, no one looked any further. As you already discovered, the needle had been removed but wasn't picked up at the scene. Last night, I asked Harper in the lab to run a quick check on the injector. I just wanted to make sure there was only one set of fingerprints. I asked him to do a rush job, and the results are in."

"There were more than one person's prints?" Le Claire asked hopefully.

"No, sir. There weren't any prints at all. The damned thing was all but polished to a shine. The doctor said that given Kate Avery's slight frame, the massive insulin overdose would have started affecting her almost immediately. This backs up what the specialist said the other day. Plus, we know the disposable needle had been unscrewed and removed. Would an elderly woman in the throes of a hypoglycaemic reaction really have the time to remove the needle, discard it somewhere—as it wasn't on the balcony—and then needlessly wipe the injector pen?"

A broad smile lit Le Claire's face. "Well done, Dewar. Come on. We've got work to do. The case of Kate Avery's death is officially open and marked suspicious."

CHAPTER TEN

After his shock at hearing of Harriet Bellingham's death, Ray Perkins had been in no fit state to be interviewed the day before. Dewar had spoken to Perkins and organised for them to visit him this morning. Le Claire hadn't expected their meet to take place at the Three Bells pub.

The morning sun was swept away by the gloom of the dark-panelled bar. The barmaid, a middle-aged woman with tired eyes, had just finished opening up and pouring a whisky for her first customer of the day.

"Bit early for all that, isn't it, Mr Perkins?" Le Claire's voice broke the quiet of the almost empty bar.

Ray Perkins turned, eyes bloodshot and colour high, and answered with a grunt. Le Claire reckoned that the drink in his hand wasn't the first he'd had this morning. "Call me Ray. I'm in no mood to stand on ceremony this morning."

Ray perched on a stool by a high, round table, and Le Claire and Dewar followed suit.

Dewar's eyes were sympathetic as she turned to Ray. "I am sorry for your loss. I can assure you that we will do all we can to catch who did this. But first we need to draw a picture of Miss Bellingham's movements on Sunday. When did you last see her?"

"When she got out the taxi at her place, and I went home to mine. That bitch Ellen kicked us out of her place so she could keep sweet with the hoity-toity Averys and that little niece of Harriet's. I was glad to see the back of them. All they did was upset Harriet. We got in a taxi to go back to Harriet's, and she was going to make us some lunch there."

Le Claire picked up on the first point. "But you last saw Miss Bellingham getting out of the taxi. You didn't join her?"

Ray's face gave nothing away. "No. We had words, all right? Harriet kept going on and on about the will, and I said that if she hadn't been such a cow, asking her sister for cash every five minutes, then maybe old Kate would still have left her the place. I gave Harriet enough money—she didn't need any from that old misery. "

"Miss Bellingham really believed that she was going to inherit the property?"

"Harriet saw a copy of the will by accident. It was just before we met. She was watering Kate's plants whilst she was away for a few days."

Le Claire flicked a glance at Dewar and resisted the impulse to roll his eyes. He wondered how many drawers and cupboards Harriet Bellingham had rooted through to find a copy of her sister's will.

Dewar asked, "Did Miss Bellingham have any enemies that you knew of?"

"My Harriet was a lovely woman, but you know what people are like. They were jealous of her, and sometimes there would be the odd little argument, but nothing serious."

"Thank you. We're just trying to gauge who may have had a reason to harm Miss Bellingham," said Le Claire.

Ray's face reddened in rage. He banged his empty whisky glass on the table and spat out his words. "It's bloody obvious, isn't it? That girl and Sam Avery—either one of them would want Harriet out the way. Stands to reason, doesn't it? She was going to contest the will and get her due. Why haven't you arrested them yet?"

Le Claire kept his voice calm. "We are looking at all angles, and I can assure you we will determine who did this. Thank you for the information."

#

Grace headed towards the wooden gazebo. The white paint was peeling, but that didn't detract from its beauty. The little summerhouse had sat there for a very long time, an additional small haven in an already idyllic place. She sank into one of the cushioned chairs, leaned her head back against the wooden panelling and closed her eyes. Just for a moment... or two. Just to have a little peace and quiet.

"Hello there, how are you?"

Grace jerked upright as the voice crashed into the blissful silence that had washed over her. "What?" Blinking her eyes rapidly, Grace peered in the direction of the piercing voice, recognition in her eyes—followed by irritation.

Grace stood and walked towards her uninvited guest. "How may I help you?"

Emma Layzell smiled broadly. "It's more how I can help you, Grace. By the way, I was sorry to hear about Harriet. They say it was murder?"

Grace couldn't really do anything other than reply, but she did so coolly. "Yes, so they do."

Emma seemed to get the message and changed the topic. "Grace, I know you said Rocque View wasn't for sale, but my client—the one I told you about—has upped the offer quite a bit. So we were thinking—"

Grace cut her off, a New England frost in her voice. "I truly don't know how to make this any plainer. This property is simply not for sale. You really need to listen to me. There may be an opportunity in a few months, but right now there's nothing. So I am afraid you are wasting your time."

"Okay, okay. Can I ask that you keep my number and give me a call if you do want to sell this place?" Emma looked around wistfully, as if calculating the commission she'd receive on a unique property of this size.

"Of course," Grace said. "Now if you'll excuse me?"

"Sure, sorry to bother you." Emma turned to go and then paused. "Look, I am sorry about Harriet. She didn't deserve to go that way. Poor Ray. I was going to pop in on him on the way here to see how he was, but I thought maybe it was a bit too soon."

Grace paled. She had not given a single thought to Ray Perkins. He must be devastated about Harriet. She asked, "Does Mr Perkins live near here?"

"Yes, five minutes away. He owns one of the new apartments in the big white-and-grey block. It's on this side of the road down to your left. Ray's in number seven."

Grace was curious. "Do you know him well?"

"Not really. We sold him the apartment, and I've met him a couple of times."

"Oh, okay. Well, thanks for coming round."

"Have a good day, Grace, and let me know if you do decide to sell this place. My buyer is desperate to own Rocque View."

Grace watched as the estate agent walked to the front of the house. A few moments later, she heard the car roar off.

With a shake of her head, she walked into the house. She had better get changed. She had a visit to make.

#

Just under an hour later, Grace stood outside Ray Perkins's apartment block. The building looked new but was in the style of a Victorian seaside villa, the white-painted brick offset by grey-trimmed windows and door frames. It looked attractive and fresh. Unlike the man who answered the door to number seven.

Ray Perkins's eyes were red-rimmed and bloodshot, his face covered in greying stubble, which contrasted with his completely bald head. An old T-shirt strained across his stomach, which protruded over khaki shorts.

His eyes hardened as he recognised her. "What the hell are you doing here?"

Grace swallowed. She couldn't bear confrontation; but Ray Perkins was obviously hurting. "Mr Perkins, I'm Grace Howard. Harriet was my great-aunt. I just wanted to say how sorry I was to hear about Harriet and to see if you needed anything?"

Ray sneered. "Sorry? Are you? Well, that's a fine one from the New York princess. That's what Harriet used to call you. Said you were born with a silver spoon in each hand, and more just keeps coming to you, doesn't it?"

"I didn't come here to argue. I just wondered if you needed any help with the arrangements."

"What arrangements?"

"I meant the funeral. My family will be happy to cover any reasonable costs you have in giving Harriet an appropriate send-off. Or I can help with the organisation." It was the least she could offer.

Ray laughed. But it wasn't from joy or genuine amusement. His mirth was vicious and slightly threatening. "Typical. All you lot think about is throwing money at a situation. Well, that isn't any good to Harriet now. Some bastard killed her, and your money isn't going to fix that."

Grace turned to leave. "I am sorry. Perhaps you would be kind enough to let me know when the funeral will be?"

"There won't be a funeral; not for a while at least. The police won't release the body yet. So you can keep your precious money—Kate's money that should by rights have gone to Harriet. We waited a long time for that old bitch to die. Now fuck off. You're not wanted here." The door slammed in Grace's shocked face.

Sam arrived home around 5:00 p.m. He had plans for the evening, and he hoped they involved Grace. Just as he started to climb the stairs, the doorbell rang. It was Paul Armstrong.

"Sam, thank God you're in. I just got back from London—been there since yesterday morning—and I've just heard about Harriet."

"Come in, Paul. Take a seat, and I'll try and hunt down Grace."

A noise behind him made him turn. "I'm here. Sorry, I didn't realise we had company. I was just taking a nap." Grace looked distracted.

Paul came forward with outstretched arms and drew Grace into one of his bear hugs. He gave her a long, intense look. "Tough times, Grace. Both your great-aunts gone within a few weeks of each other."

"I just find it so hard to believe. I mean, murder? I just can't get my head around what reason another human being would have to murder Harriet."

Sam said, "Paul, you were saying you've been away?"

"Yes. I flew to London on yesterday's red-eye. On the way back, I got to talking to some of the other passengers whilst I was waiting to board. You know what it's like, you always recognise someone on these flights. And one of the chaps told everyone the terrible news. Everyone was shocked. I mean, you can count the number of murders we've had in Jersey in my lifetime on your fingers. And to hear it was Harriet..." Paul's voice was slightly shaky as his words trailed off.

No one spoke as they contemplated the fact that a murderer was on the loose. The ringing of the house telephone broke into the silence. "I'll get it," said Sam.

He left the others quietly talking as he answered the call. Grace and Paul stopped talking as he spoke. "Oh, hello, Chief Inspector. Yes, Grace is here. Actually, we have company. Paul Armstrong, Kate Avery's lawyer."

Sam was quiet as he listened to the policeman on the other end of the line. "Yes, that will be fine. See you then." He put down the phone.

"You probably heard, but that was the police. DCI Le Claire wants to talk to us, Grace. He's on his way. It's about Kate."

#

Barely ten minutes later, Le Claire and Dewar arrived. He introduced himself to the lawyer. "It is a happy coincidence that you are here, Mr Armstrong. We've been wanting to speak to you. But we can get to that later."

Le Claire carefully looked at all three of them. Grace Howard had opened the door to them, and now she sat on one of the long sofas. "Miss Howard, we have an update for you regarding Kate Avery's death."

She looked puzzled. "Please call me Grace."

He accepted the informality. "Grace, I am afraid I have some disturbing news. The States of Jersey police have officially opened the case into Kate Avery's death, and we are now treating it as suspicious."

Sam Avery said, "Jesus, you think Kate was murdered?" His face was ashen as he walked across to Grace and, sitting next to her, took her hand in his. Pale and shocked, she did not demur.

Paul Armstrong said, "This is shocking. Why do you think Kate was murdered? Is this connected to what happened to Harriet?"

Dewar kept his face noncommittal. "It is an avenue we are exploring."

Grace gasped and slowly shook her head from side to side. "This can't be true. Why? Why would someone do this? And to Kate, of all people." She turned into Sam Avery's arms and started to sob. He ran a consoling hand down her back as Le Claire spoke.

"I won't keep you further at the moment, but we will need to speak to you again. Please do let us know if you think of anything, no matter how small, that could be helpful to our investigation. Mr Armstrong, I would like to talk with you—sooner rather than later."

"Of course. Actually, I've just come from the airport. But there is no time like the present. If you follow me into town, we can speak in my office."

Le Claire rose, motioning for Dewar to do the same. "That's perfect. Shall we?" He cast a hand towards the front door.

Grace had composed herself and stood to shake their hands. Her voice trembled a little. "Please forgive my outburst. Just such a shock."

"We'll let you know more tomorrow. I just wanted you to be aware of this development as soon as possible."

As Sam closed the door, Grace turned towards the stairs. "I can't take this in. I think I'll lie down for a little while."

Sam stalled her with a hand to her wrist. "There's something I wanted to ask you, but the timing seems off now." Sam looked almost uncertain. "I'm meant to be meeting some friends for a beach barbecue tonight. They live nearby, so we're only going up the beach a bit. I wondered if you'd like to join us?"

Grace was shaking her head in refusal before Sam had finished speaking.

"Oh no, thanks, but I couldn't. I really don't want to intrude. Anyway, I don't fancy being out two nights in a row, and I am already going out tomorrow night."

"Really, who with?"

"James Grayling. He called yesterday and suggested some dinner. Said he thought it might do me good."

"Oh, right. Hope you enjoy yourself. Anyway, see you later. I better go get ready."

#

Le Claire and Dewar followed Paul Armstrong into town and he quickly showed them to his office.

"I'm finding this hard to understand. Why is Kate's death considered suspicious?"

Le Claire answered, "A few things don't add up, and we just need to see if we can satisfy ourselves as to what actually happened."

"But who would want to harm Kate?"

"That's what we would like to know. Can you think of anything that might help our investigation?"

"Not at all. Quite frankly, the one person I believe could have done something to Kate would have been Harriet. She always did have a nasty streak. But that doesn't seem likely, does it?"

"Was Mrs Avery close to her late husband's relatives?"

Paul Armstrong's glance was sharp. "Very. They're good people and would never have hurt Kate. Never."

"Did she have any arguments with anyone or negative issues recently?"

"Kate was getting on. She tended her garden, went swimming most days and met friends for lunch or supper. The only controversy she had over the last few months was some damned estate agent hounding her to sell Rocque View."

"What happened?"

"The estate agent was overzealous. Kate wasn't young anymore, and she was being hounded by this girl."

"Miss Howard said the estate was split equally between herself and Sam Avery. Had that always been the intention?"

"Kate and Samuel originally left almost everything to their nephews, but as the boys grew into successful men, it was decided to leave the majority of their assets to Grace and Sam."

"The majority?"

"Yes, until a few months ago, Kate still intended to leave Rocque View to Harriet. The sisters had grown up with their widowed mother, who I understand wasn't the easiest of women. I got the impression that Kate felt guilty for moving to Jersey and leaving Harriet alone. The eldest sister, Grace's grandmother, had long since moved to the States."

"But she changed her will—why?"

"Harriet was a bitch. Always with a sob story and her hand out. Kate had enough of being treated like a cash cow. Especially after Harriet started a relationship with Ray Perkins. He runs a high-end car dealership and also does a roaring trade in secondhand cars. Knowing Harriet, he'd have paid dearly for her company. Harriet was swanning off on exotic holidays with him whilst still pleading poverty to Kate. I think she finally opened her eyes and saw her sister for what she really was. She'd never told Harriet she was going to leave her anything, but, as we found out, Harriet had her assumptions."

CHAPTER ELEVEN

Bang! BANG! A persistent and increasingly louder knocking had Grace come awake with a start. She sat up groggy and disoriented. "What?"

She stumbled to her feet and yanked her bedroom door wide open. Sam stood there, looking impossibly handsome. He had changed from his usual working gear of dress shirt and smart trousers. The baggy cargo shorts and brightly coloured T-shirt screamed of relaxation and fun, which were slightly at odds with the anxious look on Sam's face.

"I called Mum and Dad and told them what the police said about Kate. They're in bits. You okay?"

"Yeah, I guess. It's just so unexpected."

"Look, I can understand you not feeling up to socialising tonight, especially after the news about Kate. I just think that being so introspective isn't good for either of us. I am only going for a few hours to show face. It's really casual. Just a few friendly people hanging out together on the beach, watching the sunset and chilling. Are you sure you won't change your mind?

Grace replied without thinking. "No thanks. Really kind of you, but I am happy just being alone this evening. Thanks anyway."

Sam drew back from the door and turned to leave. "Okay. Well, I better be off. See you." As Grace made to close the door, she heard Sam call her name. He was halfway down the stairs peering back up at her. "If you do change your mind, just come and join us." He held up the canvas bag in his hand. "I've got enough food for two. Just go down the steps to the beach, turn left and keep walking. You won't miss us. The bay ends with a rocky outcropping that leads out to the lighthouse. You can't walk any farther, and that's where we'll be."

Grace just smiled. There was no need to refuse yet again. She'd told him she wasn't going, and that was that.

#

Le Claire sat alone in his office. Not that he would ever dignify the cramped space with so grand a term. The police headquarters were fit to bursting at the seams, and everyone longed to move into the new purpose-designed station currently being built at the other end of town. However, there was still space to be found for urgent matters. He had set up the MIR in a seldom used conference room. The makeshift incident room was now filled with desks, high-tech computer equipment, investigating and administrative staff. He'd escaped to his office for some thinking time.

His serviceable wooden desk groaned under a mound of neglected paperwork and A4 files. These were all his current cases, and they all required his attention. But he couldn't focus on any of that at the moment. He leaned back in his cleverly padded and flexible chair, the only piece of new furniture he had insisted on when he moved back to the island. If he was going to spend more time sitting at a desk, then he wanted to at least be comfortable. His feet were up on the desk, resting on what he suspected were the files on an unexplained fire that had razed a failing hotel to the ground. He thought, as did everyone else on the island, that it was a deliberate action and an insurance job. However, the problem, as usual, was that you had to prove guilt—not just think it.

And that was the rub of his current problem. Dewar had found the evidence that said Kate Avery had probably been murdered. The specialists they had spoken to all agreed that there was no way anyone could have taken such a massive dose of insulin and then calmly wiped the pen clean of fingerprints and disposed of the needle.

But who had killed her and why? There had to be money involved in this somewhere. Why get rid of Harriet? She was killed after the contents of Kate's will were common knowledge, so it wasn't as if someone was trying to get an inconvenient heir out of the way. Harriet wasn't a beneficiary of the will, so that motive held no water.

Le Claire's mind strayed back to the witness statements from the scene at the restaurant. Harriet had argued with the Averys and Grace Howard and had threatened to contest the will. Was that what had put her in the murderer's sights?

#

Grace was lying on her bed staring at the ceiling. She felt out of sorts, and her nerves were jangled. Only to be expected, she thought, after the last few days—especially today. The policeman's revelation had devastated her. Two members of her family murdered within days of each other—this didn't happen to people like them; this was the stuff you read about as breaking news on the national channels. Could the police be wrong? Grace could not think of a reason why anyone would want to kill Kate. In fact, if one thought about it hard enough, one would think that Harriet—with her cast-iron assertion that Kate would leave her a bundle of money—would have had more reason than anyone to wish Kate ill. But Harriet was dead as well. So who killed *her*?

Grace shook her head. On top of all that, there was Sam. She felt drawn to him, but she certainly wasn't going to open that can of worms. Grace thought about her refusal to join Sam this evening. He was no doubt just being friendly, but she felt uncomfortable meeting new people. That was why her refusal had been so swift and adamant. She was fine on her own.

She'd felt differently yesterday. She had been empowered by the possibilities of her new life, by her decision to start living life her way. She had said a final, irrevocable good-bye to Carter, her job, her old life—in her mind at least—and had happily accepted the invitation from James Grayling. She had seen her willing acquiescence as a clear example of how she was going to be in the future. Exploring new opportunities and not slamming doors shut before they had even begun to open.

A mere twenty-four hours later and Grace had reverted to type. She was closed off, and all spontaneity had been doused—as evidenced by her abrupt refusal of Sam.

She cast a swift glance at the bedside clock. It was nearly six o'clock. Did she really want to spend the night alone? What harm would it do to join Sam? Before she could think of a thousand excuses, Grace leapt to her feet and pulled on a pair of casual navy linen shorts, a plain blue T-shirt and some flat sandals. A quick brush of her hair, a flick of mascara and speedily applied lipstick and Grace was ready. Going downstairs and into the kitchen, she grabbed a slouchy shoulder bag and threw in some money and her keys.

She took out a bottle of wine and a couple of cans of soft drinks from the fridge. These were popped into the roomy bag, and Grace was ready. She paused for a moment and wondered what she was doing. With a wry smile, she mentally stiffened her spine. *Just do it, girl,* she thought. *What harm can it do?*

#

Grace followed Sam's directions and simply headed towards the lighthouse. In front of the rocks, there was a group of people standing, chatting in small groups or huddled around what looked like a small smoking fire pit.

She hoped Sam was still there. What if he had left and gone off with some of his friends or maybe some girl? What if, even worse, he didn't look pleased to see her? Perhaps Sam had only asked her tonight to be polite? Blowing out a breath of air to steady her nervousness, Grace kept walking.

She need not have worried. She could see Sam in the near distance. He was standing with his back to her, but he turned around moments after her eyes locked on to his frame.

His hand rose in welcome, and, after turning to speak to the man standing beside him, Sam sprinted up the beach towards Grace.

As he was almost upon her, Grace saw that Sam was grinning. He looked genuinely pleased to see her. "Hey, what a great surprise. Come on." Grabbing Grace's hand, Sam pulled her towards the group, and within moments, her head was buzzing from the round of introductions.

A pretty brunette laughed and said, "Don't worry if you can't remember all the names. I'm Gemma, and this is my husband, Rob.

He and Sam go back forever. So I'm sure we'll meet up again." She indicated to where Sam had been pulled aside by a black-haired, swarthy guy of average height and build with the most infectious, beaming smile Grace had ever encountered, a one-hundred-watt smile that was turned in her direction as the men came to join them. Each carried a bottle of beer and a glass of white wine.

Rob passed the glass of wine he carried to Gemma, and Sam followed suit with Grace. Gemma sipped and let out an appreciative murmur. "Perfect. So, Grace, tell me, are you married?"

A brief shadow crossed Grace's face. She'd have to get used to her un-engaged state. "No, I'm not."

"Boyfriend?"

"Nope. I guess I am, as they say, footloose and fancy free."

Grace was slightly taken aback to see what looked like keen speculation mixed with a splash of cunning cross Gemma's face. Gemma turned to Rob. "Come on, darling, let's go and grab some food and let these two have a catch up." She grabbed her startled husband's arm and virtually marched him off towards the smoking barbecue. In a moment, Grace and Sam were alone.

Sam laughed. "Sorry about that. Subtlety isn't what Gemma is known for."

Grace lifted a brow. "Subtlety?"

"Yeah, after she realised you were single, she was desperate to leave us alone. Since she and Rob got married, Gemma has been on a one-woman mission to have the rest of their friends get settled down, although it seems like I'm number one on her list. Hence her habit of leaving me alone with any suitable female that comes up on her radar."

Grace was unsure whether to be flattered that Gemma apparently thought her "suitable" for Sam or insulted that she was just what appeared to be next in a long line of Gemma's matchmaking finds. She decided to let flattery win. Quite frankly, she was too brain-tired to be insulted. It would take much more energy than she had at the moment. She was just going to go with the flow for once.

Grace took a large gulp of wine and blinked as the alcohol rushed to her brain. "Whoa! I didn't have any lunch today."

"Personally, I make a habit of never missing a meal. It's my golden rule."

Grace laughed. Sam didn't look as if he had an ounce of excess fat on him.

Sam took a sip from his beer bottle and asked, "So how come you never had lunch?"

"My mind was preoccupied." At Sam's quizzical look, Grace explained about the visit from Emma Layzell and her subsequent trip to talk to Ray Perkins.

"I can see how talking to Ray would upset you. I don't know him at all. I've just seen him out and about with Harriet. I overheard Kate talking to Mum about him once. She couldn't see what Harriet saw in him, apart from his open wallet, and felt there was something a bit devious about him."

"Well, all I know is that Ray seemed genuinely upset today."

"That's good, isn't it?" At Grace's sharp look, he continued. "What I mean is that Ray and Harriet seemed an odd, slightly mismatched pair, so it's good that he genuinely cared about her."

Grace was surprised at Sam's reading of this situation on an emotional level. She wasn't used to the men she knew thinking that way. Her dad was not one for showing any emotion, and as for Carter... Well, he was always perfectly correct, but Grace didn't think he would actually consider how emotionally attached two other people were.

Sam said, "You're a million miles away. What's up?"

"Nothing really, just thinking how our image of the world—of our life—can seem one way and then, like a mirror tilting, we have a whole new perspective."

Sam laughed. "Wow, now that is deep." He indicated his empty beer bottle hanging from two fingers. "Personally, I need another beer before I join you in philosophising. Come on, we can grab some food as well."

As they walked towards the group gathered around the food and drinks, Grace felt relaxed for the first time in days. She knew she was trying to block out the tragic news about Kate. Surely there wasn't anything wrong with that, just for a little bit.

CHAPTER TWELVE

Le Claire and Dewar waited on the Rocque View doorstep. He could hear the chiming bell through the heavy, wooden door, and within moments, Grace was beckoning them in.

Le Claire spoke first. "I am glad to see you alone. You always seen to have an Avery lurking nearby." Apparently, the sarcasm in his voice wasn't lost on her, and he noticed that she bristled slightly. She had certainly pulled herself together since yesterday.

"They have been very kind. What did you want to speak to me about?"

"I am sorry to be blunt, but we suspect that Mrs Avery may have been forcibly administered a large dose of insulin, and then, when she was in a hypoglycaemic state, thrown from the balcony. She may have been rendered unaware by the insulin, but it was the fall that killed her."

Grace winced at the harsh words, and Le Claire cursed his insensitivity. "I'm sorry, but you need to appreciate the ruthlessness of whoever committed this crime." He paused. "Or crimes, if we extend our thoughts to make this a double murder."

Grace Howard shivered. He saw her body tremble as realisation hit. Both her aunts had been killed—was it really feasible that two murderers were at large, or was it the same person?

"But why? What on earth could someone hope to achieve by disposing of Kate and Harriet? Was anything taken? Were they burgled?"

Le Claire glanced at Dewar. She had carried out an on-site review of the apartment herself and reviewed the crime scene report. He could see the compassion in her eyes as she spoke to the bewildered Grace.

"A thorough investigation has been conducted and there is no sign of any disturbance to Miss Bellingham's apartment other than in the area where she was attacked. There is nothing to give rise to a suspicion that this is a burglary gone wrong. However, we cannot rule out that Miss Bellingham disturbed someone before they were able to go through her apartment. I'm afraid we can't say any more at the moment."

As they made to leave, Le Claire's parting words hung in the air. "It is too much of a coincidence to suppose that two independent murders have taken place. They are connected; I am sure of it. Just be careful. I don't have any solid reason to think you may be in danger, but what I do know is that you couldn't have killed Kate Avery. And that could make you a victim here as well."

Once in the car, Le Claire directed Dewar to drive into town.

"Where to now sir?"

"The Averys' offices. I need to find out more about this family."

After asking to see Richard Avery, they were ushered into a spacious meeting room—modern and sleek. Offers of coffees, teas and water were all refused, and Le Claire waited impatiently. Dewar was wandering about, smelling the numerous vases of artistically arranged flowers and leaves and looking out the south-facing windows; the view stretched across town to the marina.

After an interminable five minutes of ignoring Dewar's sniffs, a tall man entered the room. His resemblance to Sam Avery gave away his identity. His face was open and his smile welcoming.

"I'm Richard Avery. I believe you met my wife, Susannah, the other day. I assume you're here about Kate. Sam called us last night and told us about your suspicions."

"I'm DCI Le Claire and this is DS Dewar—and yes, we've come to ask you about Kate Avery. And also Harriet Bellingham."

Richard Avery's face registered surprise, which was quickly concealed. "What happened to Harriet is awful. I hear she was badly beaten, but I can't help you. I barely knew the woman, so can't see that I would be of any help."

"Let's leave it to me whether you can assist or not. When I spoke to your wife the other day, she said you weren't bothered about being left out of Kate Avery's will. I find that hard to imagine. It must have been galling to be overlooked and see your own son take your place. We are talking about rather substantial sums. Were you aware of the terms of Mrs Avery's will beforehand?"

The easy smile slid off Richard Avery's face. "No, I was not. However, I am not surprised. Sam was a great favourite of Kate and Samuel. He is my only child, and I begrudge him nothing and would do anything for him. I am afraid you're barking up the wrong tree."

Dewar spoke, "It must surely have been inconvenient, perhaps even worrying, for your son that Miss Bellingham was threatening to hold up the estate. Especially as I understand your latest project has hit a financial setback."

Richard Avery replied, but his eyes were fixed on Le Claire. "I don't appreciate these insinuations. Neither Sam nor I are in need of money, and even if we were, murder is a step too far."

Le Claire stood. "If that were always the case, I'd be out of a job. Thanks for your time. I'm sure we'll be in touch."

#

Sam arrived home from work, and the first thing he did was grab a beer. He'd open the pool up and have a swim. Grace was nowhere in sight, and he figured she'd be getting ready for her date. He pushed aside the black thoughts that rose unbidden.

As he walked outside, he saw that Luca was finishing off some weeding. He called out. "Fancy a drink?"

Luca hurried over. "No thanks, I'm fine, Sam. There is something I need to speak to you about though. I found some earth disturbed the other night, clear footprints in the area. This isn't the first time."

"Kate always had issues with kids hanging about the gardens after dark. The little swines even left their beer cans scattered over the place. Could they be at it again?"

"I guess so. I'll keep an eye out."

"You do that and let me know if you find anything. We can't be too careful. Kate's sister was murdered, and now they think Kate's own death may have been suspicious."

Luca paled. "I'll pop round each morning over the next few days and have a quick look about the place."

"Thanks. It makes my blood boil thinking of them drinking and laughing in a dead woman's garden."

#

Just before seven o'clock, Grace took one last look at her reflection in the long freestanding mirror, picked up her small bag and headed downstairs. She was wearing one of her new dresses. The short-sleeved raspberry bodice fit snugly and flared from the waist into a ballerina skirt. The soft material brushed against her legs as she walked, and the knee-length hem flipped and swayed every time she moved.

Simple nude strappy sandals and a matching clutch completed her outfit. She had kept her makeup to a minimum, and her hair fell to her shoulders in gentle waves.

Used as she was to neutral, classic outfits and masculine-cut work suits, Grace felt feminine and... well... carefree. Though God only knew how that could even be possible with what she had been faced with recently. Kate's death had been shocking enough, but now that it was said to be a possible murder—along with Harriet's brutal killing... ? Any problems Grace thought she had—and she included Carter in this—faded into insignificance. She shivered as she recalled Le Claire's words that she might end up a target as well.

If Grace was going to be honest, part of her current attitude had to do with Sam. The night before had been a revelation. Sam's interaction with his friends had shown Grace a fun, caring side to him that she hadn't previously seen. They had forgotten their troubles and laughed and joked, and there had been a moment back at the house when Grace had felt a connection between them; something crackled in the air, and she had thought Sam would kiss her again. But no. He had simply dropped a chaste kiss on her cheek and headed to his bedroom with a cheerful "good night."

Which was just as well, for the last thing Grace wanted was the complication of anything happening between them. She wasn't looking for anyone, and Sam seemed happy in his bachelor life.

Hopefully, James wouldn't take her agreeing to go out with him as anything more than it was. Just a stranger in town taking up an offer of friendship and company. And with that, Grace headed to what she hoped would be a pleasant, uncomplicated evening.

#

James was already parked in the drive, standing by the passenger door of his Porsche, smart in casual dark linen trousers and an open-necked shirt. With a flourish, he bent low and opened the door, indicating for Grace to get in.

"You look lovely." Grace coloured at the compliment but nodded her head in thanks. Before she could slide into the passenger seat—why were these cars so near the ground?—a voice came from behind them.

"James. Grace. Off out, are you?"

Sam had come from the front gardens. He was wearing multi-coloured swimming shorts and nothing else. His hair was wet and tousled, and tiny droplets of water clung to his legs and chest—an extremely well-toned and muscled chest that Grace was desperately trying not to look at.

It was James who answered, "Yes, for a bite to eat. I see you've been swimming. Having a quiet night?"

"That's the plan, with a couple of beers and a pizza on the agenda."

James grinned at Sam as he walked around to the driver's seat. "Well, enjoy your evening. I'm certainly looking forward to mine."

#

What an absolute idiot was Sam's thought as his eyes tracked the car down the drive until it was out of sight. He'd felt out of sorts all day. There was a huge amount on his mind at the moment. His actions over the last weeks and the forthcoming days would quite possibly determine the course of his entire future. He had to get Grace out of his mind. He couldn't allow himself to be distracted, not when the solution to his problems was so close at hand.

#

James's car sped along the coastal road, heading east. "I've booked a restaurant which overlooks a beautiful little bay. It isn't one of my places, as I don't want to be dragged into any work issues. I'm having a night off. It's great food in a relaxed atmosphere, which is what I'm sure you could do with."

"That's exactly what I need, James. It is really kind of you to take me out. The Averys have been wonderful, of course, but it is nice to have some different company."

"It's my pleasure. I know what it's like to be shunted onto the island and not know a soul."

"I thought you were born in Jersey. You did go to school with Sam, didn't you?"

"I was born in England, but my parents moved here when I was young, so I was schooled on the island."

"Jersey certainly looks like a great place to grow up."

"Anywhere can be fun if you have money. Jersey appears an affluent society, but that's just on the surface. Those living on the edges of wealth experience a very different island."

"New York is exactly the same. Money does cushion us, but I have to say that what I've seen of the island hasn't shown me a lot of poverty."

"Then you've not been looking in the right places, or I would guess it would be more accurate to say you haven't been shown. We even have charities running food banks. There's a cycle of poverty that is hard for people to escape—and the drugs, don't get me started on that."

"I had no idea."

"Maybe I've exaggerated. There is also an issue with being on the fringe of affluence. You know, being part of it but never fitting in. Always having to worry about having the wrong blazer, the wrong shoes." James laughed bitterly, shook his head and shot Grace a sheepish glance. "Wow, don't know where that came from. You're just easy to talk to, I guess."

With that, James turned the car off the main road and drove along a small, narrow lane that opened onto a picturesque bay. After pulling into the parking area, James jumped out and opened Grace's door.

They headed towards a small wooden building with wide windows that overlooked the beach. The pale blue paint was immaculate, and tubs of colourful lavender perfumed the air. The decor was as pleasing inside as it was out. Square tables were dotted here and there, far enough from their neighbours to give diners privacy. A long bar, panelled in pale grey, lay along the interior wall, separating the cool and calm dining area from the kitchens beyond. Within moments, they were ensconced in a corner table right by the windows.

They quickly ordered, James recommending the lobster for entrees. Grace chose some simple asparagus to start whilst James went for the goat cheese.

"Grace, once again, please accept my condolences about Harriet.

"Thank you. Although, to my regret, Harriet was a stranger to me. Yes, we shared blood, but none of the brief conversations we had were particularly familial."

"Well, families interact differently, but I do know what you mean. I couldn't help but overhear Harriet letting blast at you and the Averys last Sunday."

Grace's quick bark of laughter matched the wryness in her voice. "I think the whole restaurant heard her." Grace felt guilty for talking about the deceased woman in this way, but it was the truth.

James hesitated, as if wondering whether to continue. "Well, after her kicking off at the funeral—again, quite a few people heard her verbally attacking Paul Armstrong—I guess Harriet was never going to take any slight, however deserved, lying down. I don't think anyone could hear what she was saying at the funeral, but it was pretty hard to miss at the restaurant. She was obviously really cut up about being left out of the will and seemed enraged that it was all going to you and Sam."

"Yes, I am afraid that Harriet was disgruntled." Grace sipped the cold white wine that had arrived.

"From what I hear, she was kicking off big time, saying she'd been robbed of Kate's house. That it was meant for her. And now to hear that Kate's death is being looked into is just crazy."

James paused at her look of surprise. "Sorry. I'm afraid most secrets are open ones in island life. I guess you'll be going back to the States soon?"

The starters arrived. She waited until the plates were laid in front of them, bread chosen and water glasses poured.

"I have no plans to do so. My life has, well, I guess you could say it has taken an unexpected turn." Grace sipped from the squat water glass. "And I find myself with no real reason to return to New York."

"Surely you and Sam will want to sell the place. Or do you intend on living together forever?"

Grace laughed. "It isn't so much about not wanting to sell; it's more about not being able to, not for a while anyway."

James looked intrigued; she was being a bit obtuse. But Grace simply smiled. She wasn't going to give him any more information. Apparently, he knew enough already.

They turned to their food, and Grace was grateful that James hadn't probed further. She wasn't ready to start speaking freely about what had happened with Carter or the growing feeling that she hadn't just acceded to Kate's wishes to keep a distance between Carter and herself—maybe she also hadn't been ready to leave Sam.

CHAPTER THIRTEEN

Grace rummaged in her handbag, fumbling fingers searching for keys. The outside light hadn't come on automatically, and she made a mental note to ask Luca to have a look at it. A shaft of moonlight helpfully illuminated the door lock. Now all she had to do was find her keys.

She was conscious that James sat in his car, politely waiting for her to get safely inside. Here was another indication of his thoughtfulness. Grace almost wished she was more attracted to him. He would make for an uncomplicated, brief romance.

With a sigh of relief, she felt the cold metal of the chunky key. Within seconds, aided by the helpful moon, Grace had unlocked the heavy wooden door. Turning back, she waved a last good night to James and locked the door behind her before making her way upstairs. She could hear his car revving as it headed away from the house.

Halfway up, she stopped. Balancing on one foot, she kicked the other back and hooked off one heel. Swapping feet, she dealt with the other sandal. Sweet relief surged through her as her bare feet made contact with the wooden treads. The offending high heels dangling from one hand by their straps, she finished climbing to the first floor.

About to pass the open kitchen door, she stopped and argued with herself for a moment. She had only sipped at the glass of wine that had accompanied her meal. What she fancied now was an indecently large glass of rioja and her Kindle. A relaxed hour sitting on the balcony would ease some of the inexplicable tension she felt. The evening with James had been perfectly pleasant, so it had nothing to do with that, but something had her wound tight.

A virtually full bottle of red wine lay open on the counter next to a completely empty one. Grace raised an eyebrow. Sam had certainly indulged himself in her absence. No doubt he was sleeping off the effects.

At the thought of Sam, Grace's pulse flickered and started to race. She had done her very best to keep him off her mind, and the evening with James had helped distract her from wayward thoughts. Grace knew she couldn't afford the complications an affair with Sam would bring.

She also knew that none of this was down to any latent hankering for Carter. What did it say about her that she could so easily see through the facade of her relationship with her ex-fiancé?

She grabbed a long-stemmed glass from the cupboard and poured herself a generous measure of wine. Taking a long drink, her senses were assailed with deep, heavy blackberry tones and an intoxicating aroma. This was seriously good wine. At least Sam hadn't been downing the cheap stuff.

She leaned against the glossy white island, nursing her drink, and marshalled her thoughts. She hardly knew herself. There was a restlessness within her, which sharpened her senses, making relaxation virtually impossible.

Perhaps she would just finish her wine and go to bed and give reading a book a miss; she didn't want to give her mind any more stimulation.

A sudden noise had her turning towards the balcony. She felt a tremor of fear. She stared into the darkness, her heart hammering. All she could see was a slight flicker reflected in the glass. A candle was burning. She sagged in relief. There was no intruder.

Picking up her glass, Grace walked towards the wall of glass. As her eyes became accustomed to the dark, she could see what she had missed before—the sliding doors to the balcony were slightly open.

As she stepped outside, Grace was enveloped by the balmy night air. She slowly inhaled the tang of the salty sea air and stood for a moment listening to the incessant crashing of the waves. She turned to go back inside. And then she saw him.

Sam sat on a low-slung rattan couch. His head was thrown back against the plump cushions, his jean-clad legs stretched out in front of him, ankles crossed. He wore a casual, wrinkled linen shirt that hung open and loose, the soft white material further emphasising his tanned, muscular chest.

Grace felt the air grow heavy, her senses on full alert. She moved to go back inside. Maybe it wasn't a good idea to disturb him.

"Did you have a good evening?"

She jumped as Sam's gravelly, sleep-laced voice broke the silence. "Oh yes, I did. Thank you." Feeling nervous, she decided that a strategic retreat might be best. "I heard a noise and came to investigate. I'll head off to bed. I don't want to disturb you."

Seeing Sam was unexpected. Following the pattern since she had met him, there was a visceral pull, a tightening inside whenever she saw him. Now she recognised this for what it was. Desire. She had never been one for casual encounters, but maybe, in different circumstances, she would have allowed herself to indulge her baser nature with Sam. But she had to confess that she didn't know whether her reaction was due to their living in close proximity this past week or to the sense of danger that now surrounded them. Her insides knotted—she had to stop this.

With one long movement, Sam rose and moved towards her. Grace instinctively moved back inside the house, and Sam followed.

He waved his empty wineglass in the air. "Stay. I'm just going to get a refill." Grace's eyes followed Sam as he crossed the room to pour himself another glass of wine.

Leaning against the central island that separated the kitchen from the sitting and dining area, Sam sipped his wine, contemplative, assessing eyes on Grace.

"So. How was lover boy?"

"Pardon?"

"You know who I mean, the lovely James. Show you a good time, did he?" Grace was even more amazed now. Sam sounded combative and angry, with a tinge of what she thought might be jealousy. Surely not.

She was so taken aback at Sam's words—at his tone—that it took Grace a moment to focus on something else. His speech. For Sam had slightly slurred his words.

"You're inebriated."

"No, Grace, I am not inebriated. I am, however, pissed. There is a difference."

"Well, whatever you are, I think you need to go to bed."

"Great idea. Your room or mine?" He reached out and, strong arms encircling her, pulled Grace towards him. She drew back immediately—an instinctive move. "What? Are you mad? Let me go, Sam. Don't be ridiculous!"

Sam held on tight and slowly shook his head. "Just for once, Grace—just once—don't think, don't have a discussion. Just act." And with that, he slowly lowered his mouth to hers. A part of her realised that Sam was no longer holding her tightly; his hands were just lightly resting on her forearms. She could move away easily if she wanted to. But she didn't.

Grace leaned back slightly and tilted her head to the side. They didn't break eye contact as Sam's mouth covered her own. With the first gentle touch of sensitised flesh against flesh, Grace's mind blurred. She couldn't recall why she thought this was a bad idea. Sam deepened the kiss, the previous gentle pressure giving way to a hard, determined onslaught. Grace reached up on tiptoes and curled her arms around Sam's neck, one hand at his nape, as she drew him closer still.

#

Sam hadn't meant for this to happen. He had been stewing all night, although he hadn't at first realised that was what he was doing. He'd had a beer with dinner, then he'd slouched on the sofa and tried to watch some TV, but he felt too restless. After an hour, he was sick of mindlessly flicking through channel after channel. Nothing could capture his attention.

Through the window, he had seen the setting sun as the first rays of deepening red lit the sky in vivid streaks. He had opened the wide sliders and stepped out into the cooling night air and seen loving couples strolling on the beach, hands entwined, and turned back inside and headed for the kitchen, where he had opened the first bottle of wine. A couple of beers was usually his evening max, but tonight Sam had felt reckless and more than a little on edge.

He had been on that edge for hours after Grace and James had left. He'd never really taken to the other man, but his reaction this evening was, he knew, over the top. And finally he had come to grudgingly admit that it wasn't about how he felt about James. It was more to do with what he suspected were growing feelings for Grace. And that was how he'd ended up in this situation.

Sam could sense Grace's growing desire, could taste it in her hot kisses. He was overwhelmed with the intoxication of the barriers having dropped between them. His hands roamed, unable to keep still. He touched and caressed wherever he could reach. Grace's breath was quickening, and he could feel her tentatively return his caresses. Sam's breath hitched as Grace carefully raised a hand and let one finger caress his jawline, trailing downward to rest on his upper arm.

Reality hit like an ice-cold shower. Stepping back, he drew a slightly shaky hand through his hair and looked at Grace. "God, I am so sorry. That was unforgivable." As Grace made to reply, Sam rushed on, "Please, I'm sorry. I promise that will never happen again. I must've had too much to drink after all."

#

Really, thought Grace, *so not only is kissing me an unforgivable act, he is drunk to boot!*

The words were like a vicious slap. She felt foolish and wanton and more than a little embarrassed. Moving away from Sam, she laughed—God knows how she managed that—and dismissively waved her hand. "No problem. We both had a moment of madness. It's been a tough time recently, and we all need a little release now and again. Good night and...thank you."

And with that, she headed off to bed, cloaked in bravado, leaving a bewildered Sam still standing in the kitchen.

CHAPTER FOURTEEN

Grace awoke as the persistent light crept through the slatted blinds. She had tossed and turned and counted sheep until she felt she'd seen most of New Zealand's livestock, but sleep was late in coming. All she could think about was Sam, how stupidly she'd behaved and—most worrying of all—how on earth she was going to face him.

Avoiding him was definitely not an option, not when they shared a house. Grace knew she had to somehow smooth this over. They were stuck here together for another ten weeks. And she couldn't let Kate down just because she was acting like a foolish teenager whose hormones were running amok.

With a sigh, she kicked back the covers. Best get this over with.

Sam was talking on the telephone as he leaned against the kitchen cupboards. His hair was still wet from the shower, and a dark blue shirt hung loose over his navy trousers. The phone handset was jammed between his chin and raised shoulder as he made a cup of instant coffee.

"What? It can't have come round already. Look, Mum, I'm busy tomorrow. Yeah, France." There was a pause as Sam's face looked more and more pained.

"I'll see what I can do. Yeah, I'll get on it straightaway. Yes, I'll call back soon." He hung up and looked at the phone as if he wanted to hurl it across the room. Instead, he set it down on the counter and sighed.

Grace took the opening. "Good morning. That sounded like a fraught conversation."

Blood in the Sand

Sam's head whipped around at the sound of her voice. What looked like a faint blush crept along his cheekbones. "Morning. Yeah, I forgot that Mum and Dad were going to a wedding tomorrow and planned to stay overnight at the hotel where it's taking place."

Grace was puzzled. "Why is that a problem for you?"

"Barney and Daisy. Mum's dogs. Barney is a terrier, and Daisy is a Doberman—but the softest, dopiest Doberman you could ever meet. Mum won't leave them alone for more than a few hours and never, ever overnight. Those two have never seen the inside of a kennel. I usually look after them when Mum and Dad need help."

"But you can't this time?"

"My friend Peter is having his stag-do in France tomorrow. To be honest, there's been so much going on that I totally forgot all about it."

"Stag-do? What on earth is that?"

"What? Oh yeah, I guess in the States they call it a bachelor party. Peter is getting married next month. The plan is to leave on the first boat tomorrow and get back around lunchtime on Saturday. Well, that was the plan, but now I have this issue with Mum. I don't know what to do."

Grace spoke without thinking. "I'll do it."

Sam's surprise was evident. "That's a really kind offer, Grace, but the dogs are pretty boisterous. They need to be walked twice a day and require a lot—and I mean a lot—of attention. So maybe it would be a bit too much for you."

"Seriously, Sam, I'll be fine. Shall I let Susannah know or will you?"

"Why don't you call Mum? She'll really appreciate this. So do I. Thank you."

There was a pause, which led to a definite silence. A silence which Sam eventually broke. "Grace, about last night..."

Grace was sure her face was on fire; she could feel her cheeks burning. "Please, Sam, there is absolutely no need for us to discuss this." She laughed, but even to her own ears it sounded artificial and brittle. "We both had a little too much to drink, so please just let us forget it. Okay?"

Sam looked at her, and Grace inexplicably felt that he was seeing beneath her careful veneer, that he knew she was feeling a little shaky and deeply affected by their actions of the night before. Then he looked away and picked up his mug of coffee.

"Sure. Anyway, I better get ready for work. I'll leave you to call Mum."

As Sam walked away, Grace couldn't help wondering if she had misplayed the scene. Should she have listened to what Sam was going to say?

Susannah was ecstatic with Grace's offer. "I can't tell you how happy I am. I know there has been a lot going on, but I didn't want Sam to miss Peter's event, and the wedding we are going to is really important to me. My best friend's daughter is getting married. And it will be good for us to have something to take our mind off the awfulness of the past few weeks. So I just can't thank you enough."

"Please, Susannah, it is honestly no problem. Now do I stay at your place?"

"No need. We will bring Barney and Daisy to you. Kate used to look after them sometimes, so they're used to being at the house, and we'll bring all their stuff, so you don't have to worry about anything."

They ended the call with a promise from Susannah that they would bring the dogs around early the next morning.

Le Claire and his incident team were in a briefing session when the door swung open and their main boss came in.

Chief Officer Charles Wilson was a career man. He'd worked in London for most of his life. He'd started off walking the beat, where his arrest record and case-solving abilities propelled him up the ranks. His diplomatic skills took him the rest of the way. The chief was a tall, well-built man with thick greying hair, a hooked nose and penetrating blue eyes.

Eyes that were now searching the crowded room and, when they alighted on Le Claire, sharpened ever so slightly. "Apologies for the disruption, but something couldn't wait. Le Claire, I would like a word please."

Le Claire stood and squeezed past those closest to him until he reached the door. He would like to have pretended that he didn't know what this was about. But he could think of only one recent issue that could have caused the chief's thunderous look. As he closed the door behind them, Le Claire saw the smirk that pranced across Masters's face. No doubt this had made the creep's day. He hadn't wanted him on his team, but it would have been petty, and obvious, to overlook him.

The Chief moved down the corridor, away from the incident room and eager ears, towards the stairwell.

"I am just back from a relaxing couple of days in the UK with the wife. We went to see the grandkids and had a great time. What do I return to? An accident turns out to be a murder, and we then discover the victim's sister has also been murdered in her own home. Now that is a blow, as things like that don't happen in this bloody island. But you know what really pisses me off? Do you?"

Le Claire winced. He had never had to face the Chief's legendary temper but knew he was now caught in the eye of the storm. "Sir, I can explain..."

"Explain? Go ahead then. You tell me how someone, who is supposedly one of our best officers—London training and all—manages to allow a crime scene to be contaminated by the victim's partner? Someone who could potentially be involved—whose DNA is now plastered all over the victim and the scene."

"It happened before the first response unit even got to the scene. I am so sorry."

The Chief shook his head, and Le Claire could see him deflate as the anger burned away. "I know it couldn't be helped. It was stupid of the caretaker to call a civilian before 999, but I guess he was just reacting to a stressful situation. The boyfriend quite naturally rushed round. It's just a pity that he was found in the middle of the crime scene with his arms wrapped around the deceased. Maybe he is just a clever murderer making sure any evidence is useless to us? So where are we on any of this?"

"We're getting nowhere fast. There was no forced entry into either property. Apparently, Kate Avery was in the habit of leaving the back door open, and Harriet Bellingham must have opened the door to her killer. She had a voice intercom but no video. The other apartments paid to upgrade the system, but she refused."

"Which means that we could have had a stored video image but don't. Damn."

"Exactly. We've pulled together a great team on these cases. We will find who has done this."

"You better, Jack. There's going to be interest from high up, who will not want unsolved serious crimes sullying the island's reputation. You have a week. If you're no further forward, I will have to encourage Fleming to promote someone to be your special aide until the murderer is behind bars. Maybe Masters? So you better shape up."

The Chief walked away, and Le Claire could feel the sting of that last, taunting comment. His reputation was on the line, as was his sanity if he had to work with Masters.

After a walk on the beach, Grace had settled down in front of her laptop to catch up on some correspondence. Having sent the last email on her list, she closed the computer and leaned back in her chair with a groan of boredom. What to do now? The phone rang, and Grace quickly answered it, noting the caller ID as she did so. It was Emma Layzell. Did she really have to tell her again that the place wasn't for sale?

"Hi, Emma. What can I do for you?"

The estate agent's laughter bubbled down the phone. "There's no need to be scared, Grace. I'm not going to plague you about selling Rocque View. Well, not at this precise moment anyway. No, I have a much better reason for calling. How about we grab some lunch today?"

"That is really kind of you, but—"

"I won't take no for an answer, Grace. I'm thinking you could do with a distraction to take your mind off your recent losses."

"Okay, okay. Yes. Lunch would be lovely."

"Great, I'll pick you up at twelve thirty. The weather looks like it will stay fine, so let's go somewhere out of town."

And with that, the call was disconnected. At least she had something to think about now. And that something was wondering what angle the estate agent was pulling, for Grace didn't believe for one moment that Emma Layzell didn't have an ulterior motive for wanting to meet up with her.

CHAPTER FIFTEEN

Le Claire had been in a filthy mood after his chat with Chief Wilson and had liberated Dewar from her file reviews and sent her to find out more about Harriet Bellingham. She had spent the morning with the financial unit, checking the bank records for both victims, but nothing out of the ordinary came up. Kate Avery had been a wealthy woman who lived well, but not extravagantly. Harriet Bellingham had enjoyed an average disposable income that she motored through at the speed of light. She had an income from some bonds, which were the remnants of her last divorce settlement, and also worked a few mornings a week as a receptionist at a local beautician. And that's where Dewar was now headed.

She gave a silent *hurrah* as she snagged a parking spot right outside her target, which was a pale yellow building, the bay windows shaded by candy-striped awnings. She opened the door, and a tinkling bell gently announced her arrival.

A harassed-looking teenager sat behind the glossy reception desk; a phone was wedged between her ear and shoulder as she clicked away at a computer keyboard. She caught Dewar's eye in silent apology as she spoke into the phone. "Okay, Mrs Lewis, so you are booked in tomorrow for a Brazilian wax. Pardon? Oh, sorry, that's you in for a *Polynesian* facial. Sorry again. Bye."

She disconnected the call and pasted a smile on her face as she recited her greeting in a sing-song voice, "Hello-welcome-to-Marcy's-how-may-I-help-you?"

Dewar took pity on her. "Don't worry, love, I'm not a customer. I'm here to speak to Marcy Winwood. Is she in?"

"She's out back, making a kale-and-green tea smoothie for our lunch. I'll get her."

Blood in the Sand

The teenager didn't get up—she simply leaned back in her chair, opened her mouth and yelled, "Muuuuuum. It's the police."

The door behind reception opened, and a pretty woman came rushing out. She looked at Dewar and asked, "Are you here about Harriet?"

"Yes, I'm DS Dewar. I take it you have heard about Miss Bellingham?"

The woman's eyes glistened with unshed tears. "Yeah. When she didn't turn up for work, I called her fella. You could've knocked me down with a feather when he told me she'd been murdered. What a shock."

"I won't keep you long, but I do have a few questions about Miss Bellingham. Had she worked here long? And who was she close to? Her next-door neighbour made out as if she was a loner. Said she never saw anyone but Mr Perkins at Harriet's flat."

Marcy Winwood grimaced. "That old biddy couldn't stand Harriet. She wasn't a loner; but she didn't make friends easily, and she lost them frequently. I knew Harriet for years, but I was under no illusions. She never did me any wrong, but that wasn't the case with most she met."

"Did she have any particular enemies?"

"It wasn't like that. Harriet would have a fall out with someone and then be drinking champagne with them when she next went out. These spats were never serious."

"How did she come to work here?"

"After her last divorce, Harriet ended up needing to supplement her income. I'd just opened up here and said I could give her a couple of days a week. I paid the going rate for a receptionist, and Harriet was fabulous at doing nails. I only took fifteen percent of what she charged for a manicure, so she was making a fair bit."

And I bet most of it was in cash, thought Dewar. "And what about Ray Perkins? He seemed an odd match for Harriet. She's apparently polished, sophisticated and loves champagne, and, according to the neighbour, he is a chap who makes expensive outfits look cheap and drinks fingers of neat whisky."

Marcy Winwood smiled. "Don't judge a book by its cover. Ray gave Harriet something she never got from any of her ex-husbands;

he truly loved her for who she was. He has a good business and was very generous to Harriet. He was always saying that he'd drape her in diamonds and rubies and emeralds when he made his fortune."

Dewar left none the wiser. There didn't seem to be any compelling reason for Harriet's death; so it was back to the drawing board.

#

Emma was true to her word and picked up Grace on the dot of twelve thirty. As the car sped to the west, Grace held back her hair from the rushing wind with one hand, relishing in the breeze that blew the cobwebs from her brain. She glanced at Emma.

"It's good of you to invite me to lunch, Emma. I must admit I was at a bit of a loose end, and I've been feeling a bit blue with all that's been going on."

"My pleasure. I know what it's like to feel lonely, not to know anyone. I came to Jersey at seventeen, and I've made my own way since then. I was married for a few years. Dumped the husband but kept the name."

"Oh, I'm sorry."

"Nothing to be sorry about. We were just too young."

"So you're seeing someone?"

Emma looked wary, as if she had said too much. "No. I was, but, well, he didn't have as much time for me as I thought he would. So it's finished. Anyway, here we are." Emma drove into a spacious car park opposite the beach. "We're going to cross over to the beach walkway. I've made a reservation at a new place that's just opened."

Within minutes, they were seated, their food orders taken and supplied with glasses of ice-cold water and a platter of delicious and fragrantly spiced appetisers.

Emma's gaze was open and direct. "Don't worry, I'm honestly not here to talk about Rocque View. I just thought you might like some different company."

Grace felt herself relax. There was an honesty about Emma that appealed to her.

Emma lifted her glass and indicated to Grace. "Cheers. I know you've come here for a crappy reason and that your stay got hit with more tragedy, but I hope you end up loving the island just a little bit. Most people do."

"You sound as if you've settled into island life well. You said you were married?"

As Emma winced, Grace hastily apologised. "Sorry to bring that up if it's a sore subject. I just wondered why you stayed on after the divorce."

"Exhaustion I guess. I got married at twenty-three and was divorced by twenty-five. I should just have slept with him and let it burn out. I spent the next three years building up my work reputation and partying hard, and then I met my fella." Emma seemed to falter here and, after a quick pause, carried on. "Well, ex-fella. I didn't have the energy to think of leaving. And by that time, my career had panned out, and I found I actually like living here. But that's enough of me. What have you been up to recently?"

"I guess a lot has happened. To find that one great-aunt has been murdered is shocking enough, but both of them?"

"What!" Emma's surprise was quick and unfeigned. "You mean... do you mean Kate Avery was murdered?"

"I know. It's almost unbelievable. The police just told us that they have reopened the investigation into Kate's death. They definitely think she was murdered as well." Grace's voice trembled.

Emma reached out and laid a comforting hand on Grace's arm. "I don't know what to say. I really don't. I mean, things like this don't happen in Jersey."

Grace managed a smile. "I've heard that before from numerous people. On several occasions. And no doubt I'll hear it again. People are shocked that Harriet was murdered but seem doubly perturbed that it has happened on the island."

"For all its millionaires, fancy houses and gloss, Jersey is still a bit of a backwater; but that's only one side of the island. There's a darker element, with all the usual crimes you'd get anywhere—from organised prostitution to drug smuggling and abuse and a bit of burglary thrown in. But murder is rare."

"Yet that is exactly what has happened here. And, if the police are correct, there have been two murders, and both in my family."

"God, I can't imagine how you're coping. How are the Averys taking it?"

"I don't know how much you know, but Sam Avery and his parents were related to Kate's husband. Kate was the widow of Samuel Avery. His nephew is Richard Avery. Do you know him?"

Emma waved a hand. "Vaguely."

"His son is Sam, my Sam." At Emma's raised eyebrows, Grace felt a furious blush across her cheeks. "He isn't *my* Sam—I don't mean that. But, you know, the Sam I'm living with. Not that I am living with him, but I'm sharing the house with him." Her face aflame, Grace drank deeply from her water glass.

"Well, methinks the lady doth protest too much, but it's your business."

Grace decided to keep quiet on what was going on or, as she forcibly reminded herself, not going on, between her and Sam.

"Well, Sam is obviously pretty upset about it, as is Richard. Kate was his aunt by marriage, and I believe he was pretty close to her. I don't think I'm talking out of order to say there wasn't any love lost between Richard, Susannah and Harriet. Susannah is Richard's wife. She is a really lovely lady. At least they have tomorrow to take their mind off things."

At Emma's quizzical look, Grace continued. "Sorry, I'm being a bit vague today. Susannah and Richard are off to a wedding tomorrow and, apparently, having a romantic overnight stay at some hotel. And I'm looking after their dogs. I understand that Susannah hates letting the pooches out of her sight, so it must be a special time for them both."

Emma raised her eyebrows and mocked, "How very unsophisticated; a happily married couple. Seriously though, that's really lovely after all these years. And very unusual, especially on this island, where there is a lot of temptation. People look after themselves and keep up with their social life after marriage. Well, just put it this way—the divorce rate is pretty high. Mind you, by the sounds of it, they really are still loved up. How nice."

"I know, my own parents are slightly prickly together, so it's a novelty to see anything else, believe me."

"And you, Grace, have you had any respite from all of this tragedy?"

"I did have a bit of a break last night. I went on... an outing, I guess, for I wouldn't call it a date, not really." And that was because after what had happened with Carter, she just wasn't interested in meeting anyone else. It had nothing at all to do with how Sam Avery made her heart flip. That was just a natural reaction to a handsome man. Absolutely nothing more.

Emma leaned forward. "Really? Spill the beans. Who with?"

"It was James Grayling. Do you know him?"

"Not really, although I have seen him around. Isn't he in the restaurant business? A handsome guy you don't know from Adam takes you out to dinner, but it's not a date?" Emma's smile took any sting out of her banter.

"You're way off bat there. I am definitely not interested in Sam or James, or anyone for that matter. Now tell me more about the island."

#

Emma dropped Grace off at Rocque View and steered her little sports car out of the drive and back onto the main road. The smile fell from her face.

Lying bastard! She was seething, absolutely bloody enraged. How dare he! Emma could feel her breath come in a rapid succession of short gasps. She had to calm down; otherwise she'd crash the car. She breathed in, long and deep, and slowly exhaled a couple of times.

Here she was, thinking only of him, as per usual, and he was sniffing after little Miss Perfect. Oh, but he needn't think she was going to stand for this—absolutely no way.

CHAPTER SIXTEEN

Grace was just coming in from the garden when she saw Sam drive up, flashes of red Jeep visible through the overlapping tree branches.

By the time she reached the courtyard, he was rummaging in the boot. He must have heard her footsteps, for he turned to greet her, a tentative smile on his face. "Hi, Grace. I went home to collect some gear for France. How are you? Had a good day?"

"Yes, I went out for lunch actually. With Emma Layzell."

"And what was she after?"

"Nothing. I think she was just being nice, you know, because I'm new here."

Sam snorted. "The likes of Emma Layzell are never just being nice. She was after something, I bet."

"I'll need to take your word for that. Emma has been perfectly lovely to me. I realise she probably wants to broker the sale of Rocque View, but I can't blame her for trying to earn a living. Anyway, we can deal with that when the time comes."

Grace made to walk away, but before she could take a step, Sam reached out and grabbed her. She felt the heat from where his hand encircled her wrist and pointedly stared until he released her.

"Look, I'm sorry. Sorry about slagging Emma off, sorry about hauling you back and sorry about that bloody kiss last night. I am sorry about everything, okay?"

"Don't worry about it. It's been a trying time for everyone lately. Let's start again. Friends?" Grace cocked her head to one side and smiled.

Sam's answering grin lit his face. "Okay, friends it is. Why don't I buy you supper at the pub down the road? I need to be up before dawn for the ferry tomorrow, and we could both do with an early night."

Grace knew she had to put any burgeoning feelings she had for Sam right out of her mind. This was a rough time for her on many different levels, so she knew she shouldn't blame herself if she wasn't thinking straight.

"Sure, that would be great."

#

Dressed casually in jeans and T-shirts, Sam and Grace walked along the coastal road that led to town. In only a few minutes, they reached a long, narrow slipway, to the side of which sat a large white-painted building that had obviously recently been renovated. The pristine signage and immaculately trimmed bay trees flanking the front door led them into a bright, spacious room with square, whitewashed tables set for dining. A large bar ran along the length of the room towards wide glass doors that led to an enclosed patio.

Sam pointed to a blackboard. "Choose what you want to eat, and I'll order while you grab us a table."

Grace took a moment to scan the extensive menu. "I'll have the fish and chips. And a glass of white wine, please."

"Sounds good. I think I'll have the same. Look, there's a table over by the window. Go grab a seat."

Grace did so and settled herself in front of the large picture window that looked out to the sea. Her gaze idly took in the dog walkers and families strolling along the beach. Some sunbathers were still relaxing on the sand, even though the heat had left the day. A young couple walked along the beach, the man's arm draped around the girl's shoulders as she held him tight around the waist. You couldn't have blown a puff of smoke between them.

Grace wondered what Carter was doing. When would he have told her about his affair? Actually, would he have told her? She felt like such a fool and couldn't help but wonder if she was about to make an even bigger fool of herself over Sam. The touch of his lips on hers had left an indelible mark that would take some time to forget. So caught up was she in her thoughts that Grace didn't realise Sam had joined her until the squeak of the chair next to her being drawn across the wooden floor jolted her back to the present.

Sam sat down heavily with a thump. "Sorry, just a bit difficult to balance." Grace laughed as she saw why Sam was being so clumsy. His hands and arms were full as he balanced a bottle of wine tucked under one arm—wine cooler and all—and carried two glasses, knives, forks, napkins and sachets of condiments.

"Here, let me." Grace reached across and started taking the cutlery and glasses from Sam and placing them on their table. As she took the final glass, her fingers accidentally grazed Sam's, and she felt a bolt of electricity shoot through her. She felt herself blush a fiery red as she mumbled an apology.

Sam's gaze was intent and direct. "Grace..."

Whatever he had been going to say was lost as a tall, dark-haired man approached their table. "Sam, good to see you. Are you going to France for Pete's stag-do?"

"Yes, I am. You?"

The man's laugh boomed out, causing a few of the other diners and drinkers to look their way, one showing more interest than the others. "Wouldn't miss it for the world, mate. A walk about St Malo, hitting a few of the French pubs, then lunch in the square followed by more pubs, a nice dinner and more pubs and an early lunch on Saturday—in a pub hopefully."

The man glanced at Grace and then back at Sam, but Sam made no move to make the introductions.

"I'll see you tomorrow, Dave. I'm looking forward to a few of those pubs myself." Sam's tone was pleasant, but it was obvious the conversation was over, so Dave walked over to join a group of couples who sat drinking on the patio.

Grace didn't say anything, and it was Sam who spoke into the silence. "Sorry for not introducing you, but we'd never have got rid of him. Dave fancies himself a bit of a ladies' man, and he'd have been all over you."

"Maybe I'd have enjoyed that!" Grace joked.

He shot her a look that took her aback and caused her heart to beat a little faster. A look that said a lot more than he maybe intended. A wary look, which said he didn't know if she was joking or not. And if she wasn't kidding, then where did he stand with her? A question Grace didn't have the answer to.

Blood in the Sand

A pretty waitress appeared and placed large plates of fish and chips in front of them. "Here you go. The bread's on its way. Enjoy." A second waitress took the place of the first and placed a platter of thinly sliced buttered bread triangles on the table.

Grace inhaled the smell of the freshly baked bread and hot food and smiled. "It smells great."

"Let's see if it tastes as good."

Silence reigned for the next few minutes as they ate, the quiet only broken by murmurs and sighs of appreciation. Grace laid down her knife and fork while she savoured the tender fish and perfect chips, crisp on the outside and soft and fluffy inside. "This is delicious."

Grace glanced around the room and, to her surprise, saw James standing at the bar in conversation with one of the waitresses. "Look, James is here."

Sam didn't look up from his plate. "This is one of his places, but I don't hold that against the restaurant."

Grace couldn't help but smile at his accompanying grin.

A dark shadow fell over the table, blocking out the light from the window. Glancing up, Grace shivered as she recognised Ray Perkins. His eyes were bloodshot and his face drawn. Sam inclined his head in recognition; a brief smile barely lifted his lips. "Ray, how are you?"

Ray leaned on the table, his hands heavy, as if he needed the support. The alcohol on his breath was strong and fetid. "How am I? Where do you want me to start? Not as well as you two by the looks of it. All cosy, aren't you?" He flicked a finger against the bottle of wine, making it rock precariously until Sam righted it. "Toasting your good fortune, are you? Got your greedy little paws on old Kate's money and got bothersome Harriet out of the way. Bet you little bastards are well pleased with yourselves. Eh?"

"Ray, you're drunk. I am truly sorry about what happened to Harriet, but she is gone, and we can't do anything about that."

"Yeah, she's gone all right. Made me her heir in her will, she did. Nothing for you lot. But then you've got everything anyway, haven't you? Harriet should have got Rocque View. That old bitch virtually promised it to her, and Harriet got her expectations up.

I've got rights, and you owe me. Yes, you owed Harriet, and now you owe me. You better be careful, little girl, when lover boy goes off to France. Couldn't help but overhear. All alone in that big house... anything could happen to you."

With that, Ray lunged towards Grace, grabbing her arm and dragging her out of her chair. Sam was on his feet in a second, pulling Grace out of harm's way and shoving her behind his back. Ray staggered and went to swing when his arm was caught from behind and brought down to his side. James had rushed over, and he held Ray secure as he softly spoke, "Mr Perkins, no need to make a scene. Come with me and let me buy you a drink, and we can have a nice chat."

James mouthed, "You okay?" to Grace, who nodded her head, her arms wrapped around her as she rubbed at the bruise Ray had made on her wrist. Ray Perkins hunched over, his shoulders slumped and visibly deflated as the fight left him. James put his arm around the older man's shoulders and led him through a door. The sign above proclaimed it as the pool room bar.

Sam held onto Grace's hand, his thumb distractedly tracing a soothing path over the pulse points in her wrist. Backwards and forwards he stroked as he put his arm around her and led her back to their seats. The other diners had stopped blatantly staring at them, but, from the furtive glances cast their way and whispered conversations, the argument with Ray was the talk of the evening.

"Are you okay?" Sam asked quietly as Grace settled herself down in her seat.

"I guess so. I'm just a little shaken. I don't like confrontation, and he was just, well, just so aggressive."

"Grace," Sam began and then paused, carefully weighing his words. "I'm going to cancel going to France tomorrow. I didn't want to let Pete down, but I can't leave you alone—not after what has happened to Kate and Harriet. I also don't like Ray's threats about you being alone at the house. Probably all bluster, but better to be safe than sorry."

Blood in the Sand

Grace had started shaking her head almost as soon as Sam had started talking. "No, I won't hear of it. You really want to go, I know that. And I'm not scared of some random threat. Ray seems harmless enough. I'm sure it's all bluster. I'll make sure the doors are locked and bolted, and I'll have the dogs with me. What has happened to Kate and Harriet is appalling, but we don't even know yet if they're connected."

As Sam made to speak, Grace held up a hand as if to force the words away. "No, that's final. I won't hear of anything else. I'll even lock my bedroom door, sleep with my cell next to the bed and put the cops on speed dial. Does that suit you?" Grace's tone was lighter now, and laughter lurked in her voice.

Sam filled up their almost-empty glasses and raised his in a toast. "You're a sassy woman, Grace Howard, but I am going to have to make you promise that you'll let the dogs sleep in the same room as you. Just to be safe."

Grace raised her eyebrows. "I don't think it's necessary, but okay. I agree."

#

In the no-man's-land of the dark early hours of the morning, when midnight is a memory and dawn a far-off promise, Grace lay in a twilight haze. Neither in a deep sleep nor fully awake, she—or a remote part of her that had some consciousness—heard a noise. The night was silent and calm, so the sound reverberated through the house.

A distant part of Grace's mind thought it might be the back door opening. It had a habit of sticking, and you had to give a hearty pull on the handle to prevent it from jamming. But that was ridiculous. For who'd be leaving the house at this time? It could only be Sam, but he wouldn't be leaving for the harbour until first light. She couldn't hear anything else, so with nothing better to distract her attention, heavy lids fluttered closed, and her slumberous breathing was the only sound in the room.

CHAPTER SEVENTEEN

Emma Layzell was wide awake at 3:00 a.m. She had been calling him all night, but there was no answer. She had started off by leaving breezy messages. "Hello, lover, just wanted to say hi. Gimme a call." This, after several hours and a bottle of wine, graduated to the demanding, "Are you avoiding me? I know what you're up to, you bastard. You won't get away with it."

In her drunken haze, Emma had misdialled a couple of times as she entered the first initial of the saved contact in her address book. She couldn't help but giggle at the thought she may have inadvertently left one of her irate messages on someone else's voice mail. If she had, hopefully they wouldn't recognise her number. If anyone did pull her on it, she would find a way to laugh it off. She always did.

He'd warned her not to have his details entered into her mobile, but Emma had ignored him. The number she called him on was, after all, his secret phone. The one that only she used. Secret, just like their relationship. She hadn't been stupid enough to put his real name next to the number. She didn't want his name flashing up when he called her, just in case someone in the office was looking at her callers.

No, she hadn't put his real name in her address book, but she'd had fun making up an alias. When they had first started seeing each other, they'd gone to Cornwall for the weekend. They stayed in a small out-of-the-way hotel, and to her amusement, he'd booked them in as Mr and Mrs Jones. Emma hadn't even known that a hotel would take cash only and not ask for photo identification or at least a credit card. But then she'd taken a good look at the run-down establishment, and suddenly their laxness hadn't seemed so far-fetched.

Blood in the Sand

Her Mr Jones. That's who he was. She hadn't minded the frayed sheets and old-fashioned bedspread. Even the lack of a restaurant in the hotel hadn't bothered them in the least. They'd breakfasted at a tiny cafe, basic in its menu and sparse in decor, but the fat bacon rolls, oozing thick Cornish butter, had been amazing. Lunch was taken on the hoof as they explored the surrounding beaches and coves. Dinners were cosy affairs, snuggled together in the village pub, having a carb-fest of steak pies and batter-wrapped fish with proper, chunky chips. The white-painted, half-timbered building, with its sign swinging on an iron post, wouldn't have looked out of place in a Du Maurier tale, which all added to the romanticism of their time together. All too soon, it had been back to Jersey and hurried meetings and hasty couplings as real life came crashing in on them.

Emma's last message had been over an hour ago. She had resorted to hanging up when the voice mail message clicked on. True, he'd see at least a dozen missed calls when he looked at his phone, but he wouldn't hear her increasingly slurred voice as the drink took hold.

She'd been listening to music on far too loud, but, as the nearest neighbour was a field away, who cared? Her small cottage lay on a quiet country lane. It had been screaming out for modernisation when she'd first seen it a few years ago. An elderly widow was selling up to move in with her daughter, who lived in England. Emma hadn't officially listed the property. She'd simply raced home, calculated some sums and called her bank manager. It didn't take long to persuade the old dear that the offer on the table was a good one given the condition of the cottage and the repairs required. Later, Emma could have kicked herself. The amount she'd offered was derisory, but she could have got away with offering a fair bit less.

The air quietened and stilled as the closing notes on the CD drifted into the air and the loud click indicated that was the last song. Emma stood and yawned. She couldn't be bothered changing the disk. Maybe it was time to call it a night. It was half past three now; he wouldn't call at this time. Emma turned to go to bed when she heard a car in the lane. However, it didn't drive past but stopped right outside her door. She heard it reversing into the open field beside the cottage, which she often used as an overspill car parking area when friends came round.

Curious, she crossed to the window and peeked through the venetian blind. An unmistakably male shape made its way to her door. The figure wore a jacket and had the collar up, but she just knew it had to be him. Who else would come here at this time of night—or was it morning? Emma opened the front door without thought. Surprised, she kept her face impassive as she looked up into the face of her unexpected guest.

Emma automatically stepped back to let him in. "Bit late for a social call, isn't it?" She couldn't stop the words; they just tumbled out of her mouth without thought. She knew she better watch herself as she didn't want to upset him.

"Indeed, but the matter couldn't wait until the morning." His voice was cold, and it chilled Emma. She guessed something had annoyed him, and she only hoped it wasn't her.

"What do you want?"

He had moved across the room towards the fireplace and stood looking at the photos on the mantelpiece. He stared at one of Emma from a few years back. She stood on a cliff path, bundled up in a heavy coat against the cold. Neither the weak winter sun nor the turbulent grey sea dimmed the glow of her skin or the sparkle in her eyes. She knew why. It was in the early days, when she'd first met him, the lover who consumed her attention and lit a fire in her that the years had been unable to quench. Hence her rage at his treachery.

He turned at her question. "Your phone call surprised me. It isn't often that happens." His smile was wry as he continued. "However, if I was to define the emotion it most raised in me, it would be sadness."

"Sadness?" Emma was confused. "What message caused you to feel sad?"

"Your last message, Emma. I don't know how you found out about what I've been up to, but I can't risk you being stupid enough to talk to anyone. So, believe me, that message really was the last one you will ever leave."

Emma's confusion grew, but it was fear that was uppermost in her mind as she looked into his face and, for the first time, realised that the eyes truly were the windows to the soul. For the eyes staring back at her were dark and cold and devoid of any discernible emotion. Why had she never noticed this before? He moved towards her, and she shivered as the air seemed to grow colder and she realised the predicament she was in. Beads of perspiration rose on the back of her neck, and she heard her voice shake as she spoke. "Look, you've got this all wrong. What I meant was..."

He advanced towards her, his eyes mocking as he held up a hand for silence. "Don't say anything, for I am afraid I won't hear. I am saddened that you have forced my hand, but really, Emma," and here he quirked his head to one side as he gave her a long, considering look, "I thought you prided yourself on discretion, but I was obviously very, very wrong. You brought this on yourself."

And with that, he reached out and pulled Emma towards him. Her gasp of indignation and surprise turned into a scream as savage hands encircled her throat and pressed hard, the gloved fingers cutting off her air flow, as all the while, the deadened eyes of her attacker stared, unblinking, at her. Emma struggled and tried to kick out, but her movements were ineffectual and weak. He simply laughed and forced burning fingers into her soft flesh, through to the bone of her windpipe.

Her throat was burning, on fire, and she could hear strange staccato, rasping noises. She realised they came from her as she choked and gasped, as she tried to breathe and take in the lifeblood of air.

Emma's eyes widened as she struggled to inhale one last time. The rasping of her breath ended on a choke. Lifeless eyes cast a death stare in her assailant's direction.

CHAPTER EIGHTEEN

Richard Avery dropped the dogs off just after 9:00 a.m. Two canine faces were pressed against the back window of Richard's car as he unpacked their provisions. Grace was amazed at the amount of gear he was unloading. Did they really need that much stuff for one night? Food bowls, water bowls, beds, toys (so many toys), food and treats.

Then he let them out. And everything went crazy. Barking, jumping, and running in circles, exploratory sniffs and fat wet kisses. Grace was overwhelmed. Both dogs ran up to her. Elegant Daisy, a beautiful Doberman with soulful eyes, gently rubbed her nose against Grace's hip, whilst Barney, a short, honey-coloured tornado with ratter in his blood and persistence in his nature, literally bounced and bounced and bounced. He was like a jack-in-the-box as he jumped up and slobbered over Grace's hands as she ineffectually tried to keep him down.

Richard laughed and tried to command the dogs. "Daisy, Barney, leave Grace alone. Down!" Neither dog appeared to hear him.

"I'm sorry, Grace. I've never seen them like this. Barney normally says hello to new people and then leaves them alone. He looks like he's got a bit of an obsession with you."

"I guess I'm in for an interesting day. Should I take them safely in the house before you drive off?"

"Yes, please. We'll pick them up tomorrow. I hope it goes okay." Richard looked slightly dubious.

"Thanks. Hope you guys enjoy the wedding."

Richard smiled, and he looked so much like Sam that Grace was taken aback. Susannah was a very lucky lady indeed.

#

Le Claire drove along quiet country lanes into a scene of burgeoning mayhem. The fallow field to the side of the cottage was strewn with several vans and cars. From the vehicles present, it looked like his partner plus the uniforms and honorary police were here already, as was the crime scene investigation team. An ambulance was parked nearest the cottage, its back doors wide open. It was empty inside.

Dewar was waiting for him. Climbing out of the car, he looked over at her and slowly shook his head. "I'm actually finding this hard to take in. Three sudden—and suspicious—deaths in as many weeks are more than the island has ever seen in such a short space of time. Who called it in?"

Dewar flipped open the notebook she had at the ready. "A Jackie Miller, sir. Apparently, the deceased didn't show up for work today, which was unusual. The victim, an Emma Layzell, was one of the partners in a local estate agent company."

"Who was first on the scene?"

Dewar snorted. "Constable Hunter." At Le Claire's startled look, she continued, "Hunter was in the area. He was investigating the disappearance of some of Joe Troy's cows."

"Not again. It's the joke of the station. That's why we always send the rawest recruits out. We can't afford to waste anyone else's time. When will that man realise that badly mended fences are no barrier to his herd when they want to wander?" He shook his head, but a shadow of concern crossed his thoughts. "So how has the newbie handled it?"

"Not bad, sir. He has taken preliminary statements from Sarah Welham, who found the body, and Jackie Miller. Miss Miller is the receptionist and office manager at Layzell Estates."

"What brought Sarah Welham here? Or didn't Hunter ask?"

"Now, sir, no need to be sarcastic. We all have to start somewhere. Actually, he did forget, so I sent him back in. I didn't want to start in with them until you arrived."

Le Claire waited a beat, and when no more was forthcoming, he asked with growing impatience, "So why was Sarah Welham here, then?"

"Sorry, sir. Seems that the deceased missed several important appointments today, and as this was most unlike her, Miss Miller sent Sarah Welham to the cottage to see if anything was wrong. Apparently, Welham found the body and called Miller in a panic."

"Fine, let's get on with this."

#

Sarah Welham and Jackie Miller had been inconsolable, and he'd tasked Dewar with calming them down and rechecking their statements. Now, dressed in protective clothing to prevent contamination of the scene, he stood over the reason for their distress and cursed the gods that allowed a beautiful and vibrant woman to be cut off in her prime.

John Vanguard stood alongside him, his site team having already carried out their preliminary work. "I'll report to you later, but, as is becoming habit, there was no forced entry and no evidence that the victim was entertaining. Several bottles of wine were consumed but there is only one used glass and hers are the only fingerprints."

"It looks like the victim let her killer in. She knew him or her."

"Le Claire, what have we got here, then?"

He turned at the voice and greeted the medical examiner.

"Viera. Thanks for coming down. I have an idea of the cause of death, and I'd like your sign-off so I can get on with my job. I suppose you'll say that you can't tell me anything until the Home Office Pathologist properly examines the body? How long will it take them to send someone this time?"

"The pathologist is still here. He was staying on for a few days on leave and was due to return to the UK this evening. I'll give him a call and tell him he's got another job on. First of all, let's see what we've got here."

The doctor knelt down by the side of Emma's body, using a sterile tool to gently move her hair to the side. "If your idea for cause of death was strangulation, then you'd be right. Faint marks but clearly those of two thumbprints. Strangulation often leaves so little outward trace, but the autopsy will give us confirmation. I don't think you'd be wasting any time in treating this as suspected murder."

#

Viera had confirmed what they thought. Emma Layzell's life had ended deliberately. Someone had placed their hands on her, their fingers tight around her throat, and choked the very life out of her.

There was nothing whatsoever to suggest this case was linked with the deaths of Kate Avery and Harriet Bellingham— nothing at all. Yet he did not believe in coincidences. Jersey had its issues, and they were getting worse, but three murders in as many weeks? That was extraordinary.

Dewar had agreed to drive Sarah Welham home, and Le Claire had offered to take Jackie Miller into her office. Apparently, she had work to do and arrangements to make. He left the crime scene investigators to do their job and build up a picture of who Emma Layzell had really been. Le Claire was going into her office to see what he could find there.

Jackie Miller settled into the passenger seat and cast a glance at Le Claire. She cleared her throat. "Um, look, there's something I should have said before, but I didn't want to in front of Sarah. It's about Emma."

"And what's that?"

"When Sarah was asked if Emma had a boyfriend, she replied that Em sometimes had a date or so, but that she wasn't seeing anyone special."

Le Claire felt a prickle of anticipation. This could be interesting.

Jackie carried on. "Well, I didn't say anything, but she was seeing someone. Had been for years, but it was a secret. I only found out about a year ago. Until then, I thought that she just saw people casually, concentrated on building up the business. We'd gone out for a drink. She'd said she was unexpectedly at a loose end, asked me if I fancied getting some dinner with her." She took a breath as if to steady herself.

"We went to a tapas bar, ordered too much wine and not enough food. Emma told me she'd had a date that night, but it had been cancelled. I asked if that was what had upset her, as she'd seemed a bit off during the day. She was teary and said she loved this bloke, had done for years, but he wasn't ready to commit to her and didn't want anyone to know about it. Then she must've realised what she'd said, as she clammed up straightaway and said it was a secret and I'd better not mention it to anyone. We finished up our drinks and left."

"Did she give any clue as to who he was? Did she mention him again?"

"No, but she was definitely still seeing him. Everything slotted into place. She was really secretive with her phone calls. Her mobile would ring and she'd close her office door, looking furtive and cagey. She'd sometimes disappear in the middle of the afternoon. She'd have her calendar blocked out with 'potential new client' or something innocuous. But she'd come back in and not speak about who she'd met, no file would be opened and there wouldn't be a meeting note. I figured she was sneaking some time with her fella."

"Thanks, Jackie. That's really helpful." He needed to see Emma's mobile call log as soon as possible. Perhaps he was jumping to conclusions and this case really did have nothing to do with the other murders? Time would tell.

Jackie's tongue was well and truly loosened. "Emma had a new client as well. She opened a file for him under a false name. Only she was to deal with him. She often did that."

Le Claire was surprised. "That all seems a bit cloak and dagger. And you say this was common practice?"

"Sure. Emma dealt with a lot of the wealthy on the island. They value privacy, and to be honest, I guess Emma didn't trust the other agents not to steal the big clients' details and set up on their own. Anyway, she would do everything above board. She would do the entire source of funds and due diligence herself but keep those files in her office cabinet and update the computer when the client's offer was accepted. I'd do the filing for her. I guess I was the only one she trusted."

Le Claire was curious as to why Jackie had mentioned this. "So there was nothing unusual about what she was doing with this new client? And she'd often dealt this way before?"

"Well, not exactly. Usually, the file would have a false name, but the client's real initial would be there as well. Plus full details of what they were looking for and meeting notes, together with details of what properties Emma was going to recommend and what they had been shown. In this case, the file held nothing, nothing at all except a note that the owner had refused to sell on more than one occasion, and a photo of a property. But there was nothing else."

"Thank you. That was really helpful." He'd have someone look into these mysterious files, but it didn't look like there would be much to see.

#

They pulled up to the offices of Layzell Estates, where a sign on the door said they were closed. Through the windows, Le Claire could see several people huddled around one desk. A pretty blonde saw them and came to unlock the door, giving Jackie a watery smile.

At the expectant looks from the subdued group, Jackie spoke over her shoulder to Le Claire. "I told them what Sarah had said before I went to the cottage." Turning to the group in the room, Jackie spoke quietly. "I'm afraid it's true. Emma is dead. This is," Jackie blushed, "sorry, I can't remember your name."

Le Claire stepped forward and introduced himself, though he wasn't sure his voice would be heard over the gasps and tears. "I am DCI Le Claire. We may have some questions for you later, but for the moment, I'd like to have a look at Miss Layzell's office, if that is possible?"

Jackie gestured to the red-eyed blonde. "Holly will show you the way. Everything is unlocked."

Le Claire followed Holly down a long carpeted corridor, their footsteps muffled by the plush pile. Stopping at the last door, she opened it wide and gestured for Le Claire to go in. The outer office was generally the only one that customers saw. It was neat, modern and professional—no doubt the aim was to be welcoming and not intimidating.

However, Emma Layzell's office whispered luxury and hinted at money. Thick cream rugs lay atop the polished, dark wood floor. A low glass coffee table was flanked by two sofas upholstered in cream velvet. A curved bar ran along one wall, and Le Claire lifted his eyebrows. Holly saw the gesture. "Emma uses this space to entertain wealthy clients. We often have lunches or dinners delivered here."

Le Claire was sympathetic. Holly hadn't yet started to think of her deceased boss in the past tense. It would be a shock for her when she did. "And her work space? Where is that?"

Holly crossed to the far end of the room to a linen-covered folding screen modelled on a Japanese design. The dark wood frame matched the floor. She folded it back to reveal a glass-and-chrome desk. At least he suspected it was glass; it was difficult to tell. There were files lying haphazardly atop the desk, all jumbled together with scraps of paper and Post-it notes.

Holly grimaced. "Sorry, Emma is a bit untidy. Was, I mean she was a bit untidy." At the realisation that everything to do with her boss would now be in the past tense, tears escaped and freely fell. With a mumbled "excuse me," Holly fled the room.

Le Claire was left on his own, facing the messiest desk he'd seen in a long time. No wonder it had been hidden behind a screen. Selfishly, he wished that Dewar were here. He could have set her the task of searching the office whilst he interviewed the staff. Unfortunately, his aide had sent him a text to say that Sarah Welham was hysterical and in no state to be left alone. Dewar would have to stay with her until a relative could come and take over. He didn't want to wait for another member of the team to come and assist.

He approached the desk. These files would have been the last Emma had been working on, so he needed to see if anything appeared relevant. He went to pick up a file and watched in dismay as the loose-leafed contents fell onto the desk to join similar papers. "Damn." It looked like an even bigger mess couldn't be helped.

With a sigh, he took off his jacket and placed it on the back of the desk chair—he may as well be comfortable. Settling himself, he started to try and bring some order to the jumble of papers in front of him.

Half an hour later, he had made pretty good inroads and had various neat piles of files, random documents and letters, scraps of paper and Post-it notes.

The files didn't give up much. They seemed like fairly straightforward property transaction. He'd have one of his team look at them in more detail just in case.

He'd sorted the scraps of paper into a neat pile and was flicking through them one by one. She'd had terrible handwriting, he thought as he squinted to make out the jagged scrawl. Most were to-do notes—collect dry-cleaning, pick up milk—the usual petty day-to-day housekeeping of life.

There were ones for work as well—call such and such about commission rates, chase up on an offer on a bungalow that the sellers wanted time to consider. He shook his head as he saw the little smiley or frowning faces she'd scribbled on each note. The commission had a frowning face, no doubt the clients wanted a reduction, but the bungalow had a smiley face. Maybe she thought they'd go for the offer. On and on he went through them until one scribble jumped out and caught his attention.

"Call G—Rocque View." The note was at the bottom of the pile. He'd taken the notes and papers from the top of the mess on the desk and started the piles with them; he had thought there would be a chance of working in chronological order. The notes nearer the bottom would have been the last she had made. What reason did Emma have to call Grace Howard about the house, and why was there a frowning face?

The office door opened and Jackie Miller came in, a bunch of keys in her hand. "Sorry to intrude but the file I mentioned is kept in here. I thought you might like to see it?

"Yes please." He may as well have a look whilst he was here.

There was a black lacquered cabinet in the corner of the room. It looked too fancy and ornate for file storage. But that was where Jackie Miller was headed. She selected a long, thin key, unlocked the cabinet and slid open the top drawer. She removed an envelope-style folder that she handed to Le Claire.

Le Claire looked at the label affixed to the front flap. "Mr X?"

Jackie's mouth lifted in a feeble smile. "Em wasn't that adventurous when it came to code-names."

He opened the file, and it was indeed empty except for a photograph, which was tucked into the corner facedown. Le Claire had a feeling that he knew what would be on the other side. He took out the photograph and turned it over. Rocque View. But who was the potential buyer?

CHAPTER NINETEEN

Le Claire glanced at his wristwatch and sighed. Where the hell was Dewar? He looked up as he heard a noise and saw the wide frame of Chief Wilson blocking his office doorway.

"Le Claire. What the hell is going on? I've just read the report on that young woman's death."

"Bad news, sir. On the face of it, it could be a disgruntled lover; however, there are a couple of other lines of enquiry to consider."

"Make sure you cover all the bases. I've been getting heat from above to get the Kate Avery and Harriet Bellingham cases closed. We don't need another murder to look into."

"With all due respect, I don't think the victims needed it either."

"Don't be snippy. You know what I mean. I know you'll get justice for the victims by finding their killers. It just bothers me that we have several open murder enquiries on an island that barely sees a violent death in a year. I've had sly comments from the Council of Ministers, saying surely we'll solve the crimes soon as we have a top London homicide officer in charge. I had to fight to get you on board, Jack. You know there were detractors—don't let me down."

Grace Howard was sitting on the porch when Le Claire and Dewar drove up. She rose to greet them, an anxious look on her face. "Is there news?"

"I'm sorry, there's nothing new. We've come about a different matter."

Noting her confusion, Le Claire glanced at Dewar, indicating she should get on with it. "What was your relationship with Emma Layzell?"

She didn't hear the past tense in Dewar's question. "Emma? She has a buyer for the house. We chatted a few times. I don't mean to be rude, but what is this about?"

Le Claire recited the same words he had uttered so many times in the past. All that differed was the victim's name.

"I am sorry to tell you that Emma Layzell was found dead this morning."

Grace paled and slowly shook her head. "Oh God, that's awful, just awful. We had lunch only yesterday. I had no idea she was ill, none at all. Or was it an accident? I'm sorry, this is just a lot to take in."

And there's about to be a lot more to handle, thought Le Claire.

"As far as I know, Miss Layzell wasn't ill. Or at least I can categorically state she did not die of natural causes. We believe Emma Layzell was murdered."

"What? No!" Shakily, she reached out a hand to grab on to the chair behind her. Steadying herself, her wide eyes met Le Claire's, and her voice was hoarse as she said, "Another one? I thought that didn't happen here. That's what everyone keeps telling me. Oh God, I feel sick."

Dewar moved quickly and helped her to sit back down, pushing her shoulders forward until she was staring at the ground. Le Claire knew Dewar would sense his irritation and grimaced as she rolled her eyes at him.

Le Claire waited until he felt she'd had enough time to rally herself. "We do have a few more questions, so just let me know when you're ready."

She looked up, eyes a little wild and unfocused. "Of course, please forgive me."

Le Claire indicated for Dewar to begin, thinking she may have a gentler touch.

"How did your relationship with Miss Layzell start?"

"Just after I moved into the house. She came to discuss Rocque View. Hearing that Sam and I had inherited the place, she figured we'd be looking for a quick sale. I soon put her straight and said we weren't looking for a buyer, not at this point at any rate."

"And she took that as final?"

"No, not really. She telephoned a few times, even turned up here. Then she called yesterday and asked me to lunch."

Le Claire questioned, "Why did you agree to meet? I mean, you said she was still pressuring you about the house."

"To be honest, I'm a little lonely. She said she knew what that was like. She was only being friendly. In any event, and actually—I guess this was a bit strange—she didn't talk about the house at all. We just chatted in general about our lives. It was a really nice, friendly lunch." Suddenly, there was a hitch in her voice. "I thought New York was bad, but at least you expect it there. I can't believe this bump in the sea has one murderer on the loose, let alone several."

Le Claire didn't look at his colleague, but he sensed that Dewar's eyes had shot towards him. How many murderers? That was the question.

"Thank you for your time. It is very much appreciated, and we'll let you know as soon as we hear anything regarding your late aunts."

Her eyes were bleak as the two turned to leave. "Wait. I just thought, I mean, I know it won't be important, but I didn't want you to get the wrong idea."

Le Claire turned. "About what?"

"Emma didn't want to list Rocque View and then find a buyer. She had one in place already. For quite a while, I think."

Le Claire's face was impassive. "Thank you, Miss Howard. All information is appreciated, no matter how insignificant it may seem."

Once they were back in the car, and en route to the station, Dewar spoke, "Sir, that was interesting, about the existing buyer. Whoever is interested seems really keen. Emma Layzell approached Mrs Avery, the executor and Grace Howard. She wasn't giving up—and nor was this buyer you mentioned."

"The property angle is intriguing. It ties Emma Layzell into something Kate Avery owned and Harriet Bellingham coveted. Then again, this mystery lover interests me. Could be a straightforward crime of passion. Let's get back to the station."

#

Richard and Susannah Avery had just witnessed their dearest friends' youngest daughter get married. The bride, a vision in white lace and froths of tulle, was an old girlfriend of Sam's. As the happy couple made their way up the aisle, Susanna clutched Richard's hand and whispered, "That could've been Sam."

Richard wearily shook his head at this old argument. "And I'm glad it wasn't. That girl has never had an original thought in her life. Sam's well out of it."

"But they made such a lovely couple."

"They were teenagers, Susannah. Leave it be."

Susannah looked hurt. "I don't know what's wrong with you lately. You were in a foul mood this morning."

"Don't keep going on. It gets tiresome. I told you I've got a lot on my mind."

"Please don't be like this—not again."

"Don't start on me today."

"I'm sorry, darling—don't be mad."

When Richard said nothing, she smiled and continued, "I can't believe you never came to bed and fell asleep on the sofa. You must be aching today. Guess that's why you are grouchy." Her smile was conciliatory.

Richard turned and, rubbing the back of his neck, agreed. "Sorry, love. I obviously didn't sleep well."

Exiting the church, they made the short trip by foot to the nearby hotel where the wedding breakfast was being held.

Grace was sitting on the porch when Luca de Freitas headed round the side of the house.

"Grace, how are you?"

"I'm fine, Luca. You?"

"All is well with us. I just wondered if Sam was around?"

"Afraid not. He's gone to France and won't be back until tomorrow."

Luca looked anxious and stood there as if he didn't quite know what to do or say next. With a sigh, he turned to walk away. "I'll be off, then. See you later."

Grace reached out and laid a hand on his arm. "Is everything all right?"

"Yes, yes, no problem. It's nothing really."

#

The man stood by the harbour and gazed out to sea. The crashing waves held his attention as they swept past in their never-ending ebb and flow.

The call had come the evening before. He had days left. The clock was ticking. Anxiety clutched at his stomach in sharp, piercing jabs. He had thought there would be more time. The gambling... Jesus, what a bloody fool he had been. Spiralling deeper and deeper into debt. The crowd he'd been running with had been too rich for his blood. Pity he hadn't realised before it was too late that the answer wasn't to borrow money from someone with an open wallet and a sly smile. Not for the first time, he cursed his London connections.

His plan had been so simple: own Rocque View and find the bounty. The prize that was his by right, by birth. He could pay off his debts, save the business and be set for life. But he needed no interference. It was laughable when he thought of the heartache that would have been prevented if only the old property had been used to its full potential long ago.

But the damned moneylender had toppled that particular house of cards. The reference to cards was ironic, and he smiled despite himself. Never play on credit and, dear God, never borrow from the house. There was no way he could afford to pay him back right now. He stiffened his resolve. He had done too much to give up now. If he couldn't have the right to what was his legally, then he'd have to get it by stealth. After all, a bit of larceny was nothing, not after what he had done already.

His phone rang. Noting the number, he sighed and contemplated what to do. He looked around to make sure no one could overhear. "Yes?"

"Where have you been? I've been calling for hours."

Yes, he thought, *I am well aware of that.*

"I've left loads of messages. Didn't you know it was me? I know you're a bit busy today."

He sighed. *Of course I knew it was you. Why the hell do you think I never answered?*

"Sorry, I haven't been checking my phone. As you say, I'm busy today. So what can I do for you?"

The voice on the other end of the phone rose. "Do for me? What can you do for me? I want you to do what you need to and get what is ours."

"I've got it covered. You don't need to do anything. Absolutely nothing at all is to be done. Just leave it to me."

#

The wedding party milled around the large terrace that overlooked the beach. The very beach on which the newlyweds were currently cavorting and posing as they had their photographs taken. Their guests sipped the free champagne, not caring how long the happy couple took in having their every smile and loving caress recorded for posterity. As more and more people arrived, the chatter rose to a boisterous buzz.

Richard Avery walked through the throng of guests to join Susannah, who was chatting with the bride's parents. As he gently swept an arm around her waist, Susannah leaned back into her husband's embrace. She smiled at him, and he could see she was desperately projecting all she felt for him, all they meant to each other, in her glance. Richard smiled back as he flirtatiously leaned over and took a long sip of champagne from Susannah's glass, his eyes never leaving hers. Susannah's smile was wide. "You were gone ages. Where have you been?"

"I just had to take a quick call about the Blair rebuild."

"Is everything okay?"

"Absolutely. They go on holiday tomorrow, and Steve just wanted to have a quick chat."

An attractive brunette joined their group. It was the bride's eldest sister. She looked pale, and her mother leaned out to touch her arm. "Sally, what's wrong? Has something happened?"

Sally's voice was shaky. "Oh, Mum, it's terrible. I've just heard that Emma is dead. Emma Layzell. She sold my flat last year."

Sally's voice had carried to the rest of the group, and there were shocked exclamations all around.

Susannah was the first to find her voice. "That is awful news; there seems to be tragedy everywhere you look these days."

Richard's voice broke across the others. "What happened?"

Sally turned watery eyes towards him, her voice hoarse. "Murder, they said she was murdered."

Sally's mother gasped. "Another one?"

Their loud conversation had drawn others into their circle. A couple over from London for the wedding were trying to figure out what had happened. One of the guests answered the question in their eyes. "Someone's been murdered. There was another one last weekend. It's just unbelievable."

The speaker trailed off as he realised who was within earshot, looking abashed as he glanced towards Richard. "Sorry, didn't want to gossip but... you know."

He shrugged, his mouth a thin, tight line as he acknowledged the apology. "Sure." His voice was abrupt. As he looked at the gossip's crestfallen face, he continued. "Really, I do understand." Turning to the visitors, he said, "Some family members have recently passed away. One was murdered, and the police have reopened the investigation into my aunt's death. Apparently, it's common knowledge. I'm sure you can appreciate that it's all a bit stressful at the moment."

Richard's voice was almost drowned out by shocked gasps as he revealed that Kate Avery's death may not have been an accident.

Inquisitive eyes stared; people were desperate to find out more. But they didn't dare ask, not in front of the Averys. The crowd around them dispersed, leaving Richard and Susannah with the bride's parents.

The father spoke. "I can't believe they think Kate was murdered as well. Did you guys know this Emma? Are the deaths connected?"

Susannah shook her head. "Definitely not. I doubt if Kate or Harriet ever met Emma."

"You knew her?"

"Not really, did we, Richard?" As her husband slowly shook his head, Susannah continued, "Sam went out with her a few years back. We met her once. It wasn't anything serious."

"Wait, was she the divorced one?"

Susannah had the grace to blush. "Yeah. I know I shouldn't have been so judgmental, but I want Sam to be with someone who doesn't have any baggage. Anyway, they only had a handful of dates, so all my worry was for nothing. I can't believe she's dead. Can you, darling?"

Richard said nothing as Susannah continued talking to her friend. He just stared out towards the sea. His hand trembled, just a little, as he held his champagne flute, and he hoped that no one saw.

CHAPTER TWENTY

Grace came in from the gardens as the landline phone rang. She wasn't in the mood for talking, so she let it go to the answering machine. Then she heard the voice coming out of the machine. "Hey, Grace, it's James. Just calling to see how you are. I'll try again..."

"Hi, James. I'm afraid I was screening my calls. It's been a tough day." Her voice wobbled, and she burst into tears.

"Grace, what's wrong?"

She couldn't stop crying. Her breath was ragged, and the more she tried to get the tears under control, the louder she sobbed. She could hear James's compassionate voice trying to soothe her.

"Oh, James, it's awful. Do you know Emma Layzell, she's an estate agent?"

"No, can't say I do. Why? Is something wrong?"

"She's dead, James. She's dead."

"Did you know her well?"

"Not really. I'd only just met her. She had a buyer for Rocque View. Obviously, I'd said we weren't looking to sell. We had lunch yesterday, and afterwards I was thinking she was someone I could become friends with. And then today, to hear she's dead. Murdered. It's crazy, just crazy." Her voice trailed off in bewilderment.

"Murdered? Do the police think it's the same person who killed Harriet?"

"I don't know, I guess it's early days yet. They certainly never hinted at anything like that."

"Is Sam there?"

"No, he's in France, coming back tomorrow."

"Right. I'm coming round, and I'm not taking no for an answer. I'll bring takeaway and a bottle of wine."

"I'd be rotten company. It's a lovely thought, but I'll be fine on my own, so you don't need to do this."

"I may not need to, but I want to. I'll be with you in under an hour."

"Okay, if you really want to. I'll see you then."

As she hung up, Grace reflected that maybe some company wouldn't be a bad thing. Someone to talk to and take her mind away from this nightmare she was living in.

#

Le Claire's shift had officially ended a while back, but he'd worked on, reviewing the evidence to date and trying to make sense of three brutal murders. Apart from a loose connection to Rocque View, he didn't really have anything else to tie the cases together.

When his eyes started to sting, he realised he'd been reading for far too long. Grabbing his jacket, he left the office and drove back to his apartment.

As he navigated the narrow country lanes towards his parents' home, he reflected that the dirt and grime of lowlifes and crime rarely touched people like them. People who had enough money to live in a protected bubble. People like his parents and their friends had no idea of the subculture that ran through and beneath society's respectable veneer, including on this island, where kids casually popped banned substances as if they were downing an illicit beer or wine. In his day, they'd get hauled over the coals for a few drinks and coming home worse for wear; now the kids were more likely to end up in A and E from a bad batch of something bright and shiny and very expensive.

As he turned into their private road, he figured his parents would be out. They were dinner party people, and, as his mother had said they didn't have guests this weekend, he hoped they'd be visiting friends. This was good because they'd have hangovers tomorrow, and neither of them would be in the mood for haranguing him about his wasted life.

He reached for his zapper, and the tall electric gates slowly slid open. The approach to his parents' house was long and straight, the drive bordered by rows of trees that screened the house and garage block, and therefore his apartment, from sight.

As the house came into view, his heart sank. His mother stood in the open doorway waving good-bye to a woman who was about to get into her car. That was all he needed. Sasha.

Le Claire had been playing telephone hide-and-seek with his estranged wife for a couple of days. She was seeking, and he was definitely hiding. He'd now ignored several increasingly irate voice mails from her. He guessed she'd taken matters into her hands and had turned up here looking for him. She'd have met no resistance from his mother; she'd always thought pretty, polished Sasha an ideal match for him. Maybe she had been a match for the man he had been, but they certainly weren't the ideal couple now.

She would soon be his ex-wife, all connections severed, if he ever got round to signing the damned divorce papers. He hadn't deliberately ignored them. He'd just forgotten—that was all. He had a lot on his plate.

As he got his defence ready, Sasha walked towards him, and for a fleeting moment, time shifted and he saw her as she used to be—or more correctly, what he had thought her to be. She was smiling, any trace of rancour missing from her beautifully made-up face. Her dark hair fell in soft, expensive waves and brushed her shoulders. She was tall and slim, her athletic figure the result of hours of running and yoga classes. It seemed as if the angry look she so often cast his way was gone, and she was just the funny, warm girl he'd fallen in love with. The girl with melting, chocolate-brown eyes whose love he had returned a thousandfold. He felt an ache inside him for the loss of all they had meant to each other. But the light must have been in his eyes, for as she got closer, he saw the same glare of disappointment and bubbling rage that had now replaced the easy looks of love.

"Where the hell have you been? Why don't you return my calls?"

If I did that, I'd have you screeching in stereo, he thought. He tried to be the better man, but his temper was roused. "The day you kicked me out and filed for divorce was the day when what I do, or where I've been, ceased being any of your business."

"Don't give me that. If you'd only sign the fucking papers, I'd never need to contact you ever again." She was shouting now, and her voice trailed off. When she spoke again, her voice was softer. "I don't want to be this person, Jack, I really don't, but you drive me to it—I swear you do."

"Look, I forgot. I'm up to my eyes in work with two suspicious deaths and another one today."

"Three? Are they connected?" She was quieter now, all discord gone.

Le Claire had a surge of memory—of the two of them lounging side by side on the sofa, dinner eaten and kitchen tidied, as they sipped coffees and talked about their day and brought each other up to speed on how they'd spent their time apart. He wondered if they'd stopped talking. If that was what had started their problems, or had it been the death knell? He spoke on impulse. "Why don't you come inside for a bit? To be honest, I could do with someone to talk to."

He saw her hesitate for a moment.

"Sure, but I can't stay long."

#

They walked towards the garages. On one side of the rectangular block, a set of white-painted wooden stairs ran to the first floor. The bottom of the building was concrete and steel, but the first floor was covered in planks of weathered wood turned beaten silver by the elements. Sasha followed Le Claire as he climbed the stairs. At the top, he unlocked the door and gestured for her to go in.

"I see the place hasn't changed much."

Le Claire looked around. Light flooded into the long rectangular space from the picture windows. At one end lay a small galley-style kitchen area, separated from the living space by a marble-topped, waist-high dining counter, bar stools tucked neatly underneath.

"I just updated a few pieces."

The furniture was the same—an old squashed sofa and armchair, although the bright red cushions and throws were new. The low wooden coffee table, scarred from propped-up boots, was still piled high with books and magazines. There was also a small shower room and quiet bedroom tucked at the back. Jack saw Sasha look at the closed bedroom before she quickly looked away. That was the one place in which they'd spent most of their time when they were first seeing each other.

Le Claire grimaced. Neither of them needed that memory. "So I'm back where I started out." He took a bottle of ice-cold white wine from the small fridge and poured two glasses—one small, the other much larger. He felt he needed it, though whether from the strains of the day or from Sasha's presence, he wasn't entirely sure.

They sat down, carefully apart, Sasha on the armchair opposite the sofa where Le Claire sat.

She took a small sip of the wine and looked at him over the rim of her glass. Her gaze was direct. "Jack, how are you? About London, I mean?"

His hand shook a little at her unexpected words, and some of the ice-cold wine spilled onto his hand. He carefully wiped the drips on his trousers, not making eye contact with Sasha. They hadn't had this conversation in a long time, and he wasn't going to have it tonight. His voice was abrupt and dismissive. "I try not to think about it too much, especially when I'm in the middle of a murder enquiry."

Sasha looked as if she was going to pursue her questioning but her next words brought them back to the present. "I am so shocked. I can't believe there's been another murder. You didn't answer before—are they connected?"

"I don't know, love. I just don't know."

"Who was killed? Can you tell me?"

He sighed. "As it's apparently all over Facebook, I don't see why not. It was a local estate agent, Emma Layzell. She—"

Le Claire stopped speaking as a shocked gasp escaped from Sasha and the colour drained from her face. "Em? Oh God, no."

"You knew her? I didn't know you knew her. You've never spoken about her."

"It was before I met you. She was Emma Blair then. We were kids, in our late teens. How did she die?"

"We're not releasing that at the moment, so I can't say. Sorry."

Sasha let out a long shaky breath. "Is it connected? Is Emma's death connected to the other two?"

Le Claire sighed. She'd always been a dab hand at putting two and two together.

"Not that I can see for sure at the moment; there are no apparent links. I don't even know if she knew Kate Avery or Harriet Bellingham."

"Well, I don't know about that, but she certainly knew Sam Avery."

Le Claire's eyes sharpened as they focused on her words. "What do you mean?"

Sasha shook her head quickly. "Oh, I didn't mean anything by that. I just remembered that Emma dated Sam for a while. Well, maybe a few weeks. But I only heard about that from another friend. I didn't really know Emma anymore by that time. I guess our friendship ran its course. We lost touch after she got married."

"Was she a bit of a wild girl?" He needed to poke and prod around in the crevices of the victim's life to find out who she really was, no matter how intrusive.

At her sharp look, Le Claire sighed. She thought he was being judgmental. He knew he was simply inquisitive. Another bone of discontent between them.

"No. She wasn't some tart. Well, not then at any rate. She only had a couple of boyfriends when I knew her. We then drifted apart and lost touch. She married. I met you. That's all history now. Anyway, if anything, she was more about the dream rather than reality. She was always mooning after someone or other."

"In what way?"

"She just had a few major crushes on people, pretty intense crushes. I mean, she was nuts, absolutely nuts, about James Grayling."

The name rang a bell with Le Claire, although he couldn't put a finger on why.

"One summer, we trailed a path from the Gunsite Beach to the bars in town, just so Em could accidentally bump into him."

Le Claire felt himself soften towards Sasha. This was the first time in a long time that they were just talking, not arguing. "So he wasn't interested?"

"I guess he may have been at another time, but he had some family issues. Some unknown relative turned up out of the blue. He went off the rails a bit and stopped hanging about with the usual crowd. Anyway, I hear he's done okay for himself, so he must've got sorted out."

Le Claire was amazed. He'd forgotten Sasha's ability to drag bits and pieces of information from her memory. "How do you collect all this stuff?"

"Because I pay attention to what is happening to me, around me, and not just the police file on the desk."

And that, he knew, was the root of their problems.

Sasha set down her barely touched glass of wine. "I better be going." She made for the door and turned round as she opened it, with what looked like a whisper of regret in her eyes. "Jack, sign the papers, love."

Sam sat slightly apart from the stag party. As soon as they had arrived in St Malo, they had dumped their bags at the hotel. Sam hadn't joined the others in their liquid breakfast; it was all a bit too early for that. But several hours later, after a good lunch, he sat nursing a beer as raucous laughter floated around and past him. Lost in his thoughts, he realised he was having to force himself to be part of the group, to join in. It wasn't easy. He'd thought his troubles might seem farther away with some physical distance, that he could let it all just slip away for a while.

As he gazed out to the sea, the voices around him seemed to dull to a distant hum as his thoughts clamoured to be heard.

Time was rushing past, and he felt out of control. This was the most challenging situation he had ever had to face. He had to tie everything up soon, but—and this made him feel the clammy clutch of a cold sweat—he didn't entirely know how this would all end. But end it would. Time—and fate—was rushing towards him. He had to take what opportunities came his way, even if he had to help them on a bit.

CHAPTER TWENTY-ONE

Grace opened the door, a welcome for James in her wobbly smile. He held a bulging bag of what she presumed was takeaway, and two bottles of red wine dangled precariously from one hand.

She reached out. "Here. Let me help." Taking the bottles, Grace led the way upstairs. "I hope these aren't both for us?"

"Well, it's a good wine, so if we don't drink it, promise me you won't let Sam have any, and you'll keep it to yourself."

At Grace's sharp glance, he held up a hand in mock surrender. "Hey, only kidding. Honest."

Grace led the way into the kitchen and set the two bottles on the counter. James stood behind her, one arm snaking past and reaching around her as he placed the takeaway bag beside the wine. For a moment—just a moment—James pressed against her, and Grace couldn't exactly tell if it was an accident or deliberate. But she thought it was on purpose and felt a sense of unease. She tensed, and he quickly moved away, his voice breaking the silence. "Show me where the glasses and bottle opener are, and I'll get us going."

Grace smiled. She must have imagined it, and no wonder she was on edge, imagining what wasn't there—she'd had a hell of a time recently. She pointed towards the table in front of the open glass doors that led to the balcony. The table was set for two, complete with wine glasses and a fancy bottle opener.

Grace busied herself laying out the food. She stood back, looked at the table and grimaced. Her mother would have a fit at seeing the foil containers sitting in full view. But surprisingly, Grace found she really didn't give a damn. She turned to James and smiled. "Sorry, this is all a bit casual, but it is takeout food."

James held two glasses filled with dark red wine and passed one to Grace. "Perfect. The fun of takeout is just serving straight from the cartons. The table looks lovely. You shouldn't have gone to all this trouble."

Silence reigned, broken only by murmurs of appreciation. Grace sighed. "Thanks, James. It's really kind of you to do this tonight."

"It's my pleasure. You've had a really tough time recently. I just can't get my head round the fact that you knew this girl—Emma Layzell, you said?"

"Yes. I mean, I obviously didn't know her very well, but I had lunch with her only yesterday. And just like that, she is gone." Grace shivered and took a sip of her wine. "I just feel a bit shaky. Sorry."

James shook his head, a concerned look on his face. "There is nothing to apologise for. I just want to make sure you are okay, especially being here on your own with Sam in France."

"You've been a really great support. Thank you. I just can't get Emma out of my head."

"I hate to bring the subject up, but surely the police don't think this girl's death has anything to do with what happened to your great-aunts?"

Grace shrugged her shoulders. "I don't know. They didn't say as much, but I got the impression that they were trying to see if there was a connection.

"This must be a nightmare for you."

"That is what it feels like. First Kate, then Harriet. I meant to ask you, what happened with Ray Perkins on Thursday night? Was he okay?"

"Oh, that. I herded him into the bar and bought him a double. The steam had gone out of him, and he headed home after a bit."

"Do you know him well?"

"Not really. He used to come into my restaurants with Harriet. I was just coming over to say hello to you, but Ray got there first. He's a bit rough around the edges, but I've never seen him act that way before. He is a drinker though."

"I guess grief drives us in different ways. I think he really cared for Harriet."

James's look was assessing as he changed the subject. "You don't have anyone pining away for you in the States?"

"Well, I thought I had. Turns out my fiancé was too busy having an affair with my assistant. I only found out by accident when I arrived in Jersey."

"Ouch, that's tough."

"Yeah, I know." Grace sighed as she pushed back from the table. "I believe I've eaten more than enough.

"Me too. Ah, we appear to have polished the bottle off. Shall I open the other one?"

Grace was in no mood for restraint. "Sure, why not? I'll just clear the table."

They worked quietly together. With swift and economic movements, Grace disposed of the leftover food, rinsed the crockery and cutlery and loaded the dishwasher. There was a loud pop as James drew the cork on the second bottle and poured them each a fresh glass.

"Let's sit on the sofa; it's more comfortable."

They sat, one on each end of the sofa. Grace tucked her legs under her, and James relaxed back into the soft cushions. He sipped his wine and said, "So tell me, who is Grace Howard?"

"Oh, that's a tough one. I'm a lawyer—or I was as I've quit my job due to the scummy ex-fiancé and the bitch of an assistant. So I guess I'm an unemployed lawyer. I live in an apartment in New York and spend the weekends at my parents' place by the beach. I don't have any real hobbies as I spent most of my time working. And my social life centred around Carter and my parents. I guess what I'm trying to say is that I don't know who Grace Howard is. Maybe now I'll have the time to find out."

"I wish you luck with that. Personally, I've never wanted to look too closely at myself." James's wink took any deep emotion from the words.

"So who is James Grayling, then?"

"I'm not very interesting. My dad died when I was young, and my mother passed away a few years back."

"I'm sorry. Do you have siblings?"

"No, my parents didn't have any other children."

"I certainly know what it's like to be an only child. My mother can be a little intense sometimes, and that's saying the least of it. And your mother, were you close?"

A shadow flitted across his eyes, dimming them for just a second. "For a long time, we were all each other had. It got a little rough once my dad was gone. But let's not dwell on that tonight. Are you going to stay on the island for a while?"

"I have to stay for the next three months to see out the terms of Kate's will."

She answered the question in James's eyes. "Kate's will stipulated that if Sam and I didn't stay in the house, together, for three months, then the house was to be demolished, the gardens razed and the land sold to developers."

"Isn't that rather controlling? I mean, just to try and throw you and Sam together."

Grace's eyes widened in shock. "Oh no. That wasn't her plan at all. No, what Kate wanted was for either Sam or I to make our permanent home at Rocque View."

"And is that in the cards?"

"It's a beautiful place, and I'm sure I'd be enjoying it more under different circumstances. But I'm really staying to honour Kate's wishes and to see her murderer, and Harriet's, get their due. Then I'll decide where to go and what to do. But I won't be going home for a while. I may just travel around."

James raised his glass in a toast. "To Grace Howard, the intrepid traveller. I envy you."

"Really? You don't seem the type to envy anyone. I mean, you've pretty much got it all." She silently enumerated: good looks, fit body, successful business...

"It's the freedom. And, forgive me, but you seem a little more relaxed than when I first met you."

"Ah, the uptightness would have been learned at my mother's knee. I do feel freer here, less controlled." Grace grimaced as she had a moment of clarity and realised the wine was loosening her tongue. She really had drunk too much.

"And Sam, where does he fit into all this?"

Grace felt the hot, fiery blush race across her cheeks. "Sam? I don't know what you mean."

"Really? Come on, Grace. I've noticed how he looks at you. I've also experienced his aggressive, protective stance whenever I'm around."

Grace was lost for words. Did he mean that Sam felt something for her and that Sam saw James as a threat, a rival? Surely not? She wasn't sure if James was trying to discredit Sam or promote himself.

"Sam and I are just sharing this house, waiting to find out who killed Kate and Harriet," *and*, she silently added, *perhaps Emma*, "and see out the three months. Sam will either take on Rocque View, or it'll be sold. Either way, we'll go our separate ways."

"Think what you will, Grace, but I think Sam looks at you as much more than a temporary housemate."

"I think you're turning it into too much of a romantic situation. It's real life, not a movie."

"So you don't think rom-coms are reality? What movies do you like?" The conversation turned and twisted around likes and dislikes, and Grace suddenly realised this felt like a date, and she was enjoying herself.

James picked up the bottle to pour them more wine and grimaced as a trickle of wine dropped into Grace's glass. "Whoa. I guess I'd better go. Looks like I've outstayed my welcome."

"Absolutely not. It's been a pleasure," Grace said and realised she meant it. "You've certainly taken my mind off what's been going on." *Or was that the wine she'd drunk?* whispered the devil on her shoulder. For she had a horrible feeling that she'd drunk more of the two bottles of wine than James had. She'd have to blame it on the stress.

James stood, as did Grace. But she stumbled, and as she tried to regain her balance, James put out steadying hands. His touch wasn't unpleasant, and Grace didn't push him away. Nor did he remove his hands, which rested gently but firmly on her shoulders. The heat of his palms seared through her top, and she gently swayed towards him.

James steadied her, removed his hands and took a step back. "Sorry, Grace, I think I plied you with too much wine. At least you'll sleep well tonight."

Grace walked slowly down the stairs, holding tightly to the banister, wishing everything would stop swaying. Or was that her? Once she reached the bottom of the stairs, she steadied herself and opened the front door. Unfortunately, she did so a little too enthusiastically, and the door landed hard, and loud, against the wall. "Sorry, that was clumsy of me."

Suddenly, the air was filled with a scrabbling of claws and canine howling. The dogs, who'd been in an exhausted sleep for hours, came bounding out of the downstairs garden room, grinding to a halt as they saw Grace and James.

Both dogs immediately moved to Grace's side, eyes never leaving James, Daisy leaning heavily against Grace's thigh and Barney sitting almost on top of her feet.

"James, meet Barney and Daisy, my houseguests for the night."

James moved forward, as if to kiss Grace good-bye, but as he reached out, both dogs growled, low and menacing. He took a fast step back and held up both hands, palms out in surrender. "Hey, guys, I'm not going to hurt your girl. Guess that's my cue to leave." He gestured towards the dogs sitting like sentinels by Grace's side. "Maybe you should keep that posse close by you. They are definitely great guard dogs." And with that, he walked down the steps and disappeared into the darkness.

Grace stood holding the open door for a moment. She'd had a lovely evening and hadn't really expected to feel that way. With a sigh, she closed the door and turned to make her way upstairs. However, she stopped short when she saw two doleful pairs of brown eyes staring at her. Grace gave in. "Come on, you two, let's go to bed."

Ears pricking, Daisy and Barney raced up the stairs, Barney's short legs working furiously to keep up with Daisy's long, elegant gait.

Grace awoke with a violent start. Her eyes shot wide open, and then she winced and shut them tight against the glare of the brightness streaming through the windows. She must've slept in, as the sun was pretty high. The next thing she noticed was the pounding in her head and the dryness in her throat. Damn. This was why she usually stopped after having a single glass of wine. She had a raging hangover, and she hadn't even stood up yet.

Blood in the Sand

Squinting against the brightness, she saw two shapes silhouetted against the uncovered windows. The dogs sat side by side, staring out into the gardens as if mesmerised. Sharp barks vibrated across the room. It was this noise that had woken Grace up. Thank heavens something had. "Come on, you two, keep the noise down. Come back to bed." Neither dog moved or even acknowledged her presence.

Grace sighed and, throwing the duvet back, got out of bed and crossed to the windows. The dogs weren't moving, just staring straight ahead, their growls now low and menacing. "Oh, for heaven's sake, guys. What's up?"

Daisy's soft brown gaze focused on Grace as she shuffled backwards and pressed herself heavily against Grace's legs in a protective stance.

"What's wrong? You okay?"

Grace felt a shiver as her senses heightened and her heartbeat raced. She looked outside, but all she could see was the garden—nothing unusual. But weren't dogs known for having some form of additional awareness? She shook her head to rid herself of fanciful notions. She was a lawyer, for Christ's sakes.

Bending down, she stroked the Doberman's head as the dog snuggled closer. Who was protecting whom? Barney had lost interest in whatever was outside and started bouncing up and down, trying to catch Grace's attention. Soon, the two dogs were happily vying for who could get the most cuddles from Grace and, in return, give the wettest kisses and licks. Standing up, Grace pulled herself away from the dogs, who immediately followed her. She mentally numerated her tasks. Throw on some clothes and walk and then feed the dogs. Have a shower. Eat breakfast. Get rid of her hangover before Sam came back.

CHAPTER TWENTY-TWO

Le Claire sat alone in the thankfully empty police cafeteria, nursing a mug of coffee, wincing as he took another tentative sip of the bitter, murky brew. He wished he'd taken the time to get someone to run out to the nearby coffee bar, but he hadn't thought of it. And that was no wonder because the recent murders were occupying his every waking thought. All he had was three dead bodies, a group of loosely connected people and barely a motive in sight.

He looked forlornly at his coffee cup, debated having another sip and was just about to give in when a steaming takeaway cup was placed in front of him. Looking up, he quirked a brow as Dewar sat down opposite him, sipping at her own drink. "To what do I owe this pleasure?"

"I saw you walk in here, sir. I was on my way to speak to you, so I thought I'd do you a favour and get you a decent cup of java."

"So the favour to me is having a great cup of coffee and the favour to yourself is that it might—just might—lighten my mood?"

A dark flush spread over Dewar's cheeks. "And has it?"

"Out with it. What's the issue?"

She took a breath and plunged straight in. "It's the warrant, sir, for Emma Layzell's phone records."

Le Claire didn't say anything. He just stared and waited, although he figured his eyes betrayed the impatience he felt. Dewar took another breath and continued. "It's just proving a bit difficult to get in touch with the duty jurat, sir. So I haven't actually got the warrant yet, but I will. Soon."

"See that you do. We have little enough to go on, so it would at least be a start to know who the victim was talking to during her last hours on earth."

"Yes, sir, I'll try harder." She briskly rose as she spoke and made to leave.

Le Claire's impatient words made her halt. "Oh, for God's sake, don't be so bloody sensitive. I know you're doing your best. I just need it to be better."

"Thanks, sir. I'll go and get onto it again."

Le Claire stood and shrugged on his jacket. "Come with me first. We've got a visit to make."

#

Grace heard a taxi come up the drive and opened the door just as Sam was juggling bags and searching his pockets for his keys.

He looked up and grinned. "Now that's what I call a welcome home. A gorgeous girl waiting at the door. Miss me?"

Grace wasn't in the mood for Sam's flirting right now. She didn't comment. Sam dumped his bags in the hall and followed her upstairs. "So how were the dogs?"

"Fine. I tired them out so much on the beach that they slept all through the evening and didn't even realise James was here until he was leaving."

Sam stilled. "James was here?"

"Yes, he popped over with takeout to try and cheer me up."

"Cheer you up? What was getting you down?"

"Oh, Sam, it's awful. Emma Layzell has been killed. It's another murder."

"I can't believe this. What happened?"

"I don't know, just that she was found by one of her employees at her home. The alarm was raised when Emma didn't turn up to the office and missed a couple of appointments."

"I can't get my head around this. Poor girl. Do the police think the murders are connected?"

"I don't know, but it all seems very odd. When your dad came to pick the dogs up earlier, he said you'd be shocked, but I didn't think you knew Emma that well."

Before Sam could answer her, the doorbell rang, loud and shrill.

Sam said, "I better get that. Won't be a moment."

He made his way downstairs, leaving Grace awaiting his return. Had Sam known Emma a lot better than he had let on? It hadn't seemed that way when Grace had first mentioned Emma. In fact, he'd been pretty dismissive about her the first day she had turned up at the house. Why would his dad have thought Sam would be upset? Grace pushed the thought aside—there was enough to think about without conjuring up any more issues.

As Grace walked down the stairs, she heard voices in the hallway. One voice made her stop and stand still and silent. Le Claire.

"Mr Avery, sorry to interrupt you just as soon as you've got off the boat from France, but I need to speak to you about another recent death."

Sam's voice was noncommittal. "Yes?"

Grace was straining to hear. She slowly made her way past the landing and, crouching, perched on the top stair, leaning forward to try and capture every word.

"We are investigating the death of a young woman whom we believe you know, Emma Layzell."

"I hardly knew Emma, so I'm afraid there's nothing I can say to help."

Le Claire queried, "You don't seem surprised at the news. And I understand that at one time you knew Miss Layzell rather well. You dated for a while."

Sam spoke, and there was a combative edge to his voice, "Look, I went out with Emma Layzell for about two weeks years ago. She was a complete nightmare, calling me nonstop, often in the middle of the night, hanging about and waiting for me outside the office when she knew we didn't have a date that night. She even turned up one afternoon when she knew I was going to a small family barbecue. She bordered on being a complete stalker. I dumped her as soon as I could. I've barely spoken a word to her in years. I'm sorry she's dead, but I just didn't know her anymore. I really can't help you."

Grace rammed a fist against her mouth to prevent any sound escaping. Sam had never indicated that he knew Emma as anything other than a passing acquaintance. Why would he not say anything?

Le Claire's voice rose up the stairs loud and clear. "When was the last time you saw Miss Layzell?"

"Maybe a week or so ago, but I didn't speak to her. She was leaving here. She came to ask Grace about putting this place on the market."

Dewar asked, "So you can't think of anyone who would want to harm her?"

Grace grimaced at Sam's harsh laugh. "Emma was driven, with an obsessive personality. I'm sure she aggrieved any number of people on a regular basis. But enough for anyone to kill her? That's extreme."

There was a pause. Sam continued in a gentler tone, "Emma and I had a bad breakup. We had only been casually dating, but she put me through the wringer. She is—was—a bad memory. But I'd never have wished this on her, never."

Le Claire asked, "When did you leave for France?"

"Yesterday's early boat."

"Where you were from 1:00 a.m. on Friday morning until the boat left?"

"I suppose I asked for that. I was here, Chief Inspector, in bed. And no, I don't have anyone to alibi me."

"Very well. We'll be in touch if we need to know anything else."

Grace heard leather soles on the ceramic tiles; they were leaving. She carefully stood and went to the top of the stairs. Le Claire and Dewar came into view, but they couldn't yet see past the corner to where she was.

"Wait." Sam came up behind them. "What about Kate? Have you found out who killed her yet? Or Harriet?"

Le Claire turned. "No, those investigations are ongoing."

"That all you have to say? You're no closer to solving the case? What about Emma? Are they all connected?"

"I really couldn't say at the moment, Mr Avery. As I said, we'll be in touch if we have any more questions."

And with that, they left. And Grace silently made her way to her bedroom.

#

She didn't know what to think. Sam had seemed so aggressive when he'd spoken about Emma, completely unlike his usual self. Then

Kelly Clayton

again, did she really know him? Grace had always thought she was a good judge of character, but wasn't she the one who had thought Carter was a loving fiancé? And he'd turned out to be a faithless toad.

The harsh sound of the house telephone ringing dragged her from her thoughts. The sound quickly stopped.

Just as Grace was wondering who had been on the phone, she heard a knock on her bedroom door. What did Sam want now? "Come in."

"You never came down after the police arrived. That's who was at the door, by the way."

Grace decided to play dumb. "What did they want?"

"Oh, just a few questions about my whereabouts in case they could put me in the frame for Emma Layzell's murder."

Grace waited, but Sam didn't elaborate further, so she prodded. "How strange. I mean, it's not as if you knew her that well. Why would they think to question you?"

Sam shook his head. "I don't know. I guess they maybe think it's connected to the deaths of Harriet and Kate, which, by the way, they don't seem to have a clue about."

Grace didn't know how to process his words. He was still going to make out that he hadn't known Emma. Just as she was trying to decide what to say next, Sam spoke up, "That was Paul Armstrong on the phone."

"What did he want?"

"He wanted to ask if seven or seven thirty was okay for tonight? For dinner."

"Dinner—what? I can't believe he is asking us to dinner at such late notice. I don't really feel like..." Grace's words trailed off, and she opened her eyes wide as realisation struck. "Oh no, I forgot."

"Don't worry, so did I. But I made out that I knew exactly what he was talking about, and luckily the penny dropped pretty soon. Anyway, I said that would be fine. You okay with that?"

"Of course, we can't let him down at this stage."

"Okay, so I'll catch you later?"

"Sure. I'm just going to rest for a bit."

Sam turned and walked out of the room. The moment the door closed behind him, the smile fell from her face. How was she going to get through the evening ahead knowing that Sam was lying to her? But was he only lying about knowing Emma? Or was he hiding something else?

#

An hour later and Grace was rested, showered and changed. Grabbing her handbag, she made her way downstairs. The first floor was quiet, and Sam was nowhere to be seen. The sounds of the TV were in the background, and she followed them to the downstairs lounge, where she found Sam relaxing on the couch.

He jumped to his feet when he saw her. "You look lovely, Grace. That colour is really good on you."

Grace blushed at the compliment. She knew the emerald-green top looked good with her skinny, dark jeans, but it was still nice to hear the words. She almost forgot that Sam wasn't her favourite person at the moment. Only almost though.

He gestured towards the door. "If you're ready, shall we go?"

Sam unlocked the Jeep and opened the door for Grace. She slid into the passenger seat and saw Sam walking up the drive, away from the car, towards someone who had just come through the gates. Luca.

#

"Hi, Luca, how you doing?"

"Fine, Sam. I came to see you yesterday, but Grace told me you were in France."

"That's right. What did you want me for?"

"I'm still sure someone has been wandering round the garden at night. After what happened to Kate, it's got me worried."

Sam frowned. "You don't think it's the same kids as before?"

"No. The kids usually hung out beneath the trees deep in the borders. What I saw is disturbed ground in the open. Do you think the killer is hanging about here?"

Sam shook his head. "Christ, I hope not. It doesn't make sense."

Luca grimaced. "I know but it just seems so odd."

"Leave it to me, Luca. I'll keep my eyes open, and we'll be careful."

At Sam's final words, Luca nodded, waved to Grace in the car, and made his way to the road.

# #

Sam jumped into the car and fired up the engine. Once they reached the road, he blasted the horn as they drove past Luca. The gardener lifted his arm and waved in response.

Grace asked, "So what did Luca want?"

"Nothing important. Just some questions about the gardens."

"Oh, okay. He looked a little strained. Do you think the gardens are too much for him on his own?"

"He's fine. Don't worry about it. I know the last thing you feel like is going out tonight, but Paul is good company and always great fun."

Grace settled down for the short car journey. Maybe different company was just what she needed to keep her discordant thoughts at bay.

CHAPTER TWENTY-THREE

Le Claire was at his desk in the incident room, his entire focus on the massive white board that dominated one wall. It was covered in scribblings of timelines, opportunities and alibis. No crime was perfect. There had to be something they had missed. His desk phone rang, and he considered ignoring it, especially when he recognised the caller ID. But he couldn't. What the hell did he want?

"Chief, what can I do for you?"

"My office, now. We have a visitor." As the call disconnected, Le Claire sighed and headed to see the top boss. He had a feeling this wasn't going to be pleasant.

"Come on in, Le Claire. I'm sure you know Senator Groves. Senator, this is DCI Jack Le Claire, who is in charge of the murder investigations."

The man sitting in front of the chief's desk turned. "You'll be Philip's son. How are the folks?"

"Fine, thank you, sir."

Senator Bill Groves was a thin, spare man with a politician's smile and an accountant's heart. Le Claire didn't like being ambushed, yet that's what it felt like when presented to a member of the island's parliamentary body like a sacrificial lamb. He liked it even less when they referenced his father.

"Chief Wilson tells me that you are no nearer solving these terrible murders."

"Come on, Bill, that is not what I said. DCI Le Claire is following several leads and investigating all avenues."

"Bullshit. We've just had a third murder. That is two elderly sisters and a young woman who I understand knew one of them—

the estate agent girl. They have to be connected. Find what ties them together and close the cases—quickly."

Le Claire couldn't help but think how easy that made it all sound. If only. "I can assure you, sir, that we will close these cases once we have finalised our investigations."

"You better, son. This is a holiday island, and we don't want the tourists frightened away because you can't do your job properly. People come here for a good time and to relax. We can't have any more blood in the sand. So find these killers—and soon."

With that, the senator left.

Chief Wilson sighed. "I'm sorry. He is a total idiot, but he turned up here out of the blue, and I didn't want to give him anything else to complain about. Hopefully, it made him feel good to shout at a policeman, and Philip Le Claire's son at that. Maybe he'll leave us alone for a bit. There's a lot riding on this case, son—for you as well."

Le Claire understood that to mean that London was still hanging over him, and so it should. Didn't they know that he was his own worst critic? Couldn't they see that the guilt shimmered and slithered beneath the surface, ready to consume him if he let down his guard, even for a moment?

Paul Armstrong's house was a two-storey cube of glass and chrome. A mass of leafy trees grew around the building, giving Grace the feeling that she was in the middle of a forest. The lower storey was fronted by vast bifold doors, which were currently wide open; in front of them lay a painted deck area. A smiling Paul Armstrong, looking years younger in a casual shirt and pale trousers, beckoned them into the house.

They walked straight into a large open-plan lounge and kitchen and took in the vibrant furnishings—yellow sofas, a bright blue rug, emerald-green cushions. Somehow it worked.

Grace said, "You have a stunning place. Have you lived here long?"

"I got divorced about five years ago and thought I'd go for my dream. It took a couple of years to get everything finalised, but I've lived here for nearly three years now, and I never get tired of it. Let's sit down. I've laid out some drinks and appetisers on the table."

As they sat, Paul continued. "I heard about that poor girl, Emma Layzell. What a terrible tragedy."

Grace asked, "Did you know her?"

"No, but I knew of her. Kate said she'd been on at her for months to sell Rocque View. Apparently, there was a firm buyer in place. Miss Layzell wrote to me after Kate passed and said the offer—a very generous offer—was still on the table."

Sam said, "And we all know Kate didn't want to sell."

"Kate and Sam fell in love with the place the second they saw it. It was being sold by a woman who'd recently been widowed, and I think she'd been left in pretty bad financial shape, so she wanted a quick sale."

Grace smiled. "And now we have the privilege of living there for a while. It's certainly been a haven for me."

"I am so glad, my dear. Now I'm afraid I'm no great shakes as a cook, but I am a dab hand at a roast, so we've got marinated lamb and the trimmings."

Sam lifted a brow. "I am impressed."

Grace was silent as she considered that Sam had yet again let an opportunity pass by to say that he had known Emma Layzell. She just couldn't think what that might mean.

#

Several hours later, Sam parked up in front of Rocque View. The evening had passed in pleasant, inconsequential talk, and to Grace, it had been an island of calm in the tornado of the past weeks.

As Sam closed the front door behind them, he asked, "Do you fancy a nightcap? Perhaps a glass of red wine?"

Before Grace could speak, her cell rang, and she couldn't help but think that she was saved by the bell. She smiled at Sam. "Sorry!" Fumbling in her bag, she finally grabbed her phone and, noting the caller, grimaced and said, "I better take this. Excuse me."

She answered the call as she made her way to her bedroom. "Hello, Mother. This is a surprise."

"Grace, dear, how are you?" Saccharin sweetness dripped through the phone. That made Grace wary.

"I'm fine. How are you and Dad?"

"Good. Your father's case is almost at its conclusion. But I've called to talk to you about something specific."

Grace tried to be charitable, tried to dampen the thought that her mother only ever followed her own agenda. "And what would that be, then?"

"Don't be snippy. Anyway, I have marvellous news. About Carter."

Grace felt her stomach flip. "Mother, I don't believe there is anything you can say about Carter that I would want to hear. I don't want to talk about it."

"I don't expect you to talk, just listen. I saw Carter at the tennis club this morning. He was having brunch with his parents. We joined them."

"The guy has an affair behind my back, doesn't even have the guts to tell me, and then, when he's caught red-handed, gushes about how he is in love with my assistant and you join him for a Sunday morning cappuccino? It's beyond belief."

"Grace Howard! I do not know what has gotten into you, talking to me that way. I cannot imagine what kind of people you must be mixing with for this behaviour to rub off onto you. Your father and I have known the Lawsons all our married life. I am not going to stop speaking to them just because you couldn't keep their son's interest."

"What? So the breakup is my fault?"

"Carter wouldn't have looked elsewhere if you'd been keeping him happy. He would never have had the inclination to eye up that slut if all his needs, especially his male needs, were being met."

Grace blanched. "I am not having this conversation with you."

"Very well. Anyway, Carter was in good form. He was keen to talk about you. He wanted to know what was happening. He was so shocked to hear about your great-aunts. I could tell he was worried about you. If only you'd come back home. Pretty yourself up and let him see what he has discarded."

There was a pause, and when her mother next spoke, Grace could hear the slight tremor in her voice. "Grace, this isn't how things are meant to be. We should be planning your wedding. There is a lovely brownstone that your father and I thought would be perfect for your first home together. People like us don't just take offence at the slightest mishap. Goddamn it, Grace. Come back here and fight for your life."

Grace sighed, long and heartfelt. Her tone was soft as she said, "But that isn't my life any longer. And I see Carter's betrayal as more than a mishap to navigate past."

"I have said my piece, Grace, but mark my words: if you actually bothered to put your full focus into this, I know you could get Carter back. All you have to do is come home."

"Thanks for the call, Mother. I do appreciate it, but I don't want Carter back. Look, it's late here. I better go."

As she dropped her phone back into her bag, Grace pondered where this new strength came from. Perhaps it was losing Kate, maybe the Carter breakup or the realisation that life is a frail commodity. Whatever it was, she prayed that it lasted. As she climbed the stairs to her room and readied herself for bed, Grace's thoughts were of Carter and the life they'd had together. Had it been all that bad? And was her mother right? Was something there to rescue?

Rocque View lay asleep. Moonlight reflected off the white-painted walls, which were stark against the dark surrounds of the gardens. A growing breeze rustled through the trees and blew the odd leaf across the patio. The tide was high, and thunderous waves crashed against the granite sea wall.

The man stood in the shadows of a mature oak, concealed beneath its spreading branches. He glanced at the illuminated dial of his watch—almost 3:00 a.m.—and then tucked the watch, and its offending light, under the cuff of his dark jacket.

Moving forward, he pulled his baseball cap farther over his brow and hefted the heavy bag he carried higher on his shoulder. He had to finish this—and soon.

He scanned the gardens, mindful of the hidden recesses among the deep borders, his eyes alert for the slightest movement. Then he shook his head. Who could possibly be watching him? No one, that's who.

#

Luca's knees ached, as did his back and just about every other part of him. However, it was his heart that had given him the most trouble. He had felt as if it was going to leap out of his chest when the dark figure had emerged from the side of the house, their gaze slowly—excruciatingly slowly—raking over the garden, seemingly seeking out the darkest corners.

He had shrunk farther back into the deepest foliage, hoping that his dark clothes would render him invisible to the naked eye. He had even rubbed handfuls of soil on his face in an effort to blend into his surroundings. That made him feel rather foolish, but then again, what could be more absurd than his current endeavour? Lurking in his employer's garden in the dead of the night, hoping to see what? He had been half-convinced that nothing would happen. That he would spend an uncomfortable night in the damp outdoors and return home to a ticking-off from his wife, followed by an "I told you so" tirade.

But then the man had appeared—he figured it had to be a man from the height and build—and he knew his worst imaginings had been right. Sam had confirmed the rumours that Kate had been killed, and someone had been haunting her property ever since.

Luca saw the man move towards the corner of the garden nearest the house and firmed his own fist against the handle of the spade he'd brought with him for protection. He had no option; he had to do something. Shifting his grip so that he held the spade in both hands, he moved forward, carefully placing his feet on the soft grass to muffle any sound.

A loud crack behind him startled Luca enough that he dropped the spade. He turned around and reeled back as a large fist smashed into his face.

Blood in the Sand

The assailant drew back his arm, ready to launch another punch, but his victim lay dazed, eyes closed. It had turned out to be a stroke of luck that he had trodden on the twigs scattered on the grass. The noise he'd made had him cursing at first, but he'd instinctively reacted as his startled prey had turned around. One hard hit and the weakling had collapsed like a row of skittles. He was sure there hadn't been time for his face to be seen. In any event, he wore a woollen cap, the wide brim casting disguising shadows over his face.

He took a moment to look across the lawn at the man standing by the borders. He raised his hand in greeting and wondered how many times he'd have to save his sorry ass. Not that he was ever grateful.

His victim made frantic grabbing motions, using all his effort to try and reach out for the spade that lay to his side. Fingertips were within grasping distance when he kicked the wooden handle out of his way. Bending down, he picked up the spade in both hands, swung it easily above his head, and brought it crashing down on his victim's skull. The body lay still and unmoving.

He dragged the body by the arms and dumped it at the back of the borders. There was nothing he could do to conceal what had happened. He left the spade next to the body. He was wearing gloves, and there wouldn't be anything to connect him to this night's work.

CHAPTER TWENTY-FOUR

Dewar strode into Le Claire's office with a spring in her step and a wide smile on her face, clutching a sheaf of papers, which she waved in the air. The look on her face was that of a victor expecting their due tribute. *Christ*, he thought, *she looks almost girlish.* This, for the straight-faced Dewar, was quite something.

Le Claire acknowledged her smug, expectant look and gave in. "Okay, what are you so damned pleased with yourself about?"

"As you know, we've been trying to get Emma Layzell's phone logs. However," and here she rolled her eyes, "apparently telephone companies don't like giving out customer information, especially on a weekend."

Le Claire frowned. "Didn't you have a warrant? I thought you were having one signed by the duty jurat."

"I did, but I was transferred through a line of superiors, all saying they couldn't make the decision to release the records until—finally—last night I spoke to the head honcho for the Channel Islands. He arranged for one of their guys to access the records, and I've just been to pick them up." Dewar brandished the papers like a hard-won trophy.

Le Claire's smile was wide. "Okay, go and see what you can find in them and report back to me."

Dewar looked like the cat that had devoured an entire carton of cream. "I don't need to, sir. The telecoms boss was so worried that his people had upset us that he instructed his tech guy to do a thorough job. We don't just have the numbers Emma Layzell called, we've got the names those numbers are registered to. And there are some surprises."

Blood in the Sand

Le Claire knew by the look in Dewar's eyes that he was going to like what was coming next.

#

Grace lay in bed, drifting in and out of a hazy twilight sleep. She loved this time of the morning. Not quite asleep, yet not exactly awake either. She'd slept soundly, which was surprising considering that she usually felt on edge after a conversation with her mother. Grace brushed the thought aside. She wasn't going to think of that today. She snuggled deeper under the duvet, almost rolling herself into the downy folds. Closing her eyes, she willed herself to drift off, just for a little while. It was Sunday after all.

The ringing of the front doorbell brought an end to any dreams of a lie in, the shrill ring seeming to bounce off the walls and break into the slumberous quiet of the house.

With a groan, Grace hauled herself out of bed, and, pausing to throw a cotton dressing gown over her nightdress, she wrenched open her bedroom door and ran down the stairs. As Grace reached the first floor, she saw Sam disappear down the stairs in front of her. He was wearing baggy flannel shorts and a faded T-shirt, hair mussed and feet bare. Grace ignored the internal stirring at this sight and followed close behind. She may not entirely trust Sam, but her body didn't appear to care about that.

Sam blocked the open door, and Grace had to peer around him to see who it was. The tense face of Luca's wife stared back at her.

"I am so sorry to bother you both, but I just wondered if you'd seen Luca. He didn't come home last night."

Sam looked back at Grace and lifted his brows. He was obviously thinking the same as her. Why would they know? It sounded like their gardener was up to no good.

Sam's voice was gentle. "Sorry, afraid we wouldn't know where he is. Have you tried his mobile?"

Fiona lifted a shaky hand and indicated the phone she held. "Repeatedly. But it just kicks into voice mail. I thought you might know since he was in the garden last night." Fiona turned to walk away as Sam put out a hand and lightly touched her arm.

"What do you mean, Fiona? Do you mean when he came to see me before I went out last evening?"

She shook her head. "No, he came home after that and had his supper. Said he'd seen you and he was going to—as he put it—stake out the gardens to see if he could catch whoever was coming in at night."

"I had no idea he was going to do that. I said I would deal with it. Maybe he went straight to the pier?"

Fiona shook her head. "No, I thought of that. But I remembered he said the fishing club wasn't meeting this Sunday."

Grace slid past Sam until she was standing next to Fiona on the doorstep. "What were you going to deal with?"

Sam looked apologetic. "I didn't want you to be concerned. Luca thought we may have had an intruder in the gardens over the past week. I said I'd look into it."

Grace recalled how she had slept deep and heavy two nights previously. The dogs had been staring out the window when she awoke. Had they seen someone? She was being fanciful, surely?

Sam gestured towards the gardens and spoke to Fiona. "I know you're worried. Why don't Grace and I have a quick look around? He may have fallen asleep."

Grace gave Sam a disbelieving look. Who'd fall asleep in a dew-covered garden when they only lived a short walk away?

"Okay. I am really sorry to be a bother, but that would put my mind at rest."

All three walked around the back of the house, Sam poking about the borders and bushes, parting fronds and ferns to check in the undergrowth. They moved around to the front of the house, where the borders were wider, and Grace helped Sam in the search. Soon, they were almost at the top of the lawn. Fiona coloured a little. "Sorry, he can't be here. I'll just try and call him again."

It took the three of them a moment to realise what had broken the gentle quiet of the garden. A ringing telephone.

Sam pointed to the deepest border and a lush weeping willow. "It's coming from there."

Running towards the sound, the two women following, Sam leapt over the low granite wall that supported the raised area and, bending forward, swept back the drooping boughs of the willow. "Oh, Christ!"

Luca lay unmoving on the damp ground, the discarded spade to the side of him. Fiona was right behind Sam and fell to her knees, her frantic hands reaching out to touch her husband, the vicious wound on his head visible against the stark paleness of his skin. Sam gently grabbed her hands. "We better not touch anything. Grace, call an ambulance. Quick."

Le Claire and Dewar were driving to their interview. Dewar continued to fill her boss in on all she knew about the telephone logs. "One number was dialled repeatedly over a three-hour period. As I mentioned, it's registered to a company. There was one other number that was called, just once."

"We'll deal with the single call later. Turn in on the left. I think this is the Averys' address."

As Dewar turned into the drive, they saw a charming brick farmhouse sitting squarely in landscaped gardens and surrounded by fields heavy with crops. "They're doing well, sir, even if they are short of an investor."

"Yes, but it's starting to annoy me that this family is connected in one way or another to all our open cases."

Susannah Avery opened the door herself, elegant in a pale cream shift dress and holding a matching jacket. "Oh, hello, you've just caught me. I am on my way to a lunch appointment. How can I help you?"

Le Claire responded. "Actually, it's your husband I want a quick word with. Is he available?"

Le Claire noticed that Susannah Avery paused and looked as if she was going to question him, but instead she smiled and said, "Of course. Richard is in his study."

A cream-painted door lay half-open at the end of the wide entrance hall. The thick internal walls amplified the sound of their shoes on the flagstones tiles. They followed her into what turned out to be a large study, the shelved walls holding hundreds of books. Richard Avery sat at an elegant oak desk that dominated the centre of his room. He looked up from his computer as they entered. "This is a surprise. Please take a seat."

Le Claire and Dewar sat in the two matching armchairs that faced Richard Avery whilst Susannah Avery perched on the edge of her husband's desk, gently swinging one bare, suntanned leg. Le Claire couldn't help thinking what an attractive woman she was. Richard Avery was a lucky man.

"Mrs Avery, we don't want to keep you from your lunch."

She glanced at her husband, whose shuttered face gave nothing away. "Susannah, would you mind?"

The sharp look she shot at her husband spoke volumes. Yes, she did mind, but she turned to Le Claire. "I'll make some drinks. Tea or coffee?"

Le Claire could feel Dewar's eyes on him and so said, with a sigh, "I'll have a coffee, black, and my colleague will have some tea." He could sense Dewar's smile. He didn't want a coffee, but he did want Susannah Avery out of the way for more than a couple of minutes.

The door closed behind her, and silence reigned until Richard Avery cleared his throat. To Le Claire's ear, the sound was rough with nerves. "Mr Avery, we'd like to ask you a few questions about Emma Layzell. Did you know her?"

"Emma? Why, yes, although not that well. She dated my son, Sam, a few years ago. Nothing serious. I believe it only lasted a few weeks. We heard—that is, Susannah and I—we heard yesterday that Emma was murdered. Shocking, absolutely shocking."

Le Claire's thought was that the Jersey grapevine never failed.

"Yes, that is correct. We are treating the death as suspicious. May I ask if you had any contact with Miss Layzell recently?"

"No, not at all. Look, what is this all about?"

Dewar leaned forward. "In the early hours of yesterday morning, shortly before her death, Emma Layzell called a mobile number repeatedly—over a dozen times in the space of a few hours. That number was registered to your company."

"That's ridiculous."

"That scheming bitch." Susannah Avery's voice exploded from the doorway, the tray in her hands trembling a little. Dewar moved and took the heavy tray and laid it on an empty side table, looking longingly at the teapot. Red-faced and struggling to conceal her anger, Susannah Avery swept into the room and stood beside her husband's chair, one hand resting on his shoulder.

A show of solidarity, thought Le Claire. *Wonder why she thinks that is necessary?* "What did you mean by that comment, Mrs Avery?"

She was fierce as she turned and answered. "I don't want to speak ill of the dead, but the likes of Emma Layzell never could see an opportunity slip by. My son comes from a good family, and we're not badly off. That little tart must've thought she won the lottery when Sam started going out with her. Luckily, he came to his senses and dumped her." She took a breath and continued her tirade. "It's obvious, isn't it? She heard that Sam had come into half of Kate's estate, and she was trying to get him back."

Her husband's raised voice cut her off, weariness evident in his tone. "Susannah! Be quiet. That's enough. We don't know any of what you've said to be true."

Before she could say any more, Dewar said, "You certainly have strong feelings about Miss Layzell."

"Mrs Layzell—she was divorced." Her voice dripped with condemnation.

"I take it you disapproved of her?"

"We're Catholic, and, old-fashioned as it may seem, divorce has no place in our world, and certainly not in a prospective daughter-in-law."

Le Claire interjected, "If we could get back to the questions we need answered. Dewar, do you have details of the mobile number we need to allocate a user to?"

"Yes, sir." Dewar handed the paper to Richard Avery, who immediately scanned the digits.

Le Claire asked, "Do you know who that number belongs to?"

"Not immediately, no. But I can check it with the office in the morning. We have several phones that are held in a pool, and we issue them to consultants and general staff."

"Thank you. We'll wait to hear from you. In the meantime, can you let me know if your company had any dealings with Layzell Estates?"

"We tend to market through two or three agents. I'd need to review what, if anything, we do with them."

"Please do. Finally, may I ask where you were between midnight on Thursday and 8:00 a.m. on Friday morning?"

Before her husband could speak, Susannah Avery rounded on Le Claire-her face reddened in rage. "That has to be a joke. Richard barely knew the bloody woman."

Richard Avery placed a comforting hand on his wife's arm. "Please, darling, the police are only doing their job." Turning back to Le Claire, he continued, "I was at home. We stayed in on Thursday night, as we attended a big wedding on Friday. I left the house around eight thirty to take our dogs to Grace Howard at Rocque View. I came straight back here, and we both left for the hotel about an hour or so later."

In a calmer voice now tinged with frost, his wife concurred with his account. "I can vouch for my husband."

Le Claire stood. "Thank you for your time. We'll wait to hear from you about that mobile number. We'll see ourselves out." And they left the Averys in their study.

Richard stood and took his wife into his arms. She was shaking as she said, "Oh, Richard, we've seen more of the police these last weeks than in our entire life. When will this all end? I just want us to get back to normal." She finished on a sob.

Richard gently ran a soothing hand over his wife's hair. "Hush, love, hush. We've nothing to worry about."

Susannah looked into her husband's face; her gaze was direct and perhaps a little calculating. "I'm glad to hear that because, if I am truthful, I don't know if you were in the house during the time the inspector mentioned. You never came to bed, remember? Same as last night. That's a habit I'd like you to break, darling."

Richard Avery felt the power balance in his marriage quiver and ever so slightly tilt in his wife's favour.

CHAPTER TWENTY-FIVE

Le Claire and Dewar were on their way speak to the next person their list when his mobile rang. "Le Claire speaking." He remained impassive as he listened to the caller. "We're on our way" was his only comment.

"Sir?"

"Turn around. We need to get to the hospital—fast."

#

They were directed by a clinically efficient receptionist to the right floor. Le Claire pushed through wide double doors into the ward, closely followed by Dewar.

Grace Howard and Sam Avery were huddled together on hard plastic chairs the same putty colour as the sterile hospital walls.

Le Claire murmured a brief "hello" as he made his way past them to where a uniformed policeman sat. "Briars, what's the story?"

The young constable rose, took out his notebook and slowly flipped through the pages, carefully reading what was noted on each one before checking the next.

Le Claire groaned. People usually said that one of the most disturbing things in life was that as they got older, policemen seemed to get younger. *Christ,* thought Le Claire, *they should do my job.* "Get on with it, son."

With a flushed face, Briars did just that. "Sir, Mr de Freitas, Luca de Freitas, is a gardener and handyman. One of his jobs was at the property where he was found, Rocque View. He never came home last night, and his wife went looking for him this morning. According to his wife, he thought someone was trespassing on the grounds of the property at night and had gone to see what he could find out. He was discovered by his wife, a Mr Sam Avery and Miss Grace Howard. The latter two are residing at the property. Mr de Freitas was unconscious and bleeding from a head wound. An ambulance was on-site within minutes of the call, and they alerted the station that it looked a matter for investigation."

"And what has our investigation found so far?"

"Mr de Freitas appears to have been attacked on the lawn and dragged into the bushes. He was hit over the head with a heavy instrument, a spade."

Le Claire lifted a brow. "A spade? How can we be that precise?"

"It was lying on the ground beside the victim. And there were traces of blood on it."

I asked for that, thought Le Claire. "Thanks, Briars. What is the current position with Mr de Freitas?"

"He was unconscious the last time I spoke to the doctor in charge, which was about half an hour ago. However, there have been quite a few doctors and nurses rushing in and out of the room since then."

A middle-aged man wearing dark blue scrubs was walking towards them, and Briars said, "That's Dr Foster. He's in charge."

The doctor's face was grave. "Hi, Jack. I thought you might pitch up here. This is bad business. He's lucky to be alive."

"How is he? Is he still unconscious?"

"Yes, but his condition is stable. We've just had a bit of a scare as his heart rate went off the scale, but we got it back down, and it's under control."

"Okay, but I need to know as soon as he is conscious.

The doors to the room behind them swung open, and a young nurse came rushing out. She quickly glanced around and, seeing the doctor, made straight for him. "We need you, doctor."

Dr Foster turned to follow the nurse; stopping as he realised Le Claire was right behind him. "You can't come in with me. Let me deal with this, and I'll let you see him as soon as I can."

Dr Foster closed the door solidly behind him. Dewar joined Le Claire. "Is everything all right?"

"Looks like something is going on in there, and I'm hoping we'll be able to talk to our victim soon. The timing of this attack on Kate

Avery's gardener is too coincidental for my liking. So the sooner we can find out what happened, we can either use the information or discount this incident from our enquiries."

"I spoke to Sam Avery before he left to get some coffees." Le Claire glanced round and saw Grace sitting on her own, just staring into space. "He said that Kate Avery had trouble in the past with kids sneaking into her garden at night. A couple of times she found empty beer cans and cigarette butts discarded in the bushes."

Le Claire shook his head slowly. "If this is down to kids, then the little sods deserve whatever happens to them. Wait here. I'm going to try and talk to the doctor."

#

He stood alone. Rage was coursing through him as he considered how matters were spiralling out of control. What the hell had the gardener been doing there last night? The fool certainly didn't get paid enough to stick his nose into anyone else's business, so why was he creeping around in the dark and spying on him?

He'd seen the movement behind him, tracked the dark shadow as it clumsily made its way across the lawn. In seconds, he had his bag in his hand, the machine quickly thrown inside it, and was about to turn and make a run for it. It would have been simple to lose him in the labyrinth of nearby estates. Would have been, that is, if that damned idiot hadn't brained the man, and with his own garden spade of all things. Now Rocque View was a crime scene, and he'd need to lie low for a few days until the police had finished with it.

But time was one thing he didn't have.

#

Le Claire stopped the doctor as came out of the hospital room. "How is the patient?"

"He's showing some signs of awareness."

"Can I see him?"

The doctor shook his head. "I didn't say he was conscious. My patient's health comes before your investigation. You'll see him when I am sure he is fully on the way to recovery." He took pity at Le Claire's expression. "If it's any comfort, I'd expect that he'll be up to talking to you by the day after tomorrow at the latest. I'll get in touch as soon as he's fit to be interviewed."

Le Claire groaned. That long? "Fine, I guess the doctor is always right. Let me know if we can see him earlier."

Le Claire walked back to Dewar, whose face wore a slightly haunted expression as she spoke to Grace.

"Sir, I've just been telling Miss Howard that our enquiries are proceeding and we'll let her know as soon as we have any more to say about her great-aunts."

Grace was combative. "And I've been asking why the police are being so incompetent. Do you have an answer?"

"I can assure you that we are doing all that is possible, and matters are progressing satisfactorily. However, you must appreciate that it is simply not possible, or indeed appropriate, for us to discuss the specifics of an ongoing investigation. I am sorry but I cannot prejudice our investigations."

Le Claire turned and walked away, Dewar on his heels. "There's nothing else for us to do here at the moment, Dewar. Come on."

As they exited the hospital, Dewar asked, "Where to, sir?"

"To speak to the other person Emma Layzell called just before she died. James Grayling."

CHAPTER TWENTY-SIX

Grace and Sam left the hospital shortly after the police. Luca was stable, and there was nothing they could do for the moment.

Grace busied herself with her laptop as she caught up on email correspondence. She hadn't looked at her account in days. There were several missives from her mother, a much shorter one from her father, a couple of how-are-yous from friends and, surprisingly, an email from Carter.

Grace hovered the cursor over Carter's name, considered the surname she had once thought was going to be hers. She hesitated. Was she really in any fit mood for whatever it contained? She had couriered her engagement ring back to Carter. Perhaps he was emailing to say he'd received it? Or maybe it was something else entirely, especially given her mother's recent comments.

She was jolted from her musings by the ringing of her cell. She reached out to pick it up, but her hand stopped and hovered in midair as she recognised the number. Never one to run from her demons, Grace stiffened her resolve and answered the call. "Carter. This is a surprise."

"Grace, it's good to hear your voice. How are you?"

How am I? thought Grace. *Dumped, grieving and in the middle of a multiple murder enquiry.*

"I'm fine, Carter. You?" Grace was polite, but she could feel the distance between them, physical and emotional.

"Actually, that's what I'm calling about. I'm not that great."

"Really?"

The words tumbled out of him. "It's not working out with Gina. She doesn't really fit in with our crowd. I took her to a charity dinner at the Met. You know, the annual one to benefit the smaller charities in the city."

Yes, I do know, you bastard was Grace's vicious thought as she considered how many years she had attended the exact same dinner with Carter and their friends.

"Anyway, Gina said she'd meet me there, wanted to surprise me with her outfit. Christ, that she did. It was sexy as hell, but she looked like a hooker."

"Carter," Grace interrupted. "Can you get to the point?"

"Oh, sure. Anyway, Gina really wasn't dressed appropriately. We were at a table with the governor and his wife for Christ's sake. Gina's dress was so low cut no one knew where to look!"

"You knew what Gina was like, Carter. She always dresses like that. I had assumed that's what attracted you."

"Yes, I know. But at the Met?"

Grace stifled a snort as she thought of Gina at the same table, no matter what she was wearing, as the stuck-up Governor Beaufort and his equally snobbish wife.

Carter was in full flow. "I didn't know where to put myself. The crowning moment was when Gina flipped out at the waiter for serving us soup that had gone cold. When I tried to quietly explain that gazpacho is meant to be cold, she went ballistic. Said she was mortified, blamed me for not telling her and openly ignored me for the rest of the night."

"I think we both know that Gina isn't currently my favourite person. I really don't want to hear anything about your relationship with her. I have enough to deal with right now without discussing your woes."

"Oh yeah, sorry about your aunts. Anyway, that's why I called. I'm not happy."

Had he always been so selfish? She brushed the thought aside as a gnawing in her stomach evidenced her growing nervousness about whatever he was about to say. She had a compulsion to close her ears and end the call now. But Carter's voice wouldn't go away.

"I made a terrible mistake. You're the right wife for me. Please say you'll forgive me?"

"Carter, please, I don't think..."

"Don't answer me now. Think about it. I know you won't let one little mishap ruin our future together. I'll call you again in a couple of days. We can talk properly then."

And with that, Carter disconnected the call, leaving Grace confused and not quite in control.

#

The traffic had been crawling at a snail's pace as Dewar had driven them west from St Helier along the dual carriageway and then north. A distance of only a few miles had taken them well over forty minutes as the coastal road groaned under the onslaught of Sunday drivers.

Le Claire's elbow was leaning out the open window, his hand reaching up to drum impatiently on the roof. "For Christ's sake, where are all these people going? It's a good job we don't have an emergency on, or we'd be ploughing through them. Actually, maybe that wouldn't be a bad thing." For not the first time in his life, Le Claire bemoaned his honesty and wished he was reckless enough to order Dewar to bang on the sirens and send the cars in front of them scattering out of the way.

Dewar flicked a sideways glance at Le Claire. "I guess we are in a rush, sir, so maybe... ?"

He knew she was thinking the same thing and that the canny Scot would be tempted just to slam on the siren and lights and use the power of the police symbols to get to where they wanted to go as soon as possible. Le Claire ignored her.

Having left the coast behind, they slowly drove along narrow, hedge-trimmed country lanes. Dewar glanced at the vehicle's navigational system. "Sir, we're nearly there. I think it's this block of flats coming up."

As they drove into the car-parking area, Le Claire felt a surge of nostalgia. The building used to be a hotel and nightclub venue, and he'd spent a good part of his late teens here. Like so many of these buildings, this one had recently been converted to fancy apartments for the finance sector crowd and others with more money than sense. He'd never been inside one of these, but he bet it was all open-plan living, wooden floors, double ovens and built-in coffee machines. Over the top for sure, but he couldn't help but wonder how much they went for. He guessed too much for a policeman's salary, for he drew a firm, impenetrable line at taking handouts from his parents.

"Everything okay?" The car had stopped, and Dewar was staring at Le Claire, waiting for him to make a move.

Le Claire brushed aside thoughts of finding a new home, especially one he couldn't afford, and jumped out of the car. He took in the surrounding countryside, a perfect setting for the quiet grandeur of the remodelled Georgian-style building, its long sash windows and stone balconies reminiscent of a gentler age.

"Sir, does anyone live in a normal house in Jersey?" The Scots import was used to living in police staff quarters, and she hadn't been on the island that long that she was yet blasé about the wealth and comfort that a lot of residents enjoyed.

Le Claire was grateful that Dewar had never seen his parents' place. "Of course they do, Dewar, just not on this case. Now ring the damned bell and let's get on with this. We don't have all day."

James Grayling answered immediately, his voice distorted through the intercom. "The police? You better come up. It's the penthouse."

It bloody well would be, thought Le Claire as the lift doors closed behind them. Within moments, they soundlessly slid open to reveal a brightly lit internal hallway with a silver-painted mirror and low sideboard as decoration. The solitary door faced the lift, and as they walked forward, it was opened by a tousle-haired and barefoot man that Le Claire assumed was James Grayling. He stood in the doorway, dressed in soft sweatpants and a pristine T-shirt. He gestured towards himself and apologised. "Sorry, I was just chilling on the balcony with a beer, so I'm afraid I'm a bit casual. Please come in."

Le Claire could almost feel Dewar suck in her breath, and she seemed to be walking straighter. Great, hormones at play. "Mr Grayling, I am DCI Le Claire of the States of Jersey police, and this is my colleague, DS Dewar. We have a few questions for you, if we may?"

James looked surprised but indicated that they follow him. A short, narrow corridor led into a huge open-plan living space, furnished entirely in shades of oatmeal and sand. Blasts of colour came from the modern artwork, huge canvases that bled across the walls with slashes of scarlet and ochre.

Dewar couldn't help herself. "Wow, this is some place."

Le Claire grimaced while James Grayling's face lit up with a broad grin. "Thank you, although I can't take any credit for this. It came already decorated." And with a wide, expansive gesture, he indicated the living and kitchen area. "The study and bedroom are more to my taste."

Dewar grew pinker at the word bedroom, and Le Claire had to wonder, completely inappropriately, when she had last got laid.

He shook that worrying thought aside as Grayling said, "What can I do for you?"

Le Claire answered, "I'd just like to ask how you knew Emma Layzell."

"Sorry, I don't know what you mean. That's the girl who was killed? I heard about it from a friend, but I didn't know her myself."

Le Claire shot a look at Dewar, and she handed him a piece of paper. He reeled off the digits of the mobile telephone number. "That is your number, isn't it?"

He frowned. "Yes, but I don't see what that has to do with anything."

Dewar took the paper back from Le Claire. "Your number came up as having been rung shortly before she died. Why did Emma Layzell call you?"

"Look, I don't know any Emma Layzell—oh, Christ, wait a minute. It was Emma Blair, wasn't it? Oh God, she's dead? I never knew her married name. I need to sit down."

Grayling sat down heavily on the opposite sofa to Le Claire and Dewar.

"Why would Miss Layzell have called you?"

"I hadn't seen Emma in ages. I rent this place and had been toying with the idea of buying somewhere. I bumped into Emma in town. I hadn't seen her in years. When I realised she was an estate agent, I gave her my number and said to phone me if any good apartments came up."

Dewar prompted, "What did she say on the call?"

"I never spoke to her. She left a message. Pretty garbled about where I was and so forth. To be honest, she sounded drunk. I didn't even realise it was her until I played it back a couple of times. I guess she must've dialled my number by accident. Someone was talking about her last night. I had no idea it was Emma Blair though. I'm really shocked."

Le Claire stood, followed by Dewar. His tone was even as he asked, "May I ask where you were in the early hours of Friday morning, between midnight and 8:00 a.m.?"

"I'm a suspect? That is ridiculous. I hardly knew Emma. Anyway, I am afraid I don't have a neat alibi. I was in bed—alone."

"And where were you last Sunday evening?"

"At home. I had been for lunch with friends and came back here about seven o'clock."

Dewar moved in. "And can you tell us your whereabouts on the night of the fourth?"

Grayling shook his head. "I don't know what you're trying to get at, but I was in London for a couple of days."

"Very well, thank you for your time. We'll be in touch if we have any other questions."

#

Le Claire and Dewar drove back to the station in silence, Le Claire quietly staring out of the passenger window as the cogs of his brain whirred and turned as he thought of one angle, discarded another.

Dewar dutifully followed the uncommunicative Le Claire into the station. He mumbled the odd "hello" in response to greetings from his colleagues but didn't break his stride until they reached his office.

Shrugging off his suit jacket, he threw it over a hook on the wall and sat down in the chair behind his desk with a heavy thump. His eyes flicked towards Dewar. "Sit down. Tell me what you think."

"Sir, we don't have any real suspects and few clues."

His eyebrows shot up. "You think? We certainly have persons of interest, as far as I can see. Certainly for the death of Emma Layzell."

"Richard and Sam Avery. There's a good chance one of them was the person being called by Emma. Maybe one of them was the mystery lover?"

"And then there is James Grayling."

"I thought his explanation for why Miss Layzell may have called him seemed plausible."

Le Claire sighed. "You're right. However, I remembered where I recognised his name from." He slid a brown paper file across his desk. "In there. James Grayling was one of the witnesses to the restaurant scene between Harriet Bellingham, the Averys and Grace Howard on the day she died." Dewar just stared at him.

Le Claire's voice was weary. "Don't look at me like that, Dewar. It isn't much to go on, but I just feel these three deaths are connected. So I am going to take a good look at anyone who keeps popping up, and right now, that includes James Grayling. Chase up the deep background reports on all the Averys, James Grayling and Ray Perkins. Go and hassle the team who're running the police national database reports. Let me see who we're dealing with."

#

Shadowed night surrounded the man as he sat nursing a glass of whisky, the deep amber of the liquid gradually fading as the ice cubes slowly melted. The distinctive smell always reminded him of his father, a memory he pushed to the side. It was his father who had, unwittingly, got them into this mess.

Long fingers stroked around the rim of the squat, fat glass. He was seemingly mesmerised as it reflected the flames of the tea lights he had dotted around the room. He told himself that he liked the way the candlelight cast ominous shadows; the most mundane of items—a chair, a bedside table—were transformed into towering giants that seemed alive as their shadows moved and shifted in the flickering light.

In truth, he couldn't face the penetrating glare of the electric lights. It was easier to pretend that everything was fine, that the last weeks hadn't happened as he sat in the quiet dark. He didn't need a light shone on his actions. He didn't want to think about it. Not tonight.

If he were a different kind of man, he would give up now, take what cash he had and get far away. He felt nauseous as he considered what might happen. His ruination. Everything he had fought so hard to achieve was about to come crashing down like a house of cards if he didn't get what was rightfully his in time.

He felt no surprise when the telephone rang. Perhaps he had even been expecting it; he certainly felt neither trepidation nor fear. Why be scared? He had been told exactly what would happen, and he had, in truth, brought it all upon himself.

The ringing ceased as he brought the telephone to his ear. He answered in a cocky voice. He had nothing else to lose. "And how are you this evening?"

The snort of laughter barrelled through the phone, followed by an amused drawl. "Looks like you finally found some balls. Pity it's too late. Don't suppose you've got my money, have you?"

"No, otherwise I would have been banging your door down to end this nightmare. Anyway, you'll either get the money or you won't."

"Don't be a smart-arse. You've run out of time, as far as I can see. So I'll just have to take what I can of yours. What's left of your business and reputation, for starters."

A surge of anger spurred him on to careless words. "You forget I still have until Wednesday, and I'm not out of options yet."

"Don't be a fool. You'll never get anyone to lend you the money. Cut your losses and sign your shares over to me."

The last sounded like a command, and he wasn't having that. The words shot out. "I've got something that's owed to me, and its past time I collected it."

The caller's response was blunt. "Get a move on. I want the money or your business, in two days. No more time."

The call was abruptly disconnected. He sat for a moment, the phone still at his ear, the monotonous disconnection tone almost hypnotic.

With a sigh, he put the phone down and picked up his drink. Not long to go now, not long at all.

CHAPTER TWENTY-SEVEN

Grace awoke with a throbbing headache and tension cramping her shoulders. However, she couldn't lie in bed. She needed to call the hospital, find out how Luca was and see if Fiona needed her.

Sam was already up and dressed for work. He saw Grace and tilted his head towards the counter, where he had the coffee percolating. His tone was teasing. "You have me very well trained, Grace. Want a coffee?"

She felt a blush heat her cheeks but ignored it. "That would be lovely. I wonder what else I could train you to do." Where had that come from? Grace felt her face grow warmer as Sam's grin grew wider.

"I guess we need to experiment and see how far you can go?"

Sam stood up and moved towards her, and Grace could see the intent in his eyes. She felt a thrill rush through her, and her eyes widened as she realised he was going to kiss her. She stood still, waiting, anticipating.

The shrill sound of the doorbell broke the moment and caused them to quickly move apart. Sam's gaze was rueful. "I better get that."

Grace poured herself a coffee and rolled her eyes as her hand shook a little. She really had to get a grip and stop acting like a lovesick teenager whenever she was around Sam.

She went to drink her coffee, but her hand stopped halfway, and she held the cup in midair as she heard the unmistakable sound of fierce sobbing. This was followed by Sam's voice. "Mum, what's wrong? Come here." Sam's words spurred her into action, and Grace raced down the stairs.

Susannah stood in the lounge, tears streaming down her puffed-up face. Her eyes were rimmed with red, and without a scrap of makeup, she looked a broken shadow of her usual self. "Oh, Sam, it's your dad. He, oh God, I don't know how to say this."

Sam was frantic. "Mum, what is it?"

"He..." Susannah stopped speaking, and her breath came in hitching gulps. "Richard has—oh God—he's gone to the police station. He said he has a confession to make. It's about Emma Layzell." With that, a hysterical Susannah fell into her bewildered son's arms. Sam's eyes locked on to Grace's as they stared at each other in shock.

Le Claire walked the long corridor towards the interview room. Dewar was waiting for him. No anticipation showed in her face, but he could see it in her taut stance and almost feel it vibrating from her in waves. He almost expected Sherlock's "the game's afoot" to be running through her head. It was running through his. And he was itching to get going. "Tell me what happened."

She looked jubilant. "Richard Avery turned up at the station about half an hour ago, sir. Asked for you, and as you weren't here, I got called down. Mr Avery said there was something he wanted to tell us about Emma Layzell. I read him his rights and took him straight into Interview One. Then I called you."

"So you haven't started the interview."

"No, sir. Given the seriousness of the situation, I thought it better to wait until you got here."

"Okay, let's go in."

Richard Avery sat at a rectangular table that took up most of the room. He was facing the door and looked up when Le Claire walked in, followed by Dewar. His face was pale, and his eyes looked wrecked, as if he hadn't slept. He made as if to stand at their entrance, but Le Claire motioned for him to sit down. They weren't at the country club, and Dewar would only get riled at a potential suspect politely standing at her entrance.

Le Claire pulled out a chair and sat down in front of him. He looked at the still-standing Dewar. "Would you mind getting us some water, please? I'm sure Mr Avery is thirsty." He glanced at Richard Avery, who nodded in surprised thanks.

Le Claire wanted Dewar as "bad cop" today. Dewar pasted a sullen look on her face and stomped outside, returning with a plastic bottle of water and three glasses, which she dumped on the table with a terse, "Help yourself."

Le Claire picked up the bottle and poured out the glasses of water. Handing one to Richard Avery, he placed the others in front of himself and Dewar, who had settled herself down next to him.

Le Claire smiled at him, noticing the tiny beads of perspiration that were dotted along his upper lip, the eyes that darted between Le Claire and Dewar—but never making contact with either. "Thank you for coming to see us, but I have to say I am puzzled as to why you are here. Perhaps you would enlighten us?"

There was silence for a moment. Avery's mouth opened and closed as if he was trying to speak words that just wouldn't come out. All he managed was a rasped, "Sorry, just a moment, please." He gulped down the glass of water and shakily placed it on the table.

Le Claire's voice was gentle. "You wanted to tell us something?"

"I came in before you went looking for me."

Le Claire could feel Dewar stiffen next to him as Avery continued, "You'd have found out today. The phone registered to the company, the number Emma was calling, it was my number. I use that phone."

Dewar's tone was sharp. "And why was Emma Layzell calling you, Mr Avery? What was she to you?"

"We were having an affair. I loved her. Oh God, how I loved her." And with that, he broke down and sobbed, tears of wild grief running down his face.

The room was silent apart from Avery's weeping. Le Claire and Dewar exchanged a glance. Dewar took the hint and leaned forward. "You need to pull yourself together. Why was Miss Layzell calling you?"

He drew in shuddering breaths as his sobbing slowly stopped. He looked haggard as he ran his fingers through his hair. "I don't know. I guess she just wanted to talk to me. I played her messages back the next morning. She wasn't making sense. There were so many messages. So many."

Le Claire's face was impassive. "In what way was Miss Layzell not making sense?"

"She was angry. She left some messages, but there were also a lot of missed calls where she didn't wait for voice mail."

Dewar leaned forward. "Why was she mad at you?"

"I don't know. Emma had no reason to be angry with me, absolutely none. She just got a bit frustrated by the situation sometimes." He saw the sceptical look that passed between Le Claire and Dewar. "Look, you have to believe me."

Dewar's bark of harsh laughter seemed to bounce off the walls. "Believe you? Mr Avery, you lied to our faces when we last saw you. So no, I don't believe you. You hid your connection to Emma Layzell and the fact that the number she dialled—repeatedly—on the night she died belonged to you. I don't think we're really classing you as a trustworthy interviewee right now."

"I don't know what to say. I don't know why she was angry. I can only think—well, I can only think that she knew Susannah and I had gone to the wedding, that we were staying overnight at the hotel together."

Le Claire tried to look sympathetic. "She is your wife. Surely Miss Layzell knew the score and had no right to be upset."

He had the grace to colour. "I may have led Emma to believe that Susannah and I were more estranged than we actually are."

Dewar rolled her eyes and let sarcasm have free reign in her voice. "Not that old cliché. I'm-not-sleeping-with-my-wife-anymore. Couldn't you be more original? I guess men like you do and say anything to get your leg over with a younger woman."

Avery stiffened in anger as he spat his words out. "It wasn't like that. Don't make it cheap."

Le Claire asked, "What was it like, then? How was your relationship with Emma Layzell?"

"I loved her, almost from the moment I first saw her. She was with Sam. He brought her to the small barbecue we told you about.

I was drawn to her straightaway." His features seemed to soften, and his eyes had a distant look. "Emma was so beautiful and funny and stood up for herself. It was obvious that Susannah had taken a dislike to her, but Emma just rose above it. I really admired that."

Dewar probed, "She was going out with your son. How did you start the relationship?"

"Sam split up with her shortly afterwards. I saw her that weekend. I was at a dinner at the golf club. Emma was there with some friends. I approached her, said I was sorry about her and Sam, apologised for Susannah being less than kind to her. Her friends were about to leave. Emma was going in a different direction, and her taxi hadn't turned up yet. I suggested we have a drink whilst she waited. The taxi turned up ten minutes later, but we were having such a good time that I paid the taxi driver and sent him away. We talked for ages. She really understood me, you know what I mean? She really got me."

His eyes were beseeching as he glanced between Le Claire and Dewar. Dewar's look of disgust made him focus his attention on Le Claire. "We shared a taxi and stopped at her place first. I got out of the cab with her and walked her to the door. I bent to kiss her on the cheek, just as she turned around towards me. Our lips met, and that was that. I sent the taxi away and went inside. It's like a fuse was lit within me, and I couldn't dampen it no matter how hard I tried. I had no choice—none."

Le Claire suppressed a mocking smile as he thought how neatly Avery claimed the status of victim. But that was the role that had been forced on Emma Layzell.

The smile was gone from Le Claire's face as he said, "Mr Avery, please remember that my colleague read you your rights earlier. Tell me. Did you kill Emma Layzell?"

The denial was swift. "God, no! What do you take me for? I loved Emma. That is an outrageous accusation to make."

He was almost shouting, and Dewar instinctively went in for the kill. "Did she love you? I think I know why Emma was mad at you. Playing happy family with the wife, you were going to have a lovely day out together, then a romantic overnight stay at a hotel. No wonder she was pissed at you. Did she threaten you? Is that what the calls were about?"

Avery looked at Le Claire for support. "She's talking nonsense, just making things up. Emma would never, ever do that."

Le Claire just shrugged and let Dewar get on with it. "Was Emma getting fed up with being the other woman, demanding more? Did she threaten to tell your wife? Is that why you killed her?"

Avery shot out of his chair and, leaning across the table, grabbed Dewar by the shoulders. "You're not listening to me, you stupid bitch. I didn't kill Emma. I couldn't."

Dewar stood her ground but didn't make any attempt to remove her attacker's hands. That was dealt with by Le Claire. He pulled Avery away from Dewar and said, "I don't know if you killed Emma Layzell; however, I do know that you just assaulted a police officer. I'm afraid we'll have to book and detain you for that. Quite fortunate really, as it'll give us time to have a longer chat later on."

Le Claire called for one of the duty sergeants to take care of a protesting Richard Avery. As Le Claire walked away, he almost faltered as Avery called out to him. "You think you can hold me on this nonsense? I came to you in good faith so you could eliminate me as a suspect, not so you could accuse me. I'll be out of here before you know it. There are people I can call, you know, and that includes your father." Le Claire kept on walking and ignored the inquisitive gaze directed at him by Dewar.

"Well, sir. That was interesting. If only we could prove it."

Le Claire looked at Dewar, inwardly bemoaning her haste. "I have to say he is a prime suspect. He was one of the last people Emma Layzell called, he'd been having a clandestine affair with her for years and he had a lot to lose if his wife found out and divorced him. So let's keep him on our list—near the top of our list. We've bought ourselves a little more time, and I suggest we hold him overnight. We can have another go at him later. First, I want to have another look at the files. I need to try and see what we're missing."

#

"You! Chief Inspector. Stop." The shrill voice echoed through the reception area. Le Claire, on his way to his office, halted and, to his surprise, saw an irate Susannah Avery bearing towards him, her son at her heels. She looked very different from the cool, elegant blonde he had seen the day before. Her hair was a mess, her eye makeup smeared and her clothes were far from her usual style—just basic jeans and a plain, creased blouse.

Le Claire waited for them to reach him, Dewar at his side. "Mrs Avery, what can I do for you?"

"For one, you can let me see my husband and tell me what the hell is going on." Her voice had risen, and curious eyes turned in their direction. Sam Avery laid a restraining hand on his mother's arm. "Mum, please."

She furiously shook her head, short, sharp motions, but remained silent as tears welled up in her eyes.

"I don't know what is going on. Mum just said that Dad had come in to see you, and he had a confession to make. Can you tell us what this is all about?"

This suited Le Claire perfectly. He would have been on his way to see Susannah Avery later in the day to work out what she knew about her husband's extramarital activities. A cheated wife could resort to extremes, do things they would never have thought themselves capable of.

"Of course, we can talk in one of the interview rooms. Follow me."

CHAPTER TWENTY-EIGHT

The small room was bare apart from a laminated table and four plastic chairs, with matching grey-painted walls and no window. Le Claire could see that Susannah Avery, even in her distress, found it all a little beneath her to be in such surroundings. She grimaced at the moulded plastic and pointedly swept her hand across the seat, wiping away imaginary dust and crumbs before carefully sitting down. Le Claire's hackles rose, but he dampened them down. Behaviour like this reminded him of his own mother and her superior attitude—and that was enough to colour his judgment against anyone.

Sam Avery sat down beside his mother. He half turned towards her with an anxious look before facing Le Claire. "What can you tell us? Why is my dad here?"

Dewar had followed them into the room and quietly took the chair next to Le Claire. He flicked a glance her way, commanding without words that Dewar start the conversation.

"Mr Avery came to see us to provide some information on an open case."

At the Averys' puzzled looks, Dewar continued, "He had something he thought we would want to know regarding Emma Layzell. He said that they were lovers and that it was him she'd been calling repeatedly just before she died."

There was a heavy silence, and then Sam Avery exploded, shattering the quiet. "That's a bloody lie. How dare you speak about my father like that? Mum, don't listen to this crap." He was halfway out of his chair when Dewar laid a restraining hand gently on his arm.

"Mr Avery, please, we are only repeating what your father told us." She took a breath. "So I take it you were unaware of your father's relationship with Miss Layzell?"

He quickly glanced at his mother, who was sitting still, her face devoid of any discernible emotion. "This is nonsense, and I won't believe a word of it until I speak to my father. But what I can say is that, no, I didn't know about any relationship, as they were not having a relationship." He spat the words out, and his anger seemed to fill the room.

Le Claire soothed, "Sam, I understand your concern. However, we have to take seriously what your father said to us. Mrs Avery, given the changed circumstances, I have to ask you again if your husband was with you in the early hours of Friday morning."

She took a moment before she looked directly at Le Claire, and when she did, it was with an icy glare. "I already told you. My husband was with me all night, in his rightful place, which is in our bed. May I see him now?"

Le Claire had no reason to detain her. "Your husband may have one visitor. We'll have to ask him if he would like it to be you."

She shot him a sharp look, and Le Claire continued for the hell of it. "I often find that the wife is never really the last to know. They pick up on subtle changes signalling that something is wrong in their marriage. Did you? Were you aware that your husband was sleeping with Emma Layzell?"

She flicked a look of distaste towards Le Claire. "There is nothing wrong with my marriage, and I would thank you to leave my business alone."

Le Claire simply smiled as he opened the door and indicated for them to exit before him. He'd leave Susannah Avery to her illusions about her wedded bliss, but the second her business overlapped with his, he'd be on her.

#

Grace sat in the garden, an open book lying unattended on her lap and a cup of coffee by her side. The air was cooler but she had experienced an urge for fresh air to blow away the cobwebs and clear her mind. She had been waiting for Sam to come back—or at least telephone—for the last couple of hours. Now she wasn't so sure she wanted to hear whatever he had to say. Grace had no idea if she could trust him or his parents, and she felt the weight of the last few weeks settle around her in an almost overwhelming wave of pressure.

The noise of a car pulling in front of the house abruptly dragged Grace from her thoughts. She recognised the flash of red. Sam. As he walked towards the front door, she raised a hand and called. "Sam, over here."

He was pale and crumpled, with a defeated look she hadn't seen on him before. She laid a consoling hand on his arm. "What happened? Is everything okay?"

He shook his head, simultaneously shrugging his shoulders. "I don't know, Grace. I really don't. We weren't able to see Dad. He sent a message that he doesn't want either of us having to see him in custody."

"Custody? What on earth is going on?"

"Apparently, Dad confessed that he was having an affair with Emma Layzell. I mean, what bloody rubbish is that? The police seem to think that he could be in the frame for Emma's murder. Even more rubbish." Sam swore as he kicked a stone that lay by the side of the flower bed, the break in his voice betraying his struggle.

"Oh, Sam, I don't know what to say." Without any premeditation or thinking it through, Grace moved and pulled Sam towards her, her arms settling lightly around his shoulders as she hugged him. She knew it was a mistake the moment she felt the searing heat of his body as his arms reached out and he pulled her hard against the length of him. Startled, she looked up and opened her mouth to protest. Head bent, his lips settled against hers, and he kissed her. Really kissed her. There was no hesitation or restraint in the way he almost devoured her. And Grace was with him all the way.

Her head was abuzz, and all she could think of was his body against hers, the soft touch of his mouth and the gentle caress of his hands. She pressed against him, demanding, wanting more, as his hand ventured farther across her ribcage and reached higher until settling firmly around her breast. Grace pulled back with a gasp. "Sam. No. This isn't right."

He stilled but didn't move away. He simply rested his brow against hers, his hot breath fanning her face. "I would say I'm sorry, but I'm not. I can't even promise it will never happen again. All I can say is that maybe my usual controls aren't in place."

Grace knew she was equally to blame and couldn't act the injured innocent. "It must be awful to think of your dad being treated like this."

Sam's sigh was deep and heartfelt as he leaned closer towards her. "The problem is that deep down, I know it's true. Why else would he say it? Dad was sleeping with Emma Layzell. I could believe him capable of anything right now, anything but murder, that is."

#

Le Claire was tired. Dog tired and pissed off, to be more accurate. Richard Avery was sticking to his story. According to him, he was an unfaithful, cheating swine, but he wasn't a murderer. All this was delivered in the smooth tones of someone who was clearly unrepentant that he was no doubt about to break his wife's heart and shatter what remained of his marriage. Le Claire didn't like the man, but that wasn't enough to charge him. He couldn't pin anything on him—not yet. Le Claire decided to let Richard Avery cool his heels in the cell overnight. They could still charge him with assault on an officer, but neither Dewar nor he had the stomach for that, especially as they knew they had taunted him into losing control.

Shrugging on his jacket, Le Claire left his office and took the stairs to the exit. He was going to go home early, cook something relatively healthy and collapse in front of the TV with a beer. He could almost taste it.

The doors to the station opened, and two uniforms came in with a struggling man held tight between them. They were obviously keeping him upright by the way his legs kept giving way; an overwhelming stench of alcohol surrounded him and fouled the air. Le Claire thanked whoever was up there that he was years past being called to drunken disturbances. This one looked a handful, but it wasn't his problem. He flicked a rather-you-than-me look at his beleaguered colleagues as he walked past them.

The drunk stopped struggling and looked straight at Le Claire. "Hey, Mr Fancy-pants hotshot, you found out who killed my Harriet yet? No, you don't have a clue, do you, little rich boy? We all know about you. You're playing at being a copper till Daddy pops off and you get the loot."

Le Claire ignored the two smirking beat cops and turned to their prisoner. "Ray, you look a little worse for wear. Is that why we have the pleasure of your company?"

The younger of the two policemen stepped forward. "We picked him up in town, sir. He was causing a disturbance outside the Angel's Rest wine bar."

Le Claire grimaced. The Angel's Rest was many things, but the dive wasn't for angels, and it was no trendy wine bar.

"What sort of disturbance? An argument or something more physical?" Ray Perkins looked the sort that was no stranger to using his fists.

"There was a disagreement with another man. It was verbal but turned into a fight just as we turned up. As Mr Perkins appeared to be the aggressor, we thought it best to remove him from the situation."

Ray seemed to get a grasp of what they were saying and defended himself. "Too right I was the agress-agress—whatever you said. He was being a prick about my Harriet. Load of bullshit saying whoever killed Kate Avery did for Harriet as well. It's the talk of the town. There's no connection. My Harriet had nothing in common with that tight old bitch."

Le Claire ignored his rant and walked towards the doors. "Why don't these nice gentlemen escort you to one of our rooms, where you can sleep it off?" He called over his shoulder. "Sergeant, look after our guest here. Hold him overnight, and I'll see him first thing in the morning. Get him sobered up."

#

Blood in the Sand

Once outside, Le Claire called Dewar. "It's me. Cooper is booking Ray Perkins, probably for drunk and disorderly and disturbing the peace. Get down to the cells and find out whatever you need to run a bloody good search on him. The background reports I asked for are taking too long—go and kick someone's ass. Say it's from me. There has to be some dirt in someone's past. Let's make sure it's not in their—and our—present."

Le Claire could almost hear Dewar's unuttered sigh. Yes, this was really grunt work, but it needed to be done, and he trusted her to do it right.

Instead of heading straight home, he decided to grab a beer and some supper at a pub. He was in no mood for cooking tonight.

Le Claire headed for The Foxes as if on automatic. It had been a favourite haunt before he'd left for London. As he recalled, the beer was cold, the food edible and the clientele left you alone. Perfect.

CHAPTER TWENTY-NINE

An hour later and Le Claire regretted his impulse. The pub no longer served proper meals, so he'd eaten two anaemic looking hot dogs whilst he stood at the bar nursing his lager. At least that was nice and cold.

A thumping cacophony was coming from the small raised stage, where three long-haired, spotty teenagers were belting out whatever today's version of music was. Apparently, they had fans; mini-skirted girls, who looked barely legal, were jiggling in front of the stage, smiling faces shiny with sweat.

He was getting old. Looking around, he saw a woman stick her fingers in her ears and laughingly shake her head at her companions as she made to leave. Sasha.

Le Claire took a second to reach a decision as he downed his drink and followed his wife out the door.

"Sasha, wait."

She turned. Her dark hair was caught back in a patterned scarf, exposing the long, elegant lines of her neck. Her easy smile faltered as she realised who had called her name. "Hey, Jack. What are you up to?"

"Just catching a beer after work. You?"

"The same. Look, I'm in a hurry. The next bus home leaves in five minutes."

"I'll give you a lift. Come on."

Sasha looked as if she would refuse and then shrugged and walked with him back to his car. They exchanged a few words but the silences were longer than their conversation. They made inconsequential small talk as the car travelled the relatively short distance to Sasha's house. She'd bought the place when she first returned to Jersey, when she'd walked out and left him alone in London. Or it was more accurate to say her father had gifted the house to her. No doubt he couldn't contain his pleasure that, in his eyes, his precious Sasha had seen sense and dumped her loser of a husband.

The house was light and airy, tall and narrow, stretching to three floors. Le Claire pulled into the carport attached to the side of the property. He switched the engine off and half turned in his seat to face Sasha.

Her smile was soft. "How are you really doing, Jack? You look stressed."

"I guess I am. We're no nearer finding the killer, and I've got irate senators in my way. All they seem concerned about is that dead bodies are bad for tourism."

There was silence, and he saw Sasha flick a wary glance his way. Her question was hesitant and ended on a plea. "Jack, how are you really? Talk to me."

There was no point in pretending that he didn't know what she meant. Banished memories came rushing to the surface. His voice was raw and cracked slightly. "How do you think I am? I killed that girl."

Her rebuttal was swift. "It wasn't your fault. We've been through this a million times. Everyone agreed that none of the evidence pointed to Colin Chapman having abducted another girl. You couldn't have known; no one knew."

Regret and anger, and maybe a little self-pity, battled for supremacy. Anger won, and the words burst forth. "No one knew because April Baines fell through the cracks of a stressed social system. At almost fifteen she was out roaming the streets and branded yet another runaway. No one reported her missing; no one cared."

"Please don't put yourself through this again." She was all but begging, and he could see the compassion in her eyes.

His own eyes were bleak. "But she wasn't a runaway. Chapman had her locked away. He repeatedly raped her and left her broken and bleeding, tied up in a chest that he nailed shut. And then he buried her alive."

His voice wavered, and Sasha reached out and held his hand, her firm grip comforting and so familiar. "Don't torture yourself."

The images, usually firmly locked and bolted in his subconscious, came thundering back. As if watching a movie in slow motion, his mind tracked his pursuit of Colin Chapman through the maze-like industrial estate where the serial abuser and murderer had carried out his evil business; he could almost feel Chapman's savage blows as chase gave way to vicious confrontation. He still carried the scars on his body to this day. The scarring in his mind was deeper, and even he didn't know its depth.

Le Claire had defended himself, but his ultimate aim was to subdue his assailant and keep on the right side of reasonable force. And then Chapman had started the taunting, his foul words conjuring the atrocities he had unleashed on his young victims, and Le Claire lost control. His angry fists silenced the smirking Chapman; it took three weeks for Colin Chapman to regain consciousness.

He continued as if she had never spoken. "When he came round, the bastard was gleeful as he told us about April Baines. He knew we'd be too late—and we were. So how do you think I am? This will never leave me."

He recognised the raw, broken edge in his voice and pulled away from Sasha's touch. He didn't want her pity, but Sasha held on tight. "Take care of yourself Jack. You need to let this go; you couldn't have acted any other way. And you'll get whoever has done these recent murders. That's what you do. Thanks for the lift. I better go."

Sasha turned and put her hand on the door handle, and he caught a wistful glance that flitted across her face. Before she could open the door, Le Claire covered her hand with his. Sasha turned, and the words he had been going to say stopped in his throat. Then he remembered: actions really do speak louder than words.

"Jack, what—"

He acted instinctively and pulled Sasha into his arms, his mouth covering hers, teasing and coaxing a response. After a slight hesitation, Sasha relaxed and met him kiss for kiss, caress for caress.

He had a compulsion to pull her closer, to lose himself in her embrace—to forget everything except the warm body pressed against his.

She pulled away, just a little, and stroked a trembling hand across his face, her thumb tracing a pattern across his stubble-roughened jaw. "Oh, Jack, this isn't the answer." The sadness in her voice was all too clear.

He felt all the old emotions rise to the surface, crowding out the recent, bitter memories. His entire body felt on fire. His wife was a heartbeat away from him, and that was too far. He pulled her closer, moving awkwardly within the confines of the car, the space far too restrictive for what he wanted to do. He pulled back, a little breathless, and whispered, "I want to come in with you. Let me stay the night?"

"No. That's a terrible idea."

"You don't miss us being together? Bed is one place our compatibility was never in doubt. Please, Sasha, I want you so badly. I need you."

He saw the indecision on her face; she looked into his eyes, and he recognised the moment she weakened and desire overruled her. "Okay... but it can only be for tonight, Jack. This doesn't change anything."

He didn't care; right now, all he wanted was the moment, so he followed her into the house.

CHAPTER THIRTY

The morning traffic had been a nightmare, and Le Claire was unusually late as he walked into his office. He'd left Sasha lying in bed just as the sun had risen. He'd left her with a hot kiss and a confused look. How did they get here? All thoughts of London— and the past—had been firmly pushed back into the mind box labelled "do not open".

He'd driven home to get showered and changed and hoped against all hope that neither of his parents was awake early. He thought he'd seen a shadow by their bedroom curtains as he drove up but cast the thought aside. He had bigger issues to deal with than his mother interrogating him about staying out all night.

He passed Dewar's desk and was surprised to see that the surface was clear of papers and the usual general debris she surrounded herself with. He assumed she had got caught in the traffic as well.

Being late hadn't prevented him from picking up a coffee from his favourite place, and he sat the untouched, steaming-hot cardboard cup on his desk. He had just slipped off his jacket and sat down, ready to take that first sip and feel the hit of caffeine, when his mobile rang. His hand reluctantly moved away from his coffee as he picked up his phone. This had better be good. "Le Claire."

"Sir, it's Dewar. I'm at the hospital. You have to get here as soon as possible. Luca De Freitas has regained consciousness, and you need to hear what he is saying."

#

Sam had lain awake most of the night, unable to quieten the intrusive thoughts. How many lies had his dad told over the years? For Sam knew in his heart that his father had spoken the truth, and he had been having an affair with Emma for almost four years. Those business dinners that Sam wasn't needed at—was that when he had seen her? What about the speculative trips to look at potential development sites—had he taken Emma with him?

Emma had always been a bitch, but this seemed too much, even for her. Had she been trying to get back at Sam in some way? She hadn't even hinted at this the last time he had seen her. *She deserved everything she got.* The vehemence of the thought shocked him, but he realised he meant every word of it. The ringing of his mobile was a shrill reminder of the outside world.

He recognised the number, and his heart leapt in hope as he grabbed the phone.

"Graham. I didn't expect to hear from you so soon after France."

"I thought I'd keep you updated. I had a word with my dad to see if he could help out with your financial issues."

Sam waited with tightly held breath. "He's interested in having a chat. But he's just gone on holiday with Mum, and he has a golden rule that he doesn't do any business when they're away together. He'll be back in ten days."

Sam felt slightly sick as the tidal wave of emotions jostled against each other for supremacy. He had felt euphoric when he thought the answer to his problems was at hand but seconds later had come crashing down. Two weeks was too long to wait. It would all be out by then, and once his desperation was known, he'd get pennies on the pound from any investor.

"Thanks for letting me know, Graham. I look forward to hearing from your dad. Take care." As the call disconnected, Sam knew there was only one option left, and to hell with the consequences.

#

Luca De Freitas did not look well. His face was as pale as the sheets that covered him and the wide bandage that encircled his head. However, he was awake and sitting up. That was good enough for Le Claire. "Mr de Freitas, I am DCI Le Claire. How are you feeling?"

De Freitas made to sit up, wincing as he was assisted by his wife into a more comfortable position. "Call me Luca. Actually, I don't feel too bad. It only hurts when I move or talk or sit still."

Le Claire's laugh was genuine. "At least you haven't lost your sense of humour. I don't want to keep you too long." This last comment won him a grateful look from Mrs de Freitas. "But I understand from my colleague that you have something of interest to tell me."

"Well, I don't know if it's interesting or not, but it is what happened."

Le Claire gestured for Dewar to sit in the empty plastic chair next to the bed whilst he leaned against the wall. "Start from why you were at Rocque View and just tell me what you can remember."

Luca started to speak, but his voice was rasping, and he coughed a little. His wife carefully held a water glass to his lips. "Sorry, I feel a little croaky. Okay. I was worried about what was going on at Rocque View, and I just had to do something about it."

Le Claire quickly interrupted. "What were you concerned about?"

"It was the footprints in the garden, the disturbed soil, trampled flowers in the borders. After what happened to Kate—Mrs Avery, that is—I was worried that something was going on. I think Sam was worried too."

"Mr Avery never mentioned anything to us. I wonder why?" Le Claire glanced at Dewar, who gave an almost imperceptible nod of agreement. This was a point to consider when they took another look at Sam Avery.

Luca continued, "I spoke to Sam again on Saturday night. He said to leave it with him. I came home and had dinner but couldn't shake the feeling that something wasn't right. I decided to go and sit in the garden overnight and see if I could find out anything."

At this, his wife stifled a sob, shaking her head as she tightened her hold on her husband's hand. Her other hand lay in a fist on the bed, and the knuckles whitened as she fought to control herself. When she spoke, her voice was rusty and hoarse from a night of weeping. "Someone found you, more like, you old fool."

Luca smiled and patted his wife's hand. "There, there, love. Take it easy. I'm going to be okay."

Le Claire cleared his throat as he brought matters back on track. "What happened, Luca? What did you see?"

"I saw Sam and Grace come back—that would have been around midnight. The lights in the house didn't stay on for long, and before I knew it, everything was silent. It stayed that way for a while—at least a couple of hours. I almost fell asleep a couple of times, and then I saw movement coming round the far side of the house. The man—"

Dewar interrupted. "You're sure it was a man? Would you recognise him again?"

Luca shook his head. "No, sorry. It was too dark, and he wore a cap pulled down over his face, but from the build, I am certain it was a man."

"Good. Well done. Now what happened before this man attacked you?"

"Oh, he wasn't my attacker. That was the other man. At least I think it was a man."

Le Claire and Dewar snapped to attention, senses on full alert. Dewar was first to find her voice. "What other man?"

Le Claire laid a restraining hand on his colleague's arm and spoke to Luca. "Take your time, but tell us exactly what happened."

"Okay. The man I saw first walked across the lawn. He had a long bag over his shoulder, like a sports equipment bag, and he dropped it on the ground and took something out. Like a long stick. He turned and walked towards the petanque court and the herb beds, which meant he was out of sight, shielded by the side of the house. I went to follow and came out of the bushes. I was hurrying because I didn't want to lose him. I heard a noise behind me and turned. Next thing I know, I'm on the ground with a throbbing head. I don't remember anything else until I woke up in hospital." Luca raised the water glass to his lips, but his hand stopped in midair as he said, "Wait a minute. Did that bastard hit me with my own spade?"

Le Claire's voice was sympathetic. "I'm afraid so. So you can't recall anything else?"

"No, nothing. Well, apart from the noise, that is. There was a beeping noise that just kept getting louder and louder." He paused, looked at the three people around the bed and said, a little shamefaced, "I guess it was just a ringing in my ears."

Le Claire's face was impassive, but his mind was whirring. "Thank you very much, Luca. We'll get in touch if we have any further questions. I wish you a speedy recovery."

Le Claire strode out of the hospital, Dewar snapping at his heels. "Sir, where are we going? What's the hurry?"

"The hurry is that, at long last, we finally have a couple of pieces to put in the jigsaw puzzle. Let's get back to the station. There are people I need to talk to."

#

"Good morning, Ray, and how do we find you this fine morning?"

"Keep it down, mate. I don't need you shouting at me."

As Le Claire hadn't raised his voice even a whisper above a normal tone, he knew the condition of Mr Ray Perkins. "Come on, Ray. I guess you've got a sore head this morning. No wonder. You were in a bit of a state last night."

Ray's eyes were slightly unfocused, but his temper was spot on. His face reddened and tightened as he raged. "Do you bloody blame me? My Harriet's gone, and you lot aren't doing anything to find the bastard who did it. In fact, you're doing fuck all."

Le Claire felt some grudging sympathy. Ray Perkins was a bit of a lowlife, but he had obviously loved Harriet Bellingham. "Ray, we're doing all we can. It's a complicated investigation."

"Complicated? How is it complicated? A woman gets battered to death in her own home, and you can't find out who did it. It's an island. It's not complicated. You lot are just incompetent."

"You don't appear to have a lot of regard for the police, Ray."

A sly look skittered across Ray's face. "I wouldn't say that. More like I'm a concerned citizen and taxpayer wondering where my money's going. As long as you do your job right, I've got no complaints." The last was said with a magnanimous flourish.

"I'm glad to hear that. As I said, this is a complex situation. Where were you again on the night Harriet died?"

Ray's gaze sharpened at the abrupt change of subject, and his reply was as sharp as his look was black. "Don't be an arse. I wouldn't have harmed a hair on Harriet's head. You should be trying to catch the bastard who did this, not hounding me."

"That I am, Ray, that I am. And on that subject, where were you on the night of the fourth of this month? The night Kate Avery died."

"What? I was with Harriet. Got takeaway and stayed at hers that night."

"And last Thursday night? Going into the early hours of Friday morning. Where were you then, Ray?"

Ray threw back his head and laughed. "You're clutching at straws now, mate. That's the night the little estate agent died?" At Le Claire's nod, Ray's grin grew wider. "You're out of luck. I had a few too many and ended up at my mate's place. Crashed out on his sofa and got a rude awakening from his wife as she was going out on her early shift. She left the house around 6:30 a.m. Just after giving me a cup of tea and a bollocking."

Le Claire couldn't help his disappointment. He had a feeling about Ray Perkins. "We'll need your friend's name, address and contact details."

"Be delighted, but you're barking up the wrong tree if you believe these deaths are connected."

"Let's leave that to me. By the way, what brought you to Jersey?"

Ray snorted. "Ah. Giving me the old outsider business? Maybe I am, but I've paid my dues. Stayed here for a bit in the early 90s and then came back permanent a few years ago."

"Why was that?"

"What can I say—sun, sea, sand and a bit of the other. But what I'm wondering right now is what made you come back to Jersey. Local boy leaves the Met, comes home from London. You were a talking point in the pubs. As I heard it, your old man had you down as being in line for some top job in London. Yet here you are, little rich boy playing at cops and robbers in this backwater. I suppose you'll be running the force here one day, especially with Daddy's connections. That why you come back, or was your tail between your legs?"

A muscle worked in Le Claire's jaw as he held himself in check. He kept his voice mild and even. "That's enough, Ray. Remember, it's me who asks the questions. But that will do for today. Give your friend's details to the constable who comes to do your release, and we'll take it from there."

Le Claire put Ray out of his mind. Now he had to see if a night in the cells had loosened Richard Avery's tongue.

CHAPTER THIRTY-ONE

Dewar was pacing the floor in front of a closed door, her face puckered in a frown. She turned at the sound of his footsteps echoing down the hall.

"Sir, I've been waiting for you. I've got Richard Avery in here, as requested."

"Thanks, Dewar. Why the long face?"

If anything, she began to look even more belligerent. "I can't stop thinking what a bastard this guy is. He comes across as Mr Charming, loving to his wife and family, yet he'd been blatantly lying to them for years. Is no one ever safe?"

Le Claire didn't know Dewar's history, but her vehemence came from somewhere. However, that was neither his interest nor concern. "In our jobs, we don't usually mix with the innocent. The last time I looked, being a miserable, cheating, lying bastard wasn't a criminal offence. Shall we?"

As he opened the interview room door, a chastened Dewar stepped in first. She still didn't look happy though. Le Claire followed. "Good morning, Mr Avery. I trust you slept well." Le Claire's tongue was firmly in his cheek. Richard Avery presented a very different image this morning. Unshaven and with tousled hair, he held himself awkwardly. No doubt a night in a police cell instead of on a comfortable divan had played havoc with his back. He was slumped at the table and didn't make the slightest effort to stand in front of Dewar and make a show of his chivalry. Le Claire suppressed a smile. Manners may maketh the man, but baser attitudes were laid bare by adversity.

Avery responded in a clipped tone. "Slept well? Hardly. You can be assured that I will be taking your treatment of me further. I personally know the bailiff, the governor and your father."

"I am afraid the first two wouldn't interfere, and the latter doesn't influence me."

Avery shook his head slowly from side to side as he briefly closed his eyes. When he spoke, his voice was softer, gentler, as he held out his hands, palms facing upwards, and appealed to Le Claire. "I am an innocent man."

Dewar snorted, and Avery aimed a vicious look at her.

"Apologies, sir, a cough came out the wrong way."

Le Claire ignored his colleague. He didn't give a damn how many women Richard Avery slept with; he was more concerned about whether the man was capable of murder. "You said you were at home with your wife on the night Emma Layzell died." At the nod of confirmation, Le Claire continued, "Where were you on the Sunday evening that Harriet Bellingham died?"

"Oh, for heaven's sake, this is ridiculous. I have an affair with someone who ends up dead, and now I'm on the hook for every unsolved case on your books?"

Avery leaned back in his chair and, with head thrown back, closed his eyes and exhaled, long and slow. He brought his head up to face Le Claire and answered. "I was at lunch with my wife, Sam and Grace Howard. We all had a few drinks, and I organised for a driver to come and collect us. Susannah and I went home."

Dewar flicked a glance at Le Claire before she spoke. "So your wife is your only alibi yet again?"

"Yes, but as I didn't kill anyone, I omitted to make sure I had a cast-iron alibi in place."

"And on the night Kate Avery died. Where were you then?"

"What! This is ridiculous. You cannot, for even one second, think I could have killed Kate."

"Answer the question, please."

Avery sighed, and his gaze was direct and unflinching. "Emma. I was at Emma's. Susannah thought I was at a Rotary dinner, so I didn't get home until past midnight."

Le Claire smiled. "So you have no real alibi, then." He turned to his colleague. "Dewar, as you very kindly refused to press charges against Mr Avery for assaulting an officer, please arrange for him to be released. Mr Avery, I will no doubt be speaking to you again. Please don't make any plans to leave the island."

Le Claire walked slowly back to his office. He thought of the way Richard Avery had looked at Dewar when her pretend cough had interrupted his innocence plea. There had been a hint of menace in that glance, and Le Claire couldn't tell if it was because of the circumstances and the man was just at the end of his tether, or if it was something more—a glimpse into his real character. Whatever it was, Richard Avery bore watching.

Le Claire badly needed a hit of caffeine and some fresh air. He was making his way out the building when his attention was drawn to the reception area. Ray Perkins drew a few looks as he stood by the main desk, for he smelled as bad as he looked. The lukewarm shower he had suffered earlier hadn't removed the rancid smell of sour beer seeping from his pores, which mingled with the stale cigarette smoke stubbornly clinging to his rumpled clothes.

He had been formally released without charges; the man he had been fighting with apparently having disappeared into the night. Although free to leave, Ray stood under the watchful eye of the desk sergeant as he painstakingly checked his returned loose change, coin by coin. A banging door, accompanied by raised voices, had him turning towards the source of the disturbance.

Dewar was escorting Richard Avery out of the building. Le Claire could clearly hear Avery's complaining monologue; his voice was even, but twin spots of colour darkened his cheeks and betrayed his anger. "Don't think I won't take this further, because I will. Your people will be hearing more about how appallingly I've been treated. Keeping me in the cells was uncalled for. How you can even think to question me about Kate and Harriet, I don't know—"

At that, a raw roar erupted, and Ray Perkins came charging towards them like a raging bull, his face a deep, dark red, contorted into a mask of fury. "You did for my Harriet, you bastard." Ray leapt forward and punched Richard Avery, catching him on his jaw. His aim was true and his fist solid. Avery cried out in surprise and stumbled backwards, losing his feet and landing on his backside in an ungainly heap.

The reception area was in chaos. Dewar, with the help of a burly constable, pinned Ray against a wall. Another policeman solicitously helped Avery to his feet, but as soon as he was up, he angrily brushed away his helper's hands. "I'm fine. Leave me alone." Rubbing his jaw, he looked towards the restrained Ray. "Don't tar me with the brush of your criminal tendencies. You'll be hearing from my lawyers. I'll be pressing charges, but not today. Right now, all I want is to get away from the whole damned lot of you." With that, he walked out the door.

Le Claire strode through the chaos. With a gesture towards Ray, he barked out an order to the constable who'd helped Dewar. "Give him a warning and get him out of here. We've wasted enough time today."

#

Grace was alone in the house and was enjoying the solitude. Sam had gone to work and had said he didn't know when he'd be back. Even in the midst of all the unfolding drama, there was a cosy informality to their daily routine that made Grace slightly nervous. She felt as if she was falling into a sexless coupledom with Sam. Not that she wanted the sex, no way, and she brushed the thought aside before it could take hold.

She had spent the morning sipping strong coffee and sorting through her emails and paying some bills online. She hadn't received any further email communication from Carter, nor had he called again. That had to be good, was her initial thought, but she countered this with wondering whether a life with Carter, the life she had been born into, was perhaps where she was meant to be. When Carter had gone off with Gina, any decision about their relationship had been taken out of her hands; Carter's call had put her back in control. She should have been pleased that whether or not she and

Carter had a future was firmly down to her. But all she felt was the weight of responsibility without knowing what she truly wanted.

The doorbell rang, shattering the quiet. Grace sighed. What was wrong with these people? No one ever just turned up on your doorstep in New York. They called first; they made proper arrangements. The damned bell was always ringing here. She made her way downstairs, and as she opened the door, a smile lit her face as she heard the excited yapping and barking. Susannah stood on the doorstep, a leash held in each hand as she tried to keep the two excited dogs at bay and prevent them from jumping all over Grace.

The older woman's face was drawn and pale beneath the carefully applied makeup. Susannah Avery wasn't looking her best, but who could blame her? Pity must have shown on Grace's face, for Susannah visibly stiffened, and with shoulders held tight, she greeted Grace in a controlled voice. "I'm on my way to pick up Richard now. I have a feeling we're going to have quite an interesting chat, so I wondered if you would look after the dogs for me?" The glint in Susannah's eye was steely. "I don't want them getting upset; they hate loud noises."

Grace almost felt sorry for Richard. "Susannah, I don't want to speak out of place, but I do know some of what you must be going through. I mean, Carter—"

Susannah broke across Grace's words. "He was your fiancé; as I understand it, you weren't even living together. I don't want to belittle your situation, but Richard is my husband, and we've been married for over thirty years."

Grace was contrite. "I'm sorry, I didn't mean—"

Again, the older woman interrupted. "I know you didn't." The lines on her face became more marked as her mask fell and Susannah let her anguish show. "Sorry for snapping. I'm just on edge. Look after my babies, won't you?" And with that, she handed the leashes to Grace and was gone.

Grace stood and watched as Susannah's car disappeared down the drive. Bending down, she addressed her houseguests. "Come on, you two, into the garden."

#

Le Claire had been standing at his office window for what felt like an age. He wasn't concentrating on the busy scene below but staring with unseeing eyes as he tried to sort out the coincidences and connections which made up the puzzle surrounding these three deaths. He just knew, deep in his gut, that there was something or someone that drew them together. However, he had no idea what that was.

"Sir?" Le Claire brought his mind back to the present as he turned away from the window. Dewar stood in front of him, a clutch of papers in her hand.

"Yes, Dewar, what is it?"

"I did as you asked and harassed the research desk for the background checks on the connected parties. There were no hits for either of the Averys or James Grayling."

Le Claire sighed. "I guess I didn't expect anything else."

"I also got Ray Perkins's report. Now he is an interesting character. He's been arrested a few times—minor felonies—but nothing seems to have stuck. Some bad blood in the family as his father was a..." Dewar quickly checked the paper she held, "yes, here it is, a Jim Perkins. A career criminal but apparently slightly classier than his son has turned out."

"Go on."

"Perkins Senior was a good old-fashioned thief. He died in prison; he was in for a heist that took place in one of the mansions on London's Cadogan Square. Seems they cleared out the safe of some lord but got caught when they got into a fight with a fence who they accused of pulling a fast one on them. They roughed the man up when he offered them a low price for some gear he said was just costume jewellery with fake stones. Seems he'd tried to pull this one before. He shopped Perkins in return for getting let off the fencing charges. The Establishment took umbrage at a blatant crime against one of their own, and Perkins got twelve years."

"Good work, Dewar. However, if we classed everyone who had criminal parents as guilty, the prisons would be overflowing. I guess this just backs up what we already thought of Ray Perkins. Not exactly a charmer."

"There's more: Perkins was arrested for slapping about an ex-girlfriend when he lived in London. She refused to press charges, and he got off with a caution. I was about to bring the reports to you when his financial analysis came through. His car business looks okay at first glance, but he has a fair amount of debt outstanding. A deeper look and you can see that he's pretty much juggling the business day-to-day. But there was one very interesting point. Ray Perkins paid a hefty sum of money monthly as an insurance premium. The team contacted the insurance company. The death benefit was £3 million—the life assured was Harriet Bellingham."

Le Claire paled. "I knew there was something off about him." He jumped to his feet. "Let's see if the duty sergeant has finished issuing Ray's warning. We need another chat."

#

A furious Ray jumped to his feet as Le Claire and Dewar walked into the interview room. "What the fuck are you playing at? That muppet Avery better not have pressed charges."

Le Claire's tone was even and measured. "We need to ask you some questions. Sit down."

Ray swore and thumped down heavily onto his plastic chair. Le Claire sat opposite and beckoned for Dewar to sit next to him. He made a show of skimming through the sheaf of papers he held and waved them in Ray's direction. "Your dad was an interesting character. Take after him, do you?"

Ray snorted. "Is that the best you can do? My father was a jailbird so you think I'm a rotten apple? This is rubbish. That's not enough to hold me."

Le Claire shrugged. "No, it isn't, but the rest may be. You like beating up on women?"

Two red patches rose on Ray's cheeks, the only sign that he was affected. "That's old history from my London days. I had a bit of a disagreement with an old girlfriend, and she accidentally fell against a door handle. I wasn't charged."

"It's still a point of interest. And then there's the insurance. That was a tidy sum you insured against Harriet Bellingham's death.

You're all set to pocket £3 million. People would do a lot for that much cash—even murder."

Ray's temper was spitting fire from his eyes, but he somehow kept his cool. "There is no way you'll ever prove I hurt Harriet, because I didn't. I had a policy on her, and I also paid for her to have one on me. That is what people do when they're together. It isn't illegal."

Le Claire leaned over the table; he knew he had nothing on Ray at the moment. "I will find out who killed Kate Avery, Harriet Bellingham and Emma Layzell, and I will pursue them with all I have. You are a person of interest to me at the moment, so don't make any plans to leave the island. By tomorrow, we'll have put your name on the blocked list for the airport and harbours to make sure you don't make any unscheduled trips."

CHAPTER THIRTY-TWO

The sun was weakening, but the sea air was bracing and refreshing as Grace relaxed on an old-fashioned plaid picnic blanket under the dappled shade of the ancient oak tree that grew a few feet from the pool.

The dogs were careering across the lawn, each taking turns to be the chaser and then the chased. Grace smiled at their antics, as an indulgent parent would, and caught herself. She mustn't get too attached to anything, or anyone, in Jersey. She'd soon be gone.

The roar of a car engine coming to a halt in the drive had her rising to her feet and walking towards the sound. She felt a flicker of pleasure as she recognised the car and the driver.

"James, I am so sorry I didn't get back to you. I'm afraid my voice mail is full of calls to return, and it's all been a bit hectic here."

James joined Grace in the garden and bent his head to give her a kiss on each cheek. "No problem. Although I have to confess to being a little concerned when I didn't hear from you. Is everything okay?"

Grace didn't know where to start. She quickly filled him in on what had happened to Luca, but she said nothing of Richard Avery's relationship with Emma Layzell. That story wasn't hers to tell.

"Are you safe here now, Grace? Shouldn't you maybe check into a hotel? I don't mind telling you that I don't like the idea of you staying here with people being attacked in your garden."

Grace shook her head. "No, I'll stay here, but I don't feel entirely safe. At least I've got the dogs at the moment, although I guess they'll get picked up later, but Sam will be home by then."

A buzzing noise distracted them. Bending down to the rug, Grace picked up her cell. "I'm so sorry, but I need to take this call." At his nod, Grace answered. "Fiona? How is everything?"

She listened intently as she slowly paced around the pool. After a couple of minutes Grace hung up the call. James had politely looked away to give her privacy, but now he was inquisitive. "Was that the gardener's wife? Is he okay?"

"Yes, Fiona left me a message earlier to say that Luca had regained consciousness and was going to be fine. I've been trying to call her, but I think she must have switched her phone off whilst she was in the hospital."

James looked concerned. "You seemed a little taken aback by something she said. May I ask what it was?"

Grace was distracted as she replied. "Yes, of course. It seems that the police interviewed Luca this morning, and the weird thing is that he said he heard a persistent beeping noise after he was attacked. Fiona just wanted me to know in case there was something wrong with the pool pump."

"What made her think it was from the pump?"

"Oh, just that Luca thinks the noise came from that area of the garden." They both looked across the lawn towards the wooden shed that housed all the technical pool equipment. Grace was puzzled. "I can't hear anything, but there isn't anything else electrical there, just the flower beds and petanque court. There aren't even any automatic garden lights there." Grace shrugged. "I'll tell Sam; maybe he can have a look."

"Well, I better be off. I'm glad you're okay and that the gardener is on the mend."

He chastely kissed her good-bye and left. Grace sensed James's interest in her. He was a great guy, and there was something really attractive about him. In another place, and another time, he would have been a summer distraction. But there was Sam to think about... and Carter. Grace shook her head. There was enough going on without thinking of men. One had blatantly lied to her, but what about the other two? Could she really trust either James or Sam—especially when the latter was less than truthful about his past relationship with Emma?

#

Le Claire leaned forward, bent elbows resting on a spare desk in the incident room, his hands in a prayer-like position in front of his mouth. He gently rocked back and forth as he contemplated the white board in front of him. Blown-up images of Kate Avery, Harriet Bellingham and Emma Layzell stared back at him, as if taunting him, challenging him to find their killers.

The room was a hive of activity—the clicking of keyboards, the rustle of papers and the subdued voices of conversing colleagues as they sorted through the evidence and ran probabilities and key data searches on the Home Office Large Major Enquiry System. The advanced information technology system collated all relevant evidence and data, such as witness statements, and allowed those involved in investigating serious crime to swiftly access data and cross-check through other police systems.

Dewar stood beside him and waited patiently until he noticed her.

"Sit down. See if you can help me sort through this muddle." Le Claire gestured towards a hard plastic chair beside his desk.

"Sir, what can I help you with?"

Le Claire tamped down his irritation. "Dewar, I am sick to death of you calling me 'sir' at every opportunity. You're my aide; we work together, so call me Le Claire."

Dewar looked startled. "Yes, sir, I mean, Le Claire."

Le Claire indicated the board in front of them, and they took in the photographs pinned there. There was a casual Kate Avery at some sort of informal gathering; Harriet Bellingham dressed to the nines, staring defiantly at the camera and Emma Layzell, pretty in a summer frock, her heart shining in her eyes as she looked at whoever was behind the camera.

"Look, Dewar, just look at them. Three dead women—and we're no nearer finding the murderer. We have to be missing something. Ray Perkins could have disposed of Kate Avery in the hope that Harriet would inherit the property. When that transpired to be a false hope, he could have killed Harriet for the insurance money. But why get rid of Emma Layzell? What connects them?"

"Maybe it will help if we recap out loud. Sometimes that helps—shows any jarring notes."

"Okay. We start with the death of Kate Avery. It was a clever crime, made to look like an old lady having a couple of glasses of wine too many, massively overstating her insulin dose and, in her disorientation, falling over the balcony railing."

"And think, sir—Le Claire, that is—if you hadn't started becoming suspicious, especially after her sister died, and took another look at the case, then it may always have been thought to be an accident."

Le Claire nodded. "Wealthy, childless widow is murdered. Let's follow that to its natural conclusion. Who inherits? Follow the money."

Dewar chipped in. "She skips over the next generation to leave everything to the great-niece and nephew. And nothing to the sister."

Le Claire was thoughtful. "Which Harriet knew nothing about. She reportedly reacted with fury, threatening to hold up probate and the settlement of the estate. Grace Howard and Sam Avery are Kate Avery's heirs; it's their inheritance that Harriet Bellingham was threatening to delay or grab a share of. But where does Emma Layzell fit in? If at all? Logically, I know there may be no connection—but that doesn't seem right."

"But the physical crimes themselves—they don't feel related."

"I agree. Kate Avery was killed in a calculating, well-thought out manner. The others seem less careful, more passionate."

Dewar grimaced. "So we have very little to go on except to follow the money. Could Harriet Bellingham still have ended up with a share of the estate? I mean, I don't know how that kind of thing works. Would she have had a right to anything?"

Le Claire quickly shook his head. "I don't know, but I suggest we go and speak to someone who will know. We also need to work out how Emma Layzell fits into this. The only place I can think to start is with Kate Avery. Everything seems to circle back to her."

#

Le Claire and Dewar were shown into Paul Armstrong's office, and the lawyer rose to greet them.

Le Claire reached out to shake his hand. "Thanks for agreeing to see us. I just want some general information about Kate Avery, but first I do have a specific question. We understand that shortly before her death, Harriet Bellingham was threatening to contest the will and make a claim on Mrs Avery's estate. Could she have succeeded?"

"It depends on your definition of success. Could Harriet have successfully sued and won a share of the estate? I doubt it. Could she have tied the estate up in litigation and prevented anyone from getting a penny for a very long time? Yes, that she could have done. And to Harriet, there would have been a feeling of having won even if that was all she achieved."

Dewar said, "But she wouldn't have got any money from the estate and would probably have had to pay legal fees. Why would she think she had won?"

The lawyer's laugh was a sharp staccato. "Harriet was a bitter woman but very, very clever. It always annoyed Kate that Harriet hadn't applied herself to anything of value. She would rather have looked for a handout than make something of herself. Harriet wouldn't have paid any legal fees. She'd have got one of those young, hungry lawyers who are only too keen to make a name on a no win-no fee basis. Harriet always could tell a good story, so she'd have spun him some line to make herself the poor, betrayed sister."

Le Claire nodded. "I take it you didn't like Miss Bellingham."

"Not like Harriet? I couldn't stand her. She took, took and took from Kate until even she had enough and turned off the money supply. Harriet was only ever out for herself. I wouldn't have wished this on her, but I can't be a hypocrite and pretend that I care. She was a nasty piece of work, and how she could be related to Kate, I have no idea. Sorry." Armstrong's voice had risen, and his face was flushed as he finished speaking. He reached across and grabbed a small bottle of water from the table. Twisting the cap, he took a long drink. "Apologies for the rant, but it seems that Harriet can drive me crazy even in death."

Le Claire ignored the irreverent remark and forged ahead with his own agenda. "Tell me about Kate Avery. How long had she lived at Rocque View?"

"Oh, years and years, probably about twenty-five. I remember when they bought it. The seller was desperate—a young widow. I think she had a child. Samuel could have offered her virtually anything and she'd have bitten his hand off, but he was a man of honour. He gave her a fair price, and the deal was done. Samuel got his one true passion in life—after Kate, that is."

Dewar smiled. "His passion? That sounds dramatic."

"Not dramatic, just how it was. He loved that place, did most of the work on it himself. He changed or updated everything he was allowed to. Some things couldn't be changed under the covenants on the deed. The island is an absolute nightmare for archaic laws and obscure restrictions."

Le Claire pulled the discussion back on track. "And what about Emma Layzell? You said she was hounding Kate Avery to sell the place. Who was the buyer?"

"No idea. I never spoke to the girl myself. Mind you, she wasn't giving up. Even wrote to me as the executor, said there was an increased offer on the table. Before that, she contacted Kate direct, just turned up at the house one day. Said she had a firm offer to buy the place. Kate said she didn't want to sell and kept repeating that she wasn't interested every time that girl hounded her. For that is what she did. Telephoning, turning up at the door, delivering flowers with a note about the offer—the offer that kept increasing. I did say to Kate that maybe she should consider it, but Kate ended up having a bit of a to-do with the estate agent. Seemed she just lost it and shouted that the only way she'd be leaving Rocque View would be feet first in a coffin."

"And that's exactly what happened." Le Claire's comment hung suspended in the air. "We're going to find who did this—who did all of this."

"You really think the murders are connected?"

Le Claire smiled and stood. "I didn't say that, Mr Armstrong. At the moment, I am keeping an open mind, but I would like to know a bit more about Rocque View. The names of past owners would be helpful, in case they can shed any light on the property, and also maybe how much it changed hands for last time and anything that seems even a little out of the ordinary. I assume it will be quicker for you to check the ownership chain in your files rather than us ploughing through the public records."

Paul Armstrong mumbled something as he rose and followed Le Claire and Dewar back to the reception desk. To Le Claire's ear, it sounded like the lawyer was saying, "Bloody fool's errand, does he think I've got nothing better to do?"

Le Claire and Dewar made their way back to their car, which was parked across the road from Paul Armstrong's office. Le Claire was contemplative and distant.

They drove in silence back to the station. As Dewar parked, Le Claire finally spoke up. "That house, Rocque View, it has to be connected somehow, even if only incidentally. Come on, let's go there now. I have an idea."

CHAPTER THIRTY-THREE

Sam had just arrived home from work and was climbing out of his car when he saw Le Claire and Dewar drive up. He had gone into the office, but his mind hadn't been on the emails piled up in his in-box. However, he had accomplished something in that he had finalised the plans for his future. Nothing could stop him now. The sun was in his eyes as he looked at the approaching car, and he held his hand to his brow to lessen the glare. He hadn't recognised them at first, and as the car drew to a halt, Sam's jaw tightened as he realised who his visitors were.

"I'd say this was a surprise, but then again, you seem to spend more time harassing my family than catching actual criminals."

Le Claire approached Sam, his face impassive. "Mr Avery, we have something important to discuss with you. Is Miss Howard around?"

For a moment, Sam kept up his aggressive stance, then his features relaxed, and he motioned for them to follow him into the house. "I don't know if Grace is in, but I would assume she is."

Grace was indeed at home and came running downstairs in response to Sam's called request for her presence in the lounge. "The police have something to discuss with us."

Grace looked at Le Claire, and hope shone out of her eyes as she fired questions at him. "You have news? Have you found who murdered Kate? What about Harriet and Emma?"

"I'm afraid we haven't arrested anyone yet. But we would like to have some men keep an eye on the house and gardens."

Sam was quick to question. "What do you mean? How exactly will they keep an eye on us, and what is the point?"

"Mr Avery, I said my men will keep an eye on the house and its gardens, not on you. As to how, I will have the men positioned around the perimeter, within the bushes, and as to what the point is? Well, let's just say that your gardener has made me want to clear something in my mind. You could say that I want to rule out that this house is somehow at the heart of this case."

Grace slowly shook her head. "I'm sure I don't understand what you're getting at, but you're the expert, not us. When should we expect your men?"

"Not tonight. I've only just decided on this course of action, so I'm afraid I'll need a day to get everything in order. The team will be here tomorrow night, once it's fully dark."

A slow shake of his head emphasised Sam's disbelief. "Well, thanks for letting us know, but what you hope to find skulking in the gardens, I do not know. Some louts attack Luca and you try and tie this in with Kate's death?"

"We have to take any information into account, Mr Avery, and don't forget that we don't know who attacked Luca de Freitas. You do want us to catch the culprit, don't you?"

"Of course I do, and you must do whatever you think is right. However, I can't see why a murderer would be skulking in the garden."

"We will catch whoever has done this, Mr Avery. You can trust me on that."

After the police left, Sam wrapped a consoling arm around Grace. "Would you rather not stay here? You could pack some things and go to my flat. I'd feel better if you were away from here—and safe."

"No Sam. I want to see this through to the end. I'm staying."

#

Dewar was quiet until they were in the car and heading back to the station. "I don't understand why we told them we were going to mount a watch in the gardens but that we'd be starting tomorrow night. Why tell anyone in advance? We could easily divert some of the guys from their work in the incident room and start tonight."

"We are starting the watch tonight. However, if it's thought that we'll start tomorrow, then tonight is the perfect opportunity for anyone who is up to no-good at Rocque View to get it over and done with before the place is teeming with police. Sam Avery knows about it, and I'm sure he'll tell his father. And don't forget that Ray Perkins thinks we're going to stop him leaving the island from tomorrow on. If I were him, I'd do whatever I had to do and be gone on the morning boat. If it's one of them, or a combination, we'll get them tonight, either for murder or for whatever else they're up to."

Dewar's face lit with appreciation and a tiny bit of awe. "Ah, that is cunning. But you said a combination?"

"Yes. I don't think that Luca was necessarily attacked by the same garden intruder he was following. We could be looking for two separate men, and one was looking out for the other. Or maybe not; perhaps it is just one man, but we can't ignore the possibility."

Dewar let out a low whistle. "That opens up the field. I mean, if there are two of them, then we need to look at all of the alibis all over again."

"Then that will keep you and the team busy for the next couple of hours whilst I sort out some helpers for tonight."

#

Several hours later and Le Claire had everything pretty much organised. He had roped in a couple of experienced Authorised Firearms Officers from the incident team who knew how to sit through a stakeout and had the physical capacity to handle whatever came their way. All they had to do now was wait. He was convinced that they would, at the very least, find out who Luca's attacker was. Le Claire knew that there was every possibility that he had gone off on a tangent and none of this could have anything to do with the murders. He hoped that was not the case. His gut had only let him down once before. Neither he, nor his career, could take that again.

The ringing of the telephone broke into his reverie. He was surprised when he heard who the caller was. "Mr Armstrong. What can I do for you?"

"I think it's more what I can do for you. I was intrigued after your visit this morning. The more I think of it, there is a connection to Rocque View with all three murders. Kate owned and adored the place, Harriet coveted it and was convinced it would be hers one day and Emma Layzell had a solid buyer lined up, who I understand was pretty desperate to get their hands on the place. Not that I blame them, of course, it's a quite unique property. But I digress. I had a look at the history of the place. All pretty much as I remembered. Samuel and Kate bought the house from a young widow, and she had taken ownership four years previously. What I hadn't remembered before was that the covenants weren't longstanding but had been put in place by the woman herself. She actually had the deeds amended to say she didn't want certain areas ever changed by subsequent owners: the drive, the petanque court and the pool area. They had to stay exactly as they were. Samuel would have liked to have moved the drive to a more central position, but it wasn't the end of the world."

Le Claire was half listening as he typed an email to the night's team, laying out instructions for the initial briefing meeting.

Paul Armstrong continued, "Anyway, you said you wanted names. Samuel and Kate bought the property from a Karen Perkins. The deeds were only ever in her name, but her husband must have been alive when she bought the place, as she was described as the wife, not the widow, of a Jim Perkins. Bit archaic to describe ladies by reference to their marital status, but that is how it was then."

Le Claire snapped to attention, his email forgotten. "Thank you, Mr Armstrong. That is very helpful, very helpful indeed."

Le Claire hung up the phone and called out for Dewar. "Something's turned up which could be purely coincidental, but it needs to be looked at urgently, even if just to clear the point as irrelevant. The owner of Rocque View before Kate Avery and her late husband was a Karen Perkins—the wife of a Jim Perkins. Wasn't that the name of Ray Perkins's father?"

"Yes, it was. We've got him now, sir."

"We don't know anything yet, but it's a lead to follow. Go and find out all you can about Jim Perkins, especially whether he had a connection to Jersey and was indeed married to the previous owner of Rocque View."

As Dewar hurried out, Le Claire quietly muttered, "It's that damned house again!"

#

He sat in silence, staring at the telephone on the table. He knew time was running out but, strangely, simply felt a sense of calm. *When there's nowhere else to run, the path ahead is easy to follow*, he thought. It had to be tonight, for tomorrow would be too late. He had to be positive and act for what was rightfully his—*theirs*, he hastily amended. And then the devil on his shoulder whispered its insidious poison. Did he really have to share? He was the one who had done the most to achieve this. He'd worked out the plan, made the introductions and had the balls to fix it when it looked like it was all going wrong. He checked his watch. He better get ready.

He dialled the number, and the call was answered almost immediately. He spoke in a rush. "I'll have what you want tonight, but I'm going to have to go away afterwards. I won't have time to turn it into cash."

The rough voice on the other end of the line was suspicious. "What are you going to give me? I want to be paid in full, and I like cash money."

"You'll get something worth twenty times what my debt is. Yes, you'll have to sell it—and discreetly—but you'll still end up with a hell of a lot more than I owe."

There was silence on the other end of the line, and that's when he knew he had him—if not, there would have been immediate threats.

"All right, but I want it all settled by first thing tomorrow morning, so you better get round here at first light."

He laughed. "I'm off on a journey tonight, so I'll drop it by the club later. Don't worry. In the morning, you'll be all paid up."

CHAPTER THIRTY-FOUR

Sam leaned on the kitchen counter, his phone to his ear, as he stared out towards the sea and listened to the strident ring tone. When the call was answered, his voice was gentle as he asked, "How are you, Mum? Is Dad back yet?"

He heard his mother let out a long sigh and could almost visualise her struggling to keep everything together as she spoke. "We're okay, Sam, don't worry. It will be fine."

He knew his mother had gone into automatic parent mode, putting Sam and his reassurance first. Right now, he was more anxious about his parents. "I know you're putting a brave face on it, but you know I'm there for you when you want to talk, really talk about—"

Susannah abruptly cut over Sam, blocking out what he was going to say. "Sorry I didn't call you back earlier. We got your message. Here's your dad."

The low rumbling of voices, his mother calling his father, reminded Sam of a thousand times he'd called them previously, but now there was a new distance that resonated through the line."

"How are you, Dad? What's happening with the police?"

"I'm as good as can be expected after what has to rank as the worst experience of my life. Those bloody fools at the police station apparently think I'm involved in the murders. Idiots. They should be trying to catch the real culprits."

Sam's voice was weary. "They are, Dad, they are."

His father's response was quick and aggressive. "Really, Sam? Then what are they doing keeping me in one of their cells overnight? Some trumped-up charge about assaulting an officer. Ridiculous."

Sam knew his father well in this mood—pugnacious and complaining. His mother had also borne the brunt of his father's tirades. Sam wondered how his father had been with Emma

Layzell. Had he been softer, kinder with her? That brought him to the main point of his call. "What about Emma? You were having an affair with her, weren't you?"

He heard his father draw in a quick, jerking breath, and when he spoke, the bluster had left him. "Sam, I am so sorry. I don't know what came over me. Your mother, well, she isn't always easy."

Sam's voice rose. "For Christ's sake, Dad, I don't want to hear your lame excuses. But I guess your apology answers the original question. How could you do this to Mum? How could you do this to the business? This is why you've been so distracted, so off your game that you've barely tried to find another investor. You know how important this deal is. I've gone over the figures, Dad—it's the difference between us being one step away from disaster or making enough money to have a substantial cushion in the company for future deals. You've bigged it up over the investor pulling out. You've even had me repeating like a mantra that we simply don't mix our personal funds with the company, but we both know neither of us have had the money to do that in any event."

"Sam, you know it cost a fortune to buy Kate's share of the business when she inherited from Samuel. I'd lived under my uncle's and my father's shadows long enough. I just wanted to be my own man and follow my own path."

"You've certainly done that. But it's my turn now. I've got a plan, and I know you don't like it, but we have to do it anyway. I think you've lost the moral high ground in any event."

"I know, truly, I do. But it was hard juggling them both. Trying to keep two women happy isn't easy—and then to be suspected of murder by those plodding buffoons is a nightmare. They don't have any real clues, and at this rate they won't catch anyone at all."

Sam felt a hot blast of rage at his father's dismissive attitude towards his mother. He let out a slow breath to calm himself. He didn't want to anger his father—it would be his mother that paid for it when the call was over.

"They're doing all they can, even putting a watch on the house."

Richard snorted in disbelief. "That's ridiculous. Why would they think any of this has anything to do with a house? They're clutching at straws. When do they start this madness?"

"Tomorrow night."

"Well, they better get it right because I'm just about ready to make an official complaint of their handling of the entire case."

Sam's sigh was heartfelt and his voice impatient. "Dad, don't you think we've got enough to worry about at the moment?"

#

Richard stood in the conservatory doorway, watching his wife as she sat on one of the aged but comfortable couches. There was a half-full glass of whisky in his hand, and he drained the contents in one gulp. Strengthening his resolve, he called out her name.

"Oh, there you are darling. I've just been looking at the diary. We're out with Richard and Barbara tomorrow night. I hope they don't insist on paying again—it gets embarrassing."

Richard tried to interrupt, "Susannah..." But she carried on as if she hadn't heard him.

"I know they're seriously loaded, but we must treat them, don't you agree? I'll take some champagne as well. We're having drinks at theirs before the restaurant."

"Susannah!" Richard's voice had risen, but Susannah ignored him again. Her hands rested in her lap, holding an open diary, the whitening knuckles betraying how tightly she was fighting for control.

"I've ironed your blue linen shirt; it's supposedly going to be nice weather."

Richard shouted, "For the love of God, Susannah, stop it! Stop pretending everything is all right. We have to talk, and you've avoided the massive bloody elephant in the room ever since we got home."

"If we do this, Richard, if we really talk, it changes everything. Or we can just ignore it and go on as before."

"We can't ignore it. I had a fling, and we need to recognise that and see what each of us did wrong to make me do this. Then we can see if we can rebuild, start again."

A dark flush stained Susannah's cheeks, and she jumped up to face Richard. Her voice was low and laced with barely controlled rage. "You utter, utter bastard. A fling? Is that what you call it? You've been sleeping with another woman for years, wining and dining her, sneaking away on your little sordid breaks. You think I'm a fool, don't you?"

Richard shook his head and put out a restraining hand meant to calm his wife. Susannah brushed him away as she continued. "I knew. I always knew."

Richard's look of shock made her laugh, but it was a sound devoid of any mirth. "The smell of perfume on your clothes—not very easy to explain when you've supposedly spent the night at the Rotary with a load of other boring old farts." She was spitting out the words now in short, sharp bursts of fury. "The increase in business trips, never answering your mobile without checking caller ID, the sudden interest in dinners for this and that and the other, all of which you had to attend alone. And the sex—don't forget that, Richard, or shall we just say the lack of? I'm not a fool." Susannah drew a shaky breath and stood there, a middle-aged woman on the edge, forcibly ripped from her comfortable life and its carefully constructed illusions.

"Darling, you have to know it meant nothing. We can sort this out."

Susannah's voice rose until she was screaming her words. "So you never loved her and it was all my fault you strayed? So let's find out what old Susannah was doing wrong? I made you do this, didn't I? Poor, poor Richard. Well, I'll tell you this—"

His face contorted with contempt, and his words rushed out. "Oh, play it that way, Susannah, but you'll see sense and come round to my way of thinking. We've too much to lose if we don't sort this out. I'd never have left you, you stupid woman. I need some space."

And with that, he stalked out of the room and, grabbing his keys from the hall table, stormed out the front door, banging it behind him. The noise drowned out the sobbing of his wife as she collapsed onto the sofa.

CHAPTER THIRTY-FIVE

Le Claire drove into the dimly lit seaside car park. A solitary car was almost hidden in the far corner, and two men stood outside the vehicle, leaning against it as they quietly conversed. Le Claire parked in the space next to them and gave each a nod of recognition as he joined them. All three wore dark clothing and rubber-soled shoes, multi-pocketed jackets completing the look.

"Masters, Porter, thanks for getting organised at such short notice."

Le Claire cursed his luck that DI Bryce Masters was one of the Authorised Firearms Offices chosen for tonight's work. He and Porter usually worked together, and both were on the incident team. Le Claire hadn't really had an alternative option and vowed to keep his personal feelings in check.

Masters spoke first, and Le Claire subdued his initial thought that the other man just loved hearing the sound of his own voice. "No problem. Everything has been arranged as you asked. We are armed with Tasers and handguns, and will risk assess as we go along. We've two squad cars patrolling the nearby area, and we can call them in for extra support if need be. Tyler is on the beach watching the main entrance. The two occupiers appear to still be in the house. Tyler called in a few minutes ago to say that some of the lights have gone out, and he'll let us know when the place is in full darkness."

"Thanks, Masters. If anyone does approach this place tonight, I want us well and truly in position and in control."

Porter said, "Sir, I walked around the area a couple of hours ago. The main entrance into the place is the private road that runs from the coast, but there is a weak spot. There's a gap in the hedge that separates Rocque View from the neighbouring property; it comes out just before the main gates. There's a well-worn path leading up to it, and I think it's been used as a sort of unofficial right-of-way."

"Well done, Porter. We'll keep an eye on that."

The men's attention was drawn to a familiar unmarked car that drew up beside them. Dewar jumped out. She was dressed in similar style to her colleagues—unrelieved black from the top of her baseball cap to the toes of dark trainers. Her eyes were focused on her boss.

"Go ahead, Dewar. What have you found out?"

"The Jim Perkins whose wife bought Rocque View is the self-same Jim Perkins who was a London jewel thief and Ray Perkins's father. Ray was born from a previous relationship that Jim Perkins had with a nightclub hostess. She effectively brought Ray up on her own, but apparently father and son were reconciled before he passed away, ironically, just months before his sentence was due to end."

Le Claire looked puzzled. "He served the full twelve years? What was the issue? I mean, why no parole?"

Dewar lifted a brow in disdain. "Seems old Pa Perkins never gave up the location of the stolen goods from that last job, and it's never turned up to this day. Lord and Lady Hampton were old-school. They kept almost all their valuables in their apartment—didn't trust the bank vaults or safe deposit facilities. They had one of these big old-fashioned safes, which would have been easy as pie for an old rogue like Jim Perkins."

"And the Jersey connection? How did that come about?"

"You'd know more than me about this, but apparently there's a load of very respectable and wealthy people living in Jersey today who weren't quite so respectable when they lived in London."

"There's many an ex-stripper from Soho who is now a yummy-mummy flashing her husband's wealth in diamond rings and tennis bracelets as she does the school run. But get back to Jim Perkins."

"Sorry. Earlier today, I called the neighbours around Rocque View. Most have only been there a few years. However, I got lucky, and on the way here I popped in to see the old bloke who lives on the other side. He's lived in that house for nearly forty years."

Le Claire smiled in anticipation. "And?"

"He remembers them. Said the wife was there all the time, but he hardly ever saw the husband. They told him Jim Perkins was a salesman and had to work in the UK a lot. The neighbour said that whenever he was back, the walls rattled with their arguments. Not the happiest home, I think. What is interesting is that he thought it a damned shame that the husband died and the widow had to sell up and move her and the little kid out. This is interesting because the house was sold twelve years before Jim Perkins died. That's what the lawyer told you."

Masters and Porter had been avidly listening to the conversation. Masters was first on the uptake. "I get it. The old man gets sent down for a big stretch, leaving the wife to fend for herself. So she sells the house and, by the sounds of it, ditches the husband and tells everyone he's dead. What happened to her?"

"I have absolutely no idea. I can't find any trace of a Karen Perkins in Jersey. Admittedly, I haven't had much time to look."

Le Claire was impatient to move the conversation on. "That's not important. We can look later if need be. Anything else?"

"No, not really. The old boy is mad keen on his garden though and made me take a quick whizz around it. He said it was a terrible shame that Perkins died just after he'd spent a lovely summer getting his own garden sorted—seems he was out digging at all hours."

As soon as the words blithely tripped out of her mouth, Dewar turned a stricken look towards Le Claire. "You don't think... do you... I mean..."

Le Claire laughed. "Oh yes, I bloody do think. Some East End lowlife moves to Jersey but is always popping across to the UK. He's just done a massive jewellery job and spends the summer here, lying low, and—if we can believe it—burying the loot in the garden. He gets arrested and charged and spends the next twelve years in prison."

Dewar's eyes lit up. "The covenants, sir. Preventing certain areas being dug up or built on."

"Spot on." Le Claire looked at his team for the night. "Come on, let's go over everything again while we wait for Tyler's all clear."

#

Blood in the Sand

Ray Perkins sat on his favourite stool in the hotel bar and ordered another beer. Last orders were long gone, but an old-fashioned lock-in was in progress; hotel guests and very best customers could drink until the small hours if they wanted to. The young bartender popped open an ice-cold beer and handed it across to what was probably his best customer in exchange for the correct change His voice was light and teasing. "You're taking it easy tonight, Ray. You came late, and this is only your second beer. You feeling all right?"

Ray saluted the barkeep with the bottle before taking a long swig. "I'm fine, Andy. Just got a bit of business to go about. Need to keep a clear head." And under his breath, he muttered, "And I should have done this sooner. You've got to keep an eye on things. Can't trust anyone or anything."

#

Le Claire and his team waited by the bottom of the private drive. Masters held his radio in his hand, and a soft beep alerted him to the incoming message. His voice was a whisper. "Thanks. Okay. Stay where you are."

Turning to Le Claire, he said, "That was Tyler. All the lights are out. We're on."

Le Claire gestured towards the gates of Rocque View. "Let's go. You know your positions. No radio contact unless absolutely necessary, and please be careful. Remember, let this play out. We need evidence, so no heroics until I say so."

In single file, they stealthily entered the gardens, spreading out and taking cover under the trees. Le Claire watched his team disappear into the deep foliage and then did the same. All they had to do now was wait.

#

The sun had set hours ago, and Grace was lying in bed, tired but unable to sleep. She'd had another call from her mother. She had seen Carter, who was full of his conversation with Grace and how he was giving her time to come around to his way of thinking. The words, and her mother's attitude, angered her. Was Grace just a pawn as they shuffled her about the chessboard? Carter wants you, now he doesn't, now he does—this time forever.

Her head ached, and she didn't want to think about any of this. She turned over in bed and stopped as she felt a long, hard body pressed against her. Her eyes shot open, and, wide awake, she sat up in bed and heard the low rumblings of doggy dreams. Daisy lay in a long, straight line. Her head was almost on the pillow, her back turned towards Grace, and her Doberman snore was louder than any human's. Grace realised she had been pushed across the bed by Daisy and lay almost on the edge. Perhaps she'd be better getting on the other side of the dog?

With a sigh, she sat up and swung her feet to the ground. Her hand reached out for the bedside light switch but instead fell on her phone. She'd use the flashlight app. Within a second, she was holding an illuminated beam that flickered across the room as she walked around the bed. And then she realised something was missing. Where was Barney? Both dogs had bounded up the stairs after her when she had gone to bed and had lain, cuddled together, on the soft rug that covered the wooden floor. Barney was nowhere in the room.

Grace lifted her dressing gown from the chair in the corner and, shuffling her feet into her slippers, headed downstairs with the phone lighting her way. She paused by Sam's door, which was wide open. Her voice was soft and gentle as she called for the little dog. "Barney, come on, boy, are you there?" Nothing. She peered around the open door and let the flashlight beam slowly cover the room. Barney wasn't there. Nor was Sam. His bed was empty. With a puzzled frown, Grace searched the rest of the house for the little dog—and Sam.

\#

A dark-clad figure slipped through the main garden. Hugging the front of the house, they stealthily made their way to the far right side of the swimming pool. Dropping a bag to the ground, he pulled out a spade, and without hesitation, headed straight to the middle of the petanque court, the sandy gravel crunching underfoot.

Le Claire held his earpiece as he heard Porter reporting *sotto voce*, "He's there, sir, starting to dig up the bowls area."

Le Claire's response was whispered. "Stay still. Let's see what he, literally, digs up."

As he watched the figure go about his night's work, Le Claire filtered the possibilities through his head. Trouble was that he couldn't discount anyone. Someone could have left the house by either back or main door, which was actually on the side of the house, and come into the garden. Or they could have come from the coast or through the neighbouring properties.

Sweat was pouring from his brow as he dug deeper and deeper. He felt a calm detachment, as though he were watching himself carry out this work, overseeing a man who was about to get everything he deserved, all he had fought so hard for. He knew it was there. The machine had told him so. The metal detector had gone crazy at this spot. If that bloody fool gardener hadn't been lurking in the gardens, he'd have been able to finish the job days ago. But no, he'd been worried that there had been too much of a commotion, so he had quickly refilled the hole and vanished.

It couldn't be much longer now. He was so near, so close.

CHAPTER THIRTY-SIX

Barney wasn't in the house, nor was Sam. Grace stood in the utility room and wondered where they were. Then she noticed that the back door lay ajar. What if Sam had gone out for some reason and Barney had slipped out after him? Grace couldn't shake the thought that something was wrong. Pulling her dressing gown tight, she opened the back door and went outside.

Suddenly, a dark shape loomed in front of her, and she held a hand to her mouth to stop a scream escaping. What did escape was an angry accusation, whispered in response to the silent night. "Sam, you idiot. You nearly scared the life out of me. What are you doing?"

Sam laughed gently and indicated to the base of the tree that lay in the centre of the back garden. A little body was pressed against the tree with one leg cocked as nature took its course. "Barney was jumping all over me and whining. As soon as I got out of bed, he ran downstairs and started snuffling by the back door. As you can see, he needed to go out, quite urgently I imagine from how long he's been watering that tree."

Grace patted a hand against her heart and whispered, "Almost back to normal. What a shock you gave me."

"Sorry about that. I've got in the habit of having a walk around the gardens at odd times. It's a pity I didn't do that every night—I may have been able to prevent Luca being attacked."

Grace laid a soft hand on Sam's arm, and a sudden heat spiralled between them. Sam looked at her just a little longer than was polite, and she started to feel nervous, certainly not uncomfortable, but there was a definite prickle of awareness.

Sam moved closer to her. "Grace, everything that has been going on has been so strange. I guess what I'm trying to say is that I wish we had met under different circumstances. I really feel there is something between us, and—"

Just then, a short, furry figure shot away from the tree and ran around the side of the house, heading towards the front gardens. Grace was first to move. "I'll get him, Sam. You shut the door in case Daisy comes down." And she chased after the little dog as its stubby tail disappeared around the corner.

#

Le Claire saw it all and, unexpected as it was, felt paralysed as he watched the scene unfold in slow motion. A small shape ran from the far corner of the house heading directly towards the swimming pool. It let out an excited bark and drew the attention of the dark figure, which moved backwards under the branches of the nearest tree.

With mounting horror, Le Claire saw someone chase after the little dog and felt helpless as he watched Grace Howard run down the steps towards the pool, right in the line of a man who was certainly a thief, and probably a murderer.

#

Grace held her phone in front of her, the light beaming onto the little dog but blinding her to all except that which lay directly in her path. She cleared the steps and was gaining on Barney when she saw a flicker of movement to her side. Beneath the branches of an ancient tree, she could make out a moving shape, a pale face. She let out a scream as a hard, muscular arm snaked out and roughly dragged her towards him. She recoiled in horror at the words whispered into her ear as her attacker jerked her head back by a rough pull to her hair. "You silly bitch, and you've been quite pleasant so far. If you'd stayed in the house, I wouldn't have had to hurt anyone."

Grace's heart stuttered, and her voice was hesitant as she whispered in disbelief. "You?"

#

Le Claire saw Grace being grabbed by her assailant, and, making sure the catch was off his Taser holster, he moved into the open, casting a long shadow as he stood in a pool of light from the hunter's moon. When he spoke, his voice was controlled but boomed across the garden. "Stop! Don't harm her." He shone his torch at the struggling figures, momentarily blinding them both. The man turned his face, squinting, and Le Claire quickly schooled his look of surprise. This was not what he had expected.

James Grayling moved away from the light, dragging Grace after him. She stumbled, and one slipper fell off, her bare foot scraping along the rough ground. She cried out in pain, and the dog, who had been cowering by the side of the pool, jumped up and, with a ferocious growl that belied his size, ran towards the struggling pair, sharp teeth bared. He pounced on Grayling, who kicked out a leg and caught the small dog full on its side. With an anguished howl of pain, the dog fell onto its side and lay there panting.

"You bastard." Grace's voice broke the unnatural silence, and Le Claire saw her struggle as she tried to prise James Grayling's hand from around her waist. Silver flashed in the moonlight, and Le Claire's eyes sharpened as the long blade of a vicious knife was pressed against Grace Howard's throat. Grayling's voice was harsh and emotionless. "Keep still, or I swear I'll gut you from head to toe." His captive sagged against him as if fear paralysed her limbs.

Le Claire slowly moved his hand and spoke into his transmitter. "Careful, he's got a knife. Slowly move out." Holding up his hands in supplication, he called out, his tone neutral and his words conciliatory as he used Grayling's first name to try and build a connection. "James. Steady now, you don't want to hurt anyone. Put down the knife and let Grace go."

James's arrogant smile faltered a little as he saw the figures emerge from the shadows. Dewar, Masters and Porter spread out across the lawns, blocking him from easily accessing the drive. That left only one option.

CHAPTER THIRTY-SEVEN

James slowly backed up towards the house, pulling Grace with him, the serrated edge of the knife pressed firmly against her throat so that one false move would draw blood. Le Claire and his team slowly followed. Grace ignored the hammering of her heart as she desperately tried to keep as still as possible.

James quickly cleared the side of the building, and they emerged into the courtyard behind the house. Grace kept her eyes on the advancing police team—they were her only hope.

Suddenly, the back door swung open, and Sam came out. "Grace, what on earth is that racket? Where's Barney?" He stopped as he took in the scene in front of him. "Christ, James! What the hell are you doing?"

James swung round, and Grace tried to steady herself. His arm was tight around her waist as he held her to him in a parody of an embrace. "Stay where you are, Sam. You too, Le Claire. Keep your men back. Let me go, and I'll let the lovely Grace live."

Sam halted, framed in the wide open doorway, as his eyes sought out Grace. She could see his fear and concern and desperately hoped he wouldn't do anything stupid.

Grace tracked Le Claire as he moved forward, his hands held out in supplication. "Look, can't we talk about this? Right now, we've got you for trespassing and threat with a dangerous weapon. Don't make this more serious. Come on, you're not going to harm Grace. Put the knife down."

James laughed. "Don't be so foolish. I've killed before, and I'll do it again."

Grace tensed in horror and sagged against James, letting him bear her weight, hoping it might slow him down.

Le Claire sucked in his breath. "But you can't have killed Kate Avery. You were off the island."

"Of course I had an alibi, you fool. That's the way it was planned."

Le Claire slowly nodded. "But you didn't have an alibi for the time of the murders of Harriet Bellingham and Emma Layzell, did you?"

Before James could say anything else, a hoarse voice spoke from the shadows. "You little bastard. It was you. You killed my Harriet."

Le Claire's head whipped round towards the voice just as Ray Perkins emerged from the deep borders to the side of the house. His gaze swivelled back to James, who had briefly closed his eyes. When he opened them again, Ray slowly advanced towards him; in his outstretched arm was a gun. James immediately pulled Grace in front of him as a human shield. "Don't be so melodramatic. You only went with the old bag so we could get our hands on this place. But she was a misguided old cow, wasn't she? Because she got nothing, nothing." This last was almost screeched.

The words stopped Le Claire in his tracks. They were colluding in some way. He motioned behind his back towards his team, the message clear. They were to cut off any access points out of Rocque View.

"Why the fuck did you have to kill Harriet? She wasn't standing in our way."

"Yes, she was, you benighted fool. She wanted her due." The last was said in a whiny, high-pitched voice as James mimicked Harriet. "And what would have happened then? Probate would have been held up whilst the lawyers got involved. Christ knows how long it would have taken us to get our hands on the place. No. I'm sick of the pretence. She should have kept her mouth shut."

Ray kept advancing, the gun held steady. "After all I've done for you…"

"I made all the plans. I thought of everything, every single detail. All you had to do was inject a frail woman in her seventies and make it look like an accident. And you even managed to fuck that up. You were wearing gloves, or should have been. What possessed you to wipe all the bloody prints off? That doesn't look suspicious, does it?"

Le Claire saw a shadow behind Ray. Masters had made his way around the house and was now blocking that exit. Porter would be close behind him. Le Claire needed to stall James and keep him talking. "And Emma Layzell? Why her? Was it just because she couldn't get the property for you?"

"No, she may have been terrible at securing the deal, but the little bitch knew something. She left me a message that night, but it wasn't garbled. No, it was quite clear. Said she knew what I was up to and I wouldn't get away with it. So there was nothing else I could do."

As he spoke, James was slowly retreating towards the back of the property—a wide-eyed Grace held in front of him. A wooden fence and a line of trees shielded the garden from the park beyond. It would be deserted, but it was surrounded by a maze of streets and houses. Places to get lost in. With a brutal shove, he pushed Grace towards Ray. She stumbled and fell against him, and Ray's gun arm came down in an involuntary movement as he tried to prevent himself from falling. Grace screamed as Ray pushed her aside. James turned and leapt onto the wooden fence, reaching out to take a firm hold on the top, lifting his leg to vault over.

Le Claire and Dewar were the nearest. Ray ran towards James, puffing as he did so. "Dad should have had you drowned at birth, you little swine."

James was almost over the fence, one leg still dangling. He halted and laughed. "You'd be nothing without me. You'd never have worked out how to kill Kate and make it look like an accident. It was my plan, and I had to fix things when they went wrong. Good-bye, Brother."

#

Grace tried to sit up, and a sharp pain shot through her side where she had landed on the hard concrete. As James raised his leg to disappear over the fence, there was a blood-curdling howl and a scrabbling of sharp claws as the Doberman came charging out of the house. Daisy ran in a straight line towards the fence and, with a ferocious growl, leapt up and fastened her powerful jaws around James' leg. He howled in pain and struggled to pull his leg away, but the dog wasn't letting go. James reached into his jacket and pulled out his knife and, leaning down, started slashing at the dog in savage movements.

Grace felt rage course through her. "Stop it!" she shouted.

In his panic, James missed, and Sam ran forward and grabbed at the hand that held the weapon. As he did so, James stretched as far as he could and stabbed at Sam with a hard, vicious thrust. Sam cried out and fell to the ground, the handle of the knife sticking from his chest, spurts of blood staining his white T-shirt.

Grace's anguished scream rent the air as she pushed herself to her feet, ignoring the pain. "Sam! No!"

Le Claire and Dewar had wrestled the gun from Ray, who was now being restrained by Dewar in a headlock as he struggled and cussed. Le Claire slowly advanced towards the fence.

James was kicking and flailing as he tried to dislodge the dog, but he couldn't. Masters came round the side of the building at speed, his handgun raised and ready to fire. "Stay where you are, or I'll shoot."

James ignored him, and with one last effort, he kicked out hard. The dog lifted off its paws and loosened its grip. James quickly pulled his leg over the fence and made to disappear.

The gunshot was like a loud crack of thunder, intense and booming. James clutched at his chest and fell forwards, back into the garden, and landed heavily on the ground.

In a swiftness that belied his heavy form, Ray had thrown Dewar to the ground, grabbed his pistol back, and in one sure movement had shot James Grayling.

Blood in the Sand

Masters and Porter handcuffed a surprisingly docile Ray. Grace had collapsed on the ground by Sam, kneeling beside him; she rocked back and forth as hitching sobs shook her body. A limping Dewar shut the Doberman inside and then made her way to the front of the house, coming back moments later with the small dog in her arms before he too was safely placed indoors. Le Claire stood by Sam, who lay unmoving on the ground. As he reached for his radio, Grace turned her tear-ravaged face towards him. Her eyes were slightly unfocused, but he could see the anxiety and fear. "Help him. Please." Le Claire called it in. "We need an ambulance. Hurry—I don't know if he'll make it."

CHAPTER THIRTY-EIGHT

Several hours later, Le Claire and a pale-faced Dewar were in his office. The sun had risen an hour before, and a new day beckoned. Neither had slept or changed, and both looked a little worse for wear from the night's events.

Dewar's shoulder had been dislocated in the tussle with Ray. It was now tightly strapped up, and she'd been given some painkillers. Tired as they were, they had still mercilessly grilled Ray Perkins. He had two killings under his belt now, for James Grayling had died instantly, killed by his own half brother. Le Claire shook his head as he sighed. "Well, at least Perkins was accommodating enough to fill in the blanks. He may have been the one who killed Kate Avery, but he wasn't in the mood for protecting his brother's memory. He obviously wanted Grayling's guilt to be quite clear, even posthumously. No wonder we hadn't tagged them as being connected. Karen Perkins reverted to her maiden name when her husband was convicted and put in prison."

"And then Ray, all grown up and visiting his dad, finds out he has a little brother and a hidden fortune waiting for him in Jersey. But his old man's been clever and put covenants on the property to prevent any future owner of the property from accidentally digging it up."

Le Claire took a long draught of his coffee and briefly closed his eyes in pleasure as the caffeine hit. "Years later, he contacts a now grown-up James, and they form a relationship, and it all leads to this horrific situation. We still need to do some tidying up as Perkins wasn't clear why his brother was so anxious to get his hands on the jewels. However," Le Claire got to his feet, "that will wait. You get off home."

Dewar rose and made her way to the door. "Sir—I mean, Le Claire—are you going to tell Ray Perkins that we've dug up the jewellery?"

His face was grim as he replied. "Oh yes, I intend doing that right now."

# #

Grace hadn't suffered more than a couple of bruises from the night's adventures. Not so Sam. She'd been sitting by his bedside for the last half hour. He was bandaged and drugged up to the eyeballs, but he was going to be okay. His wound was deep and would take some time to heal, but the knife hadn't hit any vital organs. There was a movement from the bed, and she realised Sam was awake and looking at her, his eyes a little unfocused.

"Hey, Grace. You're a sight for sore eyes. Been here long?" His voice was hoarse, and he was obviously in a lot of pain, but a look of appreciation still flickered in his eyes. Grace had put on some makeup and felt pretty in her cool cotton dress.

"I arrived just as your mum and dad were leaving. They've gone to pick up the dogs. They seemed strained. More importantly, how are you?"

"I'll live, and you're right, things are way off between them. Guess you couldn't expect anything else though. Mind you, it works for me. I had to tell Dad that I'm adding my inheritance from Kate into the business. I know he doesn't like mixing private money into the business, but it's the only way we'll be able to do the new deal. He's so stressed out about Mum that he didn't even care." Sam winced as he struggled to sit up.

"No, don't." Grace fussed around Sam, straightening the covers and adjusting his pillow. "The doctor said you're not to move."

"I always knew James was a sleazeball. A detective came round earlier and updated me. And what a shock that he was Ray's brother. It's the situation with the jewels I can't believe."

"Nor can I. In fact..." Grace stopped speaking as her cell rang. Glancing into her bag, she noted the caller information on the lit-up screen. "Hold on. I better take this. Hello, Carter."

Sam jerked as he heard the name and looked away to the side.

Grace's voice was loud and clear. "Thank you, Carter, but I'm afraid I'm not interested. I wish you well, but I think it's best we go our separate ways."

She reached out and touched Sam's hand. He turned to look at her, a tentative question in his eyes. "I'll be staying in Jersey for a while. I need to see how something turns out."

#

Le Claire walked into the interview room where Ray's statement was being finalised. "So, Ray, you thought killing Kate would get you Rocque View and what was hidden there? Quite the treasure hunter, aren't you?"

Ray was belligerent. "It was left to me and James by our dad. It was ours by right. Did you find them—the jewels?"

Le Claire laughed. He couldn't help himself. "Oh, Ray, you fool. It isn't yours, and it never was. Yes, we dug them up, and we've had a local jeweller give everything the once over."

Ray's eyes lit with avarice as he breathed, "Tell me, what was there? What's it worth? Do you know?"

"Oh yes. It's estimated at around two and a half."

"Jesus, two and a half million."

"Afraid not, Ray. More like £2,500. There were a couple of minor value real pieces. The rest was fake—all fake. Nice copies but worth buttons. That fence your old man accused of stitching him up was telling the truth. You and James committed three murders, and you killed your brother, for nothing—absolutely nothing."

#

Le Claire knocked on his wife's front door. He had gone there straight from the station. He caught a glimpse of himself in the mirrored finish to the door panel and winced. His jaw was dark with stubble, his hair ruffled and his eyes dark-shadowed.

Before he could try and smooth his hair, Sasha stood in the doorway, a puzzled look on her face. "Jack, what are you doing here? You look terrible."

"Yeah, I know. It's been a bit of a night, and that's what got me thinking. About us. Here's the thing: I'm not sure I want to sign the bloody papers."

The colour drained from Sasha's face as she looked at her husband. "If this is just because of the other night, then don't say another word. It was a mistake, for both of us. You just needed comfort, Jack."

"It wasn't a mistake, love, and you know that deep down. It's you I need. It was my entire fault; how I reacted to what happened in London and then being so wrapped up in the job that I forgot about us. How I let it consume me. We both turned into different people; me because of my focus on the job, and all that entails, and you because I was a selfish, self-pitying fool."

Le Claire smiled, sincerity in his eyes, as he said, "Things will be different this time, Sasha. I promise you."

THE END

<<<<>>>>

About the Author

Kelly Clayton lives by the sea with her husband and several cats. An avid storyteller, Kelly originally finished this book for a dear friend who was far from home but is happily now back where she belongs.

If you have enjoyed *Blood In The Sand*, please leave a review on Amazon. Kelly would be immensely grateful for your taking the time to do so.

Please also visit www.kellyclaytonbooks.com for updates on Kelly's novels and for posts on starting, writing and finishing your novel.

Acknowledgements

No book ever gets finished without the input and support of many people. I would like to thank those who have travelled this road with me.

Louise Voss was the first to see the rough draft and gave a critique that got me on the right path. Jennifer Quinlan (Jenny Q of Historical Editorial) who is a development and copy-editor extrodinaire and goes the extra mile in everything she does. Jenny really cares, and it shows.

To Alex, Ann, Elaine, Pam and Suzie—my amazing beta readers. Thank you for taking the time to read, to comment and to help me improve Blood In The Sand.

And to Claire, who listened to this story long before anyone else read it and was, in so many ways, my inspiration.

Many thanks also to Chief Officer Mike Bowron of the States of Jersey Police who helped me differentiate my DCIs from my DSs. Any mistakes are mine and mine alone.

Thanks to Kit Foster Design for my amazing cover and to Dean Fetzer of GunBoss Books for taking the worry out of formatting and layouts.

To Drena and Clem, thank you for believing in me and for all the ways you show your love.

Finally, to my husband Grant, who put up with so much with unfailing patience and love—there simply aren't enough ways to thank you.